Checked By You

Chicago Steel
Book 2

Jessica Buss

Checked By You
Chicago Steel Book Two
Second Edition
Jessica Buss

This book contains mature content
First Edition November 2022
Second Edition July 2023

Developmental Edit by Emerald Edits

Copy Edited by Ink Machine Editing

Cover Design & Internal Formatting by Feed Your Dreams Designs

Cover Image: Licensed by Adobe Stock/Lightfield Studios/311340138

Ebook ISBN: 979-8-9863903-8-3

Paperback ISBN: 979-8-9863903-9-0

Dedication

For Zach & Kadin
My boys. My heart. My drive. My biggest blessings.
Always
Be bold. Be brave. Be you.

Chapter 1

Shiloh

Three Years Ago – 2019

My gaze flicks around the dimly lit room, landing on hundreds of knickknacks covered in dust, decorating every surface of the sitting room in my grandparents' old, dilapidated house. My grandma, the sweetest woman on the planet, became a bit of a hoarder after Grandpa died a few years back, and her trinkets are proof of that.

Grandpa's absence had left her with hours of silence that she often filled with the QVC network and their hosts peddling the latest and greatest items you just had to have. Unfortunately, their sales tactics had worked perfectly on my seventy-year-old grandma, and now that she's gone, I'm surrounded by figurines and candles. "So, so, so many candles. Why did you have to buy them all?" I groan out loud. Over the last year especially, we had talked many times about how this collection of hers was becoming a bit unruly. However,

I hadn't factored in her stubbornness, and because of that, I was sitting in the middle of a home shopping nightmare. Obviously, my talks had never made any difference. Grandma was difficult to dissuade and I couldn't fault her for that. Over the years, after Grandpa had passed, I hadn't been able to visit as often as I wanted. But those ladies of QVC had, and often, it seemed. They had made some of those lonely moments a bit more bearable for her.

Looking past the dust-scattered sunbeam, my eyes land on a bunch of water-stained banker's boxes. Standing and moving to them, I wonder what they contain. Opening the first reveals the deed to the house. "Why did you store your most important documents in boxes that look like they barely survived a flood?" I grumble to myself while lowering to the only section of the room that the sun had shown any favor. When I managed to haul the boxes from the damp, mildewy basement yesterday, I hadn't understood the condition they'd be in. Now, the stench of mold spores mixed with the all-consuming, nauseating scent of yet another cluster of candles makes my already queasy stomach lurch. Rubbing it, I say, "I think I'm going to be sick. Every. Scent. Possible? Really? Couldn't you have picked one, maybe two and stuck to it?" Reaching my hand to my nose, I plug it, hoping that will hold back the stench. Unfortunately, the garish scent has permeated my nostrils, and despite my best efforts to breathe through my mouth, I'm still trapped in an odoriferous hell. It's kind of like I'm suffocating in an incredibly dense and overpopulated field of moldy wild flowers. If I don't deal with the overwhelming smell of this room, I'll never finish cleaning it.

After hours alone, trapped in the humid, poorly ventilated room, hunting for my grandparents' paperwork, I reach my limit and go hunting for a wooden clothespin. Locating a handful of them, I rejoice. "Thank you, Grandma, for your weird sock matching obsession." I clutch the antique clothespins close to my chest. "These are going to help me survive the next few hours," I mumble in a garbled voice, my nose clogged, sounding like I've suddenly developed a severe head cold.

My grandma, who raised me after my parents died in a car accident when I was four, recently passed away after years of suffering from chronic illness. She named me the sole recipient of her estate, and losing her was beyond horrible. She was the only family I had left. Not only was she my grandma, she was my friend.

Though quite a bit older than my friends' parents, Grandma had done her best to keep up with me, but at times it hadn't been easy. My teenage years and the many disagreements we had flash through my mind. Grandma Linda was much more than just my caregiver. She was everything and had been my rock. Now knowing she's gone, I'm devastated. Despite the pain of her loss, I have to admit I'm also relieved that she was no longer in pain and would finally join Grandpa, the love of her life. But sitting in this room, filled with so many of her personal things, I swear I could hear her voice speaking to me. *"Just keep going, sweetie. It'll get easier."* Every time I try to focus and listen, her words magically disappear, leaving me with just my own scattered thoughts. The empty house is eerily quiet, it's almost deafening when a whispered cry falls from my chapped lips. "Grandma, I miss you so much. Who's going to give me advice now?" Dropping my head, I admit the last of my confession. "Because, right now, I really could use some." The stale and stagnate air surrounding me is my only companion on this journey to finally say goodbye.

A few weeks after Grandma's funeral, Trent, my husband, begins nagging me, telling me we need to move into the much larger house Grandma left me in Burr Ridge. Logically, his arguments make sense, but still, I hesitate.

"Shiloh, think about it. We'd save money because we wouldn't have any rent. The house is outside the city and much safer for our family. You know, the one you want to expand? Don't you want Samuel and his future siblings to have room to play and grow?"

Up to this point, every time I'd approached the subject of having more kids, he'd been resistant, immediately shutting down the conversation and making me feel bothersome. Now, as an incentive to get his way, he's dangling giving our two-year-old son a sister or brother over my head like a prized carrot.

So, as usual, I give in. And not even a month after we buried Grandma, we move into her house—the place where I'd been raised. Coming home feels both incredible and deceptive at the same time. Instead of feeling comforted, I feel conflicted. This house holds so many treasured memories, and I love it. It was here that I always felt safe and loved. Here I could be me without question or challenge. But being here with Trent seems wrong, almost as if we're unwelcome tres-passers. Even after all the years we've been together, he'd never earned either of my grandparent's approval. They'd always told me they wanted more for me and that I was settling with Trent. Being young and stub-born, I just dug in my heels and did what I wanted and married him. And now that they're gone and we're in their house, I constantly question whether I made a mistake agreeing to move.

Despite the uneasy feelings I have, I just bury them, refusing to deal with them, and press onward, hoping changes will be just what we need to get back on track. In all honesty, our relationship wasn't good, and it hadn't been for quite some time. I was desperate to make Trent happy. Who knows, maybe moving could do that.

Trent and I have been together since my sopho-more year of high school, and this wasn't the first time our relationship had been strained. When he graduated two years before me and left to go to college a few hours away, we kept dating, doing the whole long-distance thing.

* * *

Just after my freshman year of college, Trent had proposed. He'd convinced me we should get married right away. His plan was that I should drop out of school and support us while he finished his business degree. After all, he was closer to graduation than I was. My grandparents had begged me to stay in school and put off the wedding for a little while, but I stubbornly argued that I needed to be serious about my relationship with Trent. And marrying him and dropping out of school was the only answer. In hindsight, it had been an answer, just a terrible one that I wished I could take back.

In college, I'd chosen to study elementary education, and I was excited about teaching one day. However, when I dropped out, I'd flushed that dream down the toilet. Thankfully, I'd found a job at a daycare that had a preschool within it. It was great experience that could help me one day get a job as a teacher's aide. Sure, it wasn't the road I would have taken if I hadn't been so blinded by love. Or what I thought was love. But it was my life. The reason I had been so infatuated with Trent was because he'd given me attention. And he was my first everything. I thought we'd love each other forever.

* * *

Like years before, I squash down my uncertainty and focus on what I assume will keep Trent home and engaged—his family. For years I held on to the belief that we were only in a rut, and I hoped we could rekindle the feelings we'd once shared. When we had Samuel, I tried time and time again to prove to myself that he could be a good father and we could be a happy family. It was all I ever wanted. But in the end, I put all my loyalty, love, and faith in a man who couldn't return those feelings. And again, I'd been burned. I'd been completely wrong about him. So. Very. Fucking. Wrong.

I had a choice to make. Trent isn't the same boy I fell in love with in high school. Everything that drew me to him originally has faded away as the years passed. Where once he'd been so attractive, now he looks rough, aged beyond his years. He used to be caring, but now, the way acts toward Samuel is dismissive and detached. He doesn't even take part in his life and never really has. Samuel is a toddler and I can't rationalize Trent's lack of involvement. Although I'd been desperate for a family, I can't justify what is right in front of my face. And over our years together, he'd shown me plenty of times that his lack of regard for me and the way he treated me overshadowed any positive attributes he may have had a long-ass time ago. We're stuck. I'm too tired from caring for Samuel by myself and trying to keep Trent appeased on the rare occasions he's home. And he's too self-absorbed to realize we aren't working and need a change. For so long I've devoted myself, my love, my loyalty to him, expecting that one day he'll return it. Desperately, I want him to be part of our lives, to be a daddy to Samuel, but no matter what I do, how much I hope and pray, he doesn't seem interested. Growing up without my parents, I wanted more for Samuel than I'd had.

Proving my point, not long after moving into our "dream home," Trent returned to his old ways, leaving for work early in the morning and returning whenever he felt like it. Most nights he was at the bar late with his loser friends. Showing no consideration for us.

Months later, I text him, informing him I've been sick with what I assume is the stomach flu, and he doesn't reply. Instead, he comes home in the early morning hours and sleeps on the couch. Rather than checking on me, he avoids the house completely, acting like I infected it with the plague.

The next morning, he stumbles into our bedroom, complaining about the state of the house and remarking on how I look like death warmed over. Then, after he showers and dresses for work, he leaves without another word.

After two days of Trent's cold shoulder, I resort to texting my friend Monica and begging for her help.

ME

Hey, Monica.

MONICA

Hi, Shiloh. How are you?

ME

I'm fighting the stomach flu, and I was wondering if I could ask for a favor.

MONICA

Sure, anything.

ME

Would you have time tonight after work to run by the grocery store and grab me some crackers and Sprite?

MONICA

You bet. Can you wait until school is out?

ME

I can definitely wait. I'm not holding much down yet, so this evening is great. I appreciate it. Thank you so much.

MONICA

It's really no problem. See you in a few hours and please let me know if you need anything else. How's Samuel?

ME

Samuel is good. He doesn't seem to
have it, thank goodness.

MONICA

Glad to hear my little buddy is not
feeling miserable too. Hang in there.

ME

Thanks again.

Monica's presence in my life has been a true godsend. She and I met on a rare ladies' night, where Trent had actually agreed to watch Samuel so I could go out. My fellow nursery school mom-friend, Jenny, had arranged the night and thought Monica and I would hit it off. Jenny's intuition was right about her eldest daughter's former teacher and me. We've been tight ever since.

So, after teaching a full day of kindergarten, Monica rushes to the grocery store for Sprite and crackers. Before heading over, she also grabs a plain cheese pizza for her and Samuel's dinner, which thrills him. The meals of microwave easy mac and soup were losing their appeal after day three.

"Auntie Mo, this is the best pizza I've ever had!" Samuel exclaims.

"I'm so glad you like it. How about after we finish dinner, we help Mommy tidy up a bit before bedtime?"

"I can help with the blocks," he says.

"Sounds good, little man," Monica answers. Even from the other room, I hear the smile in her voice.

While they eat, clean, and enjoy their evening together, I'm laid out in bed, praying for relief from whatever is taking over my body.

After she tucks Samuel into his toddler bed and makes sure he's asleep, Monica throws in some laundry, cleans dishes, and changes my sweaty bedding after she pushes me into the bathroom for a much-needed shower.

Following my refreshing shower, I change into clean clothes. Stepping out into my bedroom that smells faintly like Febreze, Monica cautiously hands me a pregnancy test she brought with her.

"I'm not sure if you need this, but I grabbed one at the grocery store just in case." Monica's words are gentle and comforting, but what she said puts me on the defensive.

Terrified, I gape at her, hoping to harness some of the strength she always projects.

"Thanks for thinking of that. I was trying to avoid going there. It's not a good time, but I went off birth control a few months ago because Trent mentioned having another baby."

Knowing Monica is right and that I need to take the test, I return to the bathroom to drink some water. The entire time I force a cup of water down, I'm a complete basket case, trembling. It worsens, especially while waiting the agonizing three minutes for an answer. The appearance of two pink lines shakes my world to the core. My legs grow weak, forcing me to sink to the aged vinyl flooring below me. I sob hysterically. It isn't that I don't want another child, because I do. I'm crying because I'm not sure I want another one with Trent.

Despair, grief, and anger course through my body, making me shake. Desperate for it to all go away, I long to curl into a protective ball, ensuring my safety.

Entering the bathroom and seeing me crumpled in a heap, Monica wraps herself around me tightly. "Shhh. I've got you, Shiloh." After a while, my crying lessens and my hysteric breathing regulates. This is something I have to deal with. Knowing I have her support makes all the difference. And at this moment, it forever changes me.

In the months following my grandma's death, Trent has become an unrecognizable person. Someone I don't like. I even question if, in all our years together, I've ever known the real him. Huddled in the bathroom of my grandma's house, cradled in my friend's arms, I admit something to myself: I don't love Trent anymore. Not only does that revelation scare me, but considering the positive pregnancy test in my hand, things would have to change.

"It'll be okay, Shiloh. I promise," Monica softly whispers into my ear while she remains wrapped around me. Even though her words are fairly simple, I know that coming from her they carry so much more meaning, and at this point I'm desperate to cling to the promise I feel she's making. Words are powerful, they could change lives, and her words are full of confidence and truth, letting me know I'll be all right. Whether or not I liked the circumstances, my tribe is growing, and I choose to embrace that. Our future would be uncertain, but in the end, I know, it'll turn out fine.

After the emotional evening, where I barely have enough strength to climb into bed after Monica leaves, I wake up the next morning feeling better than I have in days. Showering, I get ready before Trent noisily stumbles up the steps. Ready to confront him, I stand waiting. When he finally enters our room, I tell him we need to talk. A smell wafts off him, permeating the surrounding space. The musty stench of stale beer, cigarettes, and poor decisions makes my stomach heave, wanting to empty itself. "Push forward," I whisper to myself.

Yes, he is off-putting. His appearance is just as repellant as the attitude he carries. He looks haggard, his clothes are wrinkled, and I spot a smudge of bright-red lipstick on the collar of his white shirt. Not even wanting to allow myself to be distracted by that obvious telltale sign of his philandering ways, I launch into my practiced speech.

"Trent, I'm pregnant," I confess nervously, unsure of how he'll react or what he'll say.

He *hmphs* loudly and aggressively shoves past me,

knocking me off balance. He tears his clothes off on his way to the closet and I stand there, just waiting. Moments later, he steps out, still rubbing the sleep from his eyes and decked out in his birthday suit, and scowls at me before heading toward our bathroom. Briefly, when he'd faced me, I'd seen something that made my skin crawl and my stomach churn: hickeys. A variety of them in different colors and sizes covered his chest, confirming that they were from multiple encounters. Obviously, the asshole hasn't been faithful to me, and I wonder how long his extramarital activities have been happening. Even though he disgusts me and I have to swallow down the bile trying to expel itself, I follow him, hoping to get more of a response to what I just told him.

While waiting, I try to remember the last time I'd seen him naked or that we'd had sex. Recently, we've been off, almost like two ships passing in the night. Then my memory registers something. The last time we'd been intimate had been about two months before.

During the chaos that ensued that night, I hadn't given any thought to contraception, forgetting that weeks before I'd gone off it because we'd talked about expanding our family.

Now that it was happening, I wait for Trent's reaction, refusing to be upset. Minutes pass, and still needing answers, I stand outside the shower's glass door with my arms crossed. "Aren't you going to say anything?" I ask impatiently, trying to control the frustration in my voice.

His head whips toward me with an angry glare shooting from his bloodshot, beady blue eyes. His weathered face wears a snarl. "What do you want me to say?" he snaps, and I flinch at his tone.

Laying a hand over my abdomen protectively, I announce, "I'm keeping this baby. And if you don't want to be a part of our lives, you don't have to be."

Still glaring, eyes pinched almost closed, lips thinned, he bares his teeth. "I'll make it easy, Shiloh. No, I don't want to be part of this. I never did." His vile words hurt, but they don't deter me.

The truth finally sinks in; Trent doesn't want to be a part of our lives. I could do this by myself, raise two kids alone. I won't deny that the thought of that scares me. But I won't let it break me. As I channel my strength, I remember a lifeline—my grandma's inheritance. Having it would make at least the financial side of being alone easier.

"Oh, and Shiloh, don't start making plans for a new life just yet. Once I'm gone, you might find it tough to get by." Had he read my mind? His warning sends shivers racing across my body. "In fact, I'll make it easy for you. I agree to walk away without a fight. You can have the kid... kids."

Why does that sound too good to be true? Because it probably is. Summoning newfound courage, I ask, "What'll it cost me?"

"Only two million dollars, Shiloh. It's your choice." An evil smirk that makes me cringe, my blood boil, and my hand fist covers the face of the person I once loved. *What a selfish asshole.*

Thankfully, because I agree to hand over the stocks, our attorneys complete our divorce in months.

Chapter 2

Shiloh

Present Day -July 2022

It'd been another hectic day. I guess that's really the story of my life these days. Being a single mom isn't for the weary, that's for damn sure. Although, if I had to choose, I'd still pick it over dealing with my lying, greedy, self-absorbed ex-husband. Three years ago, I'd thought I had the life I'd always dreamed of. But I'd been so very wrong. Apparently, I lived in the state known as denial. Now I know better. This life isn't perfect, but it's all mine.

"Pancakes, pancakes, pancakes," my five- and two-year-old sing from their chairs at the table. This morning, when I'd gone to make the boys their favorite breakfast, I realized I didn't have any eggs. When I'd run errands yesterday, I'd known that, or at least, I thought I did. Apparently, between the blur of morning and bedtime, it had slipped my overwhelmed, weary mind. If I were honest with myself, that's been happening more and more often, and it fills me with such anxiety. Probably, I need to subscribe to a mindfulness or yoga app, but honestly, who has time for them? *Not this girl.*

Like most days, being a single-parent—stretched far too thin—things had simply been missed. Yesterday, by late afternoon, I had been running severely behind with everything, including Lian's much-needed nap. In the tension-filled, grumpy afternoon, I'd overlooked my reminder note. In fact, it had been such a horrible day that I'd done the unthinkable and caved and bought them fast food. *The horror.* Last night, with two hungry, cranky boys complaining, the simple task of running to the grocery store for anything bordered on insanity. *Was it a full moon?* After the day I'd had, I didn't even consider looking in the fridge for dinner. Instead, I hustled through the drive thru of McDonald's so I could grab them dinner before heading home.

"These are soooo good, Momma," Samuel had called from the back seat after digging into his fries. The golden arches had done it again. With their magical little happy boxes, the meals transformed my boys from grumpy monsters to happy kids in mere moments.

In the privacy of my bedroom later that night, I examined my choice. Again, concluding dinner was a success and therefore a win. Even I could admit it wasn't my best mom moment, but I pushed away the guilt, reminding myself that at least I'd remembered to order milk to drink and apple slices along with the burgers and fries. Judging from the squeals I'd heard in my car on the way home, my boys thought I was the best mom ever.

Now, as I stare into my nearly empty fridge, hoping eggs will materialize out of thin air, I notice I'm almost out of milk too. With two young kids, that is simply unacceptable and something I need to rectify quickly. Hurriedly, I grab a sheet of scratch paper from the chaotic junk drawer and start a grocery list that grows longer and longer. Before I know it, my two items have grown to ten. *Ugh!* I rub my head to ward off a potential migraine. My plan is simple: run to the grocery store, then load the boys into a race car cart and pretend we're just like the cars at Talladega Superspeedway, racing for the finish line. "I can do this," I tell myself.

But before we can leave, we have to get ready. I give each boy a granola bar, an applesauce pouch, and some water. Then I run into the laundry room, grab clean clothes from the dryer, and frantically pull them on. Heading back into the kitchen, I grab clothes for the boys from where I left them yesterday evening. Looking around the kitchen, I notice my boys sitting quietly, devouring their breakfast. They probably didn't even realize I stepped away for a moment.

After finishing breakfast, we hustle upstairs to get ready.

"Let's go, boys. We need to get ready so we can run to the store," I command as we march up the stairs.

Dressing a two-year-old and five-year-old simultaneously is always entertaining. Clothes could end up backward and inside out. But, despite that, it was nothing compared to helping them brush their hair and teeth. I'm not sure it's an exaggeration to say that we go through a whole tube of children's toothpaste in one week because most of it gets on the sink and mirror, instead of in their mouths.

Once we conquer the task of making them presentable, I lead them into my bedroom and distract them with the TV.

"Can you guys watch a little TV while Mom gets ready?" I ask.

Samuel nods and asks for the show he wants. "*Paw Patrol*, please."

Lian pretends to be a puppy, hips wagging and tongue out while he says, "*Woof, woof.*"

In my attempt to look decent, I head to my bathroom, plucking my bra from the door handle as I go. After I strap the girls back, I tie my hair in a messy bun, brush my teeth, and apply ChapStick. No one at the FoodSmart needs an eyeful from me this morning.

Before we leave, I notice on the calendar that it's July 4th. *Definitely need to go before the town gets busy with holiday traffic.* I know our town has some holiday activities for the kids throughout the day. After dinner, we can head into downtown and see about getting a patriotic dessert from a local shop.

* * *

Twenty minutes later, when we arrive at the grocery store, there isn't a race car cart in sight.

"Darn, no race cars," I mutter under my breath, wondering how the boys will react.

Lian makes a *zoom* sound when he hears me say car.

"Momma, you promised we could go fast," Samuel whines.

Looking at Samuel, all I can say is, "I'm sorry. We can try next time. How about we use a regular cart and you can show me how fast you can walk next to me? You can race Lian in the cart. How does that sound? Want to beat your brother?"

Lian again makes *zoom* sounds.

"I'm going to beat him," Samuel calls out as he starts power walking away from the cart.

After some clever negotiating that involves an extra-long bath time—this kid loves bubbles and bath time—I finally get Lian in the cart, facing me. Samuel does his best power walk while still holding the side of the cart. It Isn't long before I hear him complain.

"My legs are tired. Are we almost done?" Samuel whines as he trudges down the aisle, dramatically dragging his feet as if they are incredibly heavy. No longer is he racing the cart. His whine is his telltale way of letting me know he's tired. Unfortunately, I'm not the only one he informs. A sharply dressed woman gives me a pitying look as she passes us. I'd like to tell her, "It's fine. This isn't my first rodeo."

Lian makes another *zoom* noise when he realizes we've slowed down.

"I'm sorry, bud. We need to grab a few more things and then we'll be done. Next up is cookies. Sam, do you want to go pick out a package?"

"Cookies," Samuel squeals out.

Without another word about his achy legs, Samuel lets go of the cart and jets down the snack aisle toward the prized treats. Lian and I follow closely behind. For a little guy, Samuel moves surprisingly fast. Thank goodness for toddler-sized hands, because as soon as he reaches the cookies, he begins frantically grabbing packages and tossing them haphazardly toward the cart. By the time the first package leaves his hand, I'm only steps away and able to get the cart close enough before any packages land on the floor.

"Stop," I instruct in my best stern-mom tone, and he does just that. Carefully, he sets down the package he'd been holding and slowly backs away like he's a bomb tech and the cookies are set to detonate. While he waits, watching me, I unload the few packages of cookies he got into my cart and put them back on the shelf. Just as I turn back, I realize Samuel is no longer next to me. Alarmed, I whip around and see that he's moved next to his brother, feeding him cookies. Not wanting to leave a chaotic mess for some employee, I leave the cookie packs less scattered on the shelf before I hustle over to Samuel.

"Mom, these are so good. Look, Lian likes them too. See?" Proud of himself, he flashes me the messiest smile I've ever seen. It's hard to be angry with my little cookie monster.

Then, looking over at Lian, I cringe. Crumbs have mixed with his incessant drool and he has chocolate smears marking everything. Nothing is immune to his drool art. His face, clothes, and my purse are smeared with brown slime that looks absolutely disgusting. Holding back a gag, I instead let out an exasperated sigh. Both of the boys' attention flies to me and two pairs of deep-brown eyes peer at me, heavy with worry. Thankfully, their sad puppy dog eyes are the only thing they inherited from their no-good father. Unfortunately, every time I have to reprimand them, it reminds me of Trent, and just the thought of him and his not wanting to be a part of his boys' lives angers me. These are the greatest kids ever. Looking back and forth between my boys, taking in their sad state, I shake my head. These two are the loves of my life, even if they are mischievous stinkers.

Lian reaches out and places his chubby, messy hand on mine before he says in a sweet murmur, "Momma." My heart melts instantly, completely forgetting about being frustrated.

I turn to my oldest son, who wears a sheepish grin, and I try my best to school my smile. "Samuel, we can't open items in the store because we haven't paid for them yet. Let's put the open cookie pack in our cart and clean up. We still have a few things to grab before checkout, okay?"

Samuel nods and then stuffs the cookie he was holding in his mouth and puts the package in the cart. Meanwhile, I give Lian a wet wipe bath before he can tag anything else with his chocolate/drool graffiti. After we tidy up the cookie section, grab two half-gallons of milk, eggs, and some apples, we head toward the checkout.

After the chaos of the store, I'm glad to be heading home. Thankfully, we live close by. The day has already been trying, and I'm exhausted and not sure I can handle much more excitement. I do best with normal and boring, and life with young boys is anything but that.

Returning home, Lian begins to fidget. "Out, Momma. Out."

"Lian, hold on a sec. I'll get you out once the groceries are unloaded. Okay?" History has a way of repeating itself, and I know if I let Lian free, I'll be so busy chasing him, I'll likely forget I even have groceries. Samuel, however, being older and wiser, has unbuckled himself and is patiently waiting for me. Just as I balance the last bag in my arms, I feel something creepy and crawly move over my sandaled foot. Being convinced it's just a spider, I shift my foot, hoping to kick it off. *Get off.* However, the only thing I'm successful at is throwing off my center of gravity.

As if in slow-motion, I feel the bags shift in my arms, and the one tucked high in the middle of the others—carrying the eggs, of course—tips over. For a moment, time pauses, and I see the bag tumble away from me. *No!*

Before the bag crashes to the ground, I feel someone behind me. The faintest brush against my arm when the bag is effortlessly lifted away from me confirms it. Quickly, I shuffle, tightening my arms around the remaining bags, hoping I won't drop any more. I shift slowly, turning toward the mystery person behind me. Forcing my eyes up, they land on the most attractive man I've ever seen. In. My. Life. Standing before me in nothing but running shorts. *Holy hell. This man is a god.* His lack of shirt reveals a trim waist, a perfectly sculpted hairless chest, and flawless abdominal muscles that make me want to wash clothes like a pioneer woman. I'm mesmerized and I can't help but feel giddy as I slowly trace my eyes over all the ridges of his perfectly carved abs.

Cradled in his tanned muscular arms is my escapee grocery bag. Swallowing becomes problematic as I openly gawk at the fine specimen of strong, hunky man in front of me. I have never seen anyone with a body this ridiculously amazing. My fingers twitch as I ache to reach out and touch him. *Is he real? Or just a figment of my very starved libido's imagination?* I'm desperately hoping for option A.

He stares at me with wide brown eyes that I can tell are also assessing me. But despite his watchful look, his eyes still appear soft and kind. Being under his focused stare feels amazing until I remember how I looked when I left the house this morning. When my disastrous appearance registers, I sigh and my cheeks redden with embarrassment. Looking like this, I could easily audition and win the role as the poster child for the definition of a hot mess. Cringing, I wonder why he's still looking at me. The handsome mystery man steps forward and, without saying anything, leans toward my face. Frozen in place, everything stops except my mind, which is whirling with questions. *Why is he coming closer? Is he leaning in to kiss me? What do I do?* Holding my breath, my eyes flick back and forth, desperately trying to read the situation in front of me. His large hand comes near my face and I lean into it as if I'm seeking out his touch. It grazes my cheek—that feels nice—and then it's followed by a sharp tug. "Ouch." I mutter as I peer at him, confusion marring my face. Pulling back his hand, he shows me a clump of cookie that had been in my hair. Instantly, I frown. *Thanks, Lian.* He must have put that lovely hair accessory in while I was giving him the wet wipe bath at the store. "Sorry. It's Chips Ahoy!" I mumble at him as he stares at his fingers, perplexed. We stare at each other another moment before I awkwardly thank him.

Then I hear Lian giggle and Samuel call out, "Momma, who's that?"

All I can think is, *yes, who is this delicious man standing in front of me? I'd really like to know too.* But I can't answer Samuel's question before the handsome stranger mumbles something, sets down my grocery bag, and runs off like he's taking part in a competitive sprint race. His huge body moves gracefully as he rushes to my next-door neighbors' porch. *Wait! What?* In a few quick strides, he's inside, leaving me entirely confused. *Hold on! He's my neighbor?*

Honestly, I've been too preoccupied with keeping my head above water to notice who lived next door. Until right now, I hadn't cared who lived there. But now I do. And if I'd known it was a gorgeous god, I would have paid more attention, especially with the way I looked when I left my house.

Unfortunately, before I could even make an introduction, he left me standing in my driveway, alone. What am I supposed to do now? Walk over and knock? Introduce myself and the boys? Or just forget about the unusual interaction and the undeniable way my body reacted to him? Because, honestly, it was impossible to miss that exchange when he took the grocery bag from me. Something happened between us. His touch, although faint, electrified my skin, sending a charge throughout my body, lighting all of me up. The chemistry between us was irrefutable. It was like a conduit of desire leaving me feeling heated, rattled, and off-kilter. That feeling was entirely unexpected, but it made me extremely curious.

In fact, I'm pretty sure my kids scared him away, because he'd seemed fine until he'd heard them. He must be one of those guys. You know the type, unwilling to pursue a woman with kids. To them it's considered a definite no-go. But it isn't like I'm looking for forever from him. I'm craving a man's body against mine. It's been so long. The only intimate moments I've been having for a while are with my B.O.B, so anything between us would be more like a cleaning out of the cobwebs or scratching an itch. His living next door would definitely make a hook-up scenario incredibly convenient for this busy momma. Plus, he's indisputably the sexiest man I've ever seen. Seemed like a win to me. Too bad I'd probably never find out.

Honestly, when I think about the reaction I just had to my neighbor, I realize it's been forever since I've noticed anyone remotely attractive showing me any interest. I'm not overly confident, but I know that's exactly what he was doing before he ran off. But now I'm sorely disappointed. Looks like I won't be able to get in a round with him. I'm not much of a gambler, but I'd place odds on a night with him being an unforgettable experience. In fact, one I'd probably want to repeat again and again.

Needing to shake off the weird exchange, I gather my groceries and head inside. After setting them in my kitchen, I return to free Lian and, while walking back into the house, I ask Samuel, "Now that we've gone to the store, what do you think we should do with the rest of the day?"

Without a blink of hesitation I hear, "Playground."

I laugh and Lian joins in with his toddler gibberish chanting, "Paygwnd. Paygwnd."

Once I unpack the groceries and assemble a picnic lunch, I holler to the boys in my best sing-song voice, "Time for sunscreen." *Wait for it... commence whining.*

"Momma, do we have to?" Samuel asks in a pathetic voice. Lian just stands there and shakes his head no.

"Okay, but if we don't put it on, we'll have to stay home."

"But, Momma... really?" Samuel questions.

I answer by putting my hands on my hips and waiting. Obstinately, Lian crosses his arms and pouts out his bottom lip. After another minute, the boys cave and the fiasco of applying sunscreen begins.

Wiggling and squealing, Lian cries out, "Momma, tickles."

Meanwhile, Samuel tries to put on his own cream while I'm turned away. "Samuel. Wow. It looks like you're doing a great job. Can I help a little to make sure you don't get it in your eye?" Obviously proud of himself, he smiles wide. Looking around, I don't see the sunscreen. "Where's the cream, bud?"

Stepping to the side, Samuel reveals the now nearly empty bottle of sunscreen that had been hidden behind him. Surprised, I gasp. Where'd all the cream go? That was an almost new bottle. Then I notice Samuel's hands; layers of thick sunscreen coat both of his little palms, making him look like he's turning into Frosty the Snowman. Muffling a laugh, I ask, "Do you think you've got enough?"

Holding up his hands, he laughs. "I think I squeezed too hard." *You think?* Full-on laughter falls from my lips as I snatch a towel from the diaper bag and clean up Samuel's hands.

"Sunglasses, hats, and shoes," I holler out while walking to the front door. With my bag packed full of lunch, I throw in chalk and bubbles, just in case. "Let's go," I say to the boys after I see we're ready.

Chapter 3

Mika

This season had been one for the books. We'd won the Stanley Cup! It wasn't our first, that was last year, but it was still a worthy accomplishment for the Chicago Steel. As far as I'm concerned, life couldn't get any better. I had everything I'd ever wanted. All season, I'd worked my ass off, and now it was time to relax.

All I had planned was lying low during the off season. Unlike many of my teammates, I was smart and had absolutely nothing scheduled. It was going to be amazing! I didn't have the stress of pulling off some fancy-ass vacation like our captain, Josh Logan. Rumor had it he was taking his incredibly awful girlfriend, Kayla, to Jamaica to an extremely posh and hugely expensive resort. Knowing her, the vacation was all her idea, and I suspect it's his way of appeasing her so he can push off her insistence for a ring. Yikes. To be in his shoes. No, thank you. She's hot, but damn, she's scary.

During my years in the NHL, I'd learned not all puck bunnies are like Kayla. Some were obvious; they were trying too hard with everything. Others were harder to spot. I learned quickly who to avoid. Despite the number of puck bunnies I'd hooked up with over the years, no one's showed the psychopathic tendencies Kayla does. Speaking of said psycho, I hope she won't be at the 4th of July party Lucas Bouchard and his fiancée Samantha are hosting at their house later today. If Kayla shows up, she'll ruin it with her over-the-top drama and crazy antics. This barbeque is going to be epic, for sure. Lucas promised great food and fun. I even heard Samantha mention a giant slip 'n slide, and I can't wait to let loose and relax. The entire team, coach Tristan, and our new owner, Trey McConnell, are supposed to be coming.

Leaning against the kitchen counter and drinking the last of my chocolate protein shake, I remind myself I need to get my run in. "Ugh!" Groaning loudly, I head toward my front door. Running isn't my favorite thing to do; I actually loathe it. It's boring, monotonous, and tiring. I don't care who say's it, but runner's high is complete bullshit. I'll take skating sprints any day over running. But even though it's the off season, and I despise it, I won't allow myself to check out. Come September, I know if I slack off, training camp will kick my ass hardcore and I'll end up in a ball-shrinking, air-sucking, frigid ice bath every day. For this reason, and for this reason alone, I stay firm with my diet and exercise all year long.

Let's go. After I pull on my Nikes, I tuck my AirPods in my ears and head out to my front yard. The neighborhood's quiet, other than the birds chirping. Stretching my legs in my front yard, I select my running playlist—90s rock. With Smashing Pumpkins blasting, I'm ready to get this torture over with. Thankfully, with it being early it isn't too hot or muggy yet. Regulating your breathing sucks when it's muggy out. Kind of like sucking Jell-O through a straw—tight and restrictive.

Slap, slap, slap. The sound of my feet hitting the well-groomed trails near my house centers me. I feel my body start to unwind, my shoulders relax, and my stride lengthens. Living where I do is an absolute luxury, and these trails are the proverbial cherry on top. In Burr Ridge, I still have the benefit of being relatively close to the city, but I don't deal with traffic congestion or other major big-city problems.

Following my 5K, I jog slowly up the road. Moving toward my house, something flashes in my peripheral vision and I notice my mysterious neighbor struggling with what looks like her groceries. *Oh shit. That doesn't look good.* Quickly, I pluck my AirPods from my ears and head up her long driveway. Until today, I'd never been close enough to notice much about her. *What have I been missing?* Coming upon her now, I'm completely blown away. "Beautiful," I whisper to myself. Even though I've lived here for several years, I'd never paid much attention to any of my neighbors. *That stops now. Well, at least in regard to this neighbor.*

I notice she's softly muttering something that sounds remarkably like "Not again, Satan." Being close enough to catch the tumbling paper bag from her l arms, I step forward and do that. In the exchange, our arms brush slightly and it feels like a jolt of electricity shoots through my body, leaving a hot, lingering buzzing in its wake. Suddenly recognizing it's a similar feeling to when I was shocked as a kid when I shoved a fork in an outlet, my body feels feverish and tingly all over. My eyes widen and a gasp falls from my lips. I'm shocked by my reaction to her. *Did she feel it too?*

She flails wildly while still attempting to not only recover the bag I'd already rescued but by maintaining hold of the others too. "Dammit. Arggg." Her growls are adorable, just like her. In fact, they aren't threatening at all. Even though I'd yet to see her face, I couldn't help but notice the delectable body only inches from me. She's petite and covered with soft curves that more than entice me. I want to run my fingers over each rise and fall of her delicious body. Just the thought of that makes me slightly crazed and noticeably turned on. Stifling a groan, the lyrics of a John Mayer song float into my head. He got it right when he sang about a body being a wonderland.

When she finally realizes I'm behind her, she spins

around, totally shocked. A squeak falls from her small mauve lips, and her dreamy eyes widen, taking me in. I freeze under her perusal, not wanting to alarm her further. She reminds me of a startled deer, statuesque, and immovable when surprised.

While standing there, my eyes lazily wander over every inch of her face, enjoying what I find, making note of her soft blonde hair tied in a messy configuration at the nape of her lean neck. Her eyes, which are mocha colored, are warm and captivating and framed by long lashes. They intrigue me instantly. Mostly they're subtle, except for a few enchanting bursts of hazel that remind me of dancing flames. A light dusting of freckles spreads across her high cheekbones, telling me she spends a good deal of time outdoors. Her tanned skin reinforces that, and I can't help but wonder if I missed opportunities to see her sunbathing. Just thinking of her in a bikini makes all the blood in my body rush south. I lower her grocery bag in front of my crotch, covering the obvious reaction I'm having to her. Returning to her face, I notice something unusual on her head. Reaching toward her, she freezes. When my fingers find the substance, I notice it's soft, gooey, and brown. Second guessing myself immediately, I wonder what this unknown matter is that I've removed from her hair. Her eyes widen as I pull my brown fingers back, and as they near my body, I faintly smell chocolate chip cookies. *That's weird.*

After she tells me it's cookies, I wipe my fingers on

my shorts as I continue my perusal of her. I notice she isn't wearing any makeup. *Radiant.* The siren before me is absolutely stunning; the eighth natural Wonder of the World.

After I conclude my neighbor is the most attractive woman I've ever encountered, I step back to appreciate the entire package. *Fuck me.* She's wearing jean cutoffs that aren't minis but, on her body, they're dangerous and tantalizingly sexy. A soft cotton tank that I want to tug off clings to average-sized breasts I desire to palm and caress. The mental picture I've concocted leaves me speechless and my mouth watering like Pavlov's dogs. *Does she know she's a walking wet dream?* Then I hear a pair of giggles coming from inside her car and my wandering fantasies evaporate immediately.

"S-sorry. You looked like you needed a hand. I didn't mean to intrude. I'll just set this here. Later," I mumble out rapidly before I run away from her like my ass is on fire, refusing to look back until I arrive at my front door. Nerves propel me forward the entire distance, but I'm unsure of what I left in my hasty departure. Once I key in the code, and as I push open my front door, relief hits me. Before closing it, curiosity gets the better of me and I chance a look over my shoulder. And what I see makes me edgy. My neighbor looks dazed and confused. Acknowledging her, I give a slight wave and retreat inside to hide out. Guilt plagues me as I think about our disastrous interaction. *What just happened?*

After closing the door, I lean against it, taking a moment to calm my pounding heart and rapid breathing. Once I'm regulated, I quickly take a few steps, planting myself in front of my bay windows, giving me an unobstructed view of my neighbor. *Hello, creeper.* The desire to know what was unfolding next door pushes me to inconspicuously tug the curtains to the side. *Am I acting normal?* Shrugging the question off, I resume watching.

After a few moments of spying, a loud "Momma!" called out in a small, shrill voice, stills me. The beauty whips back around, away from my gaze, and focuses back on her old, well-used 4Runner. I continue watching her every move like it's my job. And before long, she looks back over at my house. Guilt gnaws at my gut. *Can she see me? Does she know that after one brief interaction she's turned me into a desperate man, craving only one thing—her?*

As if she can hear my thoughts, she smiles to herself, and my heart stalls. *I'm so screwed.*

Reminiscing about the brief moments we were in the same space, I come to one undeniable conclusion. This woman, *my neighbor,* is undeniably beautiful. Of all her incredible features, the most amazing is her smile. It's a combination of happy, hopeful, and playful. Just thinking about it makes me smile. Then reality comes crashing back in as I remind myself that she's off-limits. Her unknown relationship status requires that of me. No matter what, though, I can't deny I'm drawn to her.

My hungry eyes watch as she climbs up into the 4Runner, and visions of her crawling up my bed toward me flood my brain. My cock hardens and I push my palm against it, warning it to chill. *Settle down, bud.* Though a few minutes later, when she shimmies back out of the vehicle, I'm about ready to blow. Seeing her wiggle her hips back and forth makes me harder than steel. My mind buzzes and my heart races, leaving me feeling woozy. *Shit, I need to calm down.* Hoping to center myself, I place my palm on the wall to settle myself. *No luck.* Even the pair of boys in her arms does nothing to squash the lust racing through my body at super speed. *They're cute.* If I had to guess, I'd say her kids are about the same age as my teammate Connor's, two and five.

Chapter 4

Mika

When I can no longer see her, I forcedly push off the windowpane and stalk into my kitchen. Feeling restless and agitated, I move to my fridge and grab an ice-cold bottle of Gatorade. Looking down, I can't help but laugh. My best friend and teammate, Lucas, is the newest spokesperson for the sports drink. As far as I know, he has his life together. *Shit.* Suddenly, I realize I'm jealous of one of my best friends. *I've never been that guy. What's happening to me?* I'm heading to his house in a few hours to celebrate his recent engagement, winning the cup, and the 4th of July. Pushing the green-eyed monster aside, I lift the cold beverage to my lips and guzzle it down, hoping it will quench my overheated body. It's hard for me to understand why I feel all hot and bothered. Why does my skin feel itchy? Is it because of my run or the temperature outside? *No.* Flashes of my sexy-as-sin neighbor cloud my mind, and I realize she is solely responsible for my body short-circuiting and overheating. Just being close to her for a moment set me ablaze, scattering my brain, and throwing my damn libido into orbit. My attraction to her was instant and completely foreign. Although I was only in her presence for a few minutes, I had to continually fight the indisputable urge to reach out and touch her. And it wasn't just want. It was need.

Draining the last of the frigid drink in seconds, my throat convulses, temporarily stalling the incessant thoughts of my neighbor. Rubbing my throat and swallowing helps ease the agony piercing my temples. When relief finally arrives, so does the continued onslaught of new fantasies of the siren next door. *Irresistible.* Never before had anyone elicited such an intense reaction in me, and the realization of that slams into me like a 175-pound forward checking me against the boards. My brain staggers. *What does it all mean?*

"Mika," I caution myself, "you've always been surrounded by beautiful women." Until now, I'd never been all that interested in any of them. "Why's she so different?" I muse. Because all those women were predictable. When they looked at me, all they saw was dollar signs and fame. Recognizing my thoughts, I shudder at the realization that none of my interactions with women had been honest. *Had that been on purpose? Was honesty what I was actually looking for?* Admitting I was just looking for a good time was more difficult than I'd thought. A wave of nausea washed over me. My previous life of hookups wasn't as appealing as it had once been.

Over the years, I'd learned that for me, a professional athlete, women were easy. Easy for me to read, to predict, to use. And after we'd both gotten what we were after, we were done. Our interaction was complete. I never did more or got serious. Stroking my chin, I wondered, *was it enough?* In the past it had been, but it didn't feel that way anymore. Lately, I'd noticed some of my teammates settling down, and I could admit that was beginning to sound more desirable and tempting. It seemed like once those guys found "the one," they finally looked settled, content, and happy. *I want that.* Unfortunately for me, it looks like the only woman I'd ever been remotely interested in appears to be off the market.

"Stop moping," I chastise myself as I run my hand through my sweaty hair.

"I need a distraction," I groan out while jogging up the stairs to shower. *Distraction?* Thoughts of an impromptu vacation fill my mind as I'm showering. Perhaps spending some time on a beach or in Vegas, good old Sin City, would rid my mind of the incessant thoughts of my neighbor?

Ding, ding.

Just as I'm stepping out of the shower, my phone dings. Retrieving it, I see a text from Jase, our team's newest rookie, offering me something I can't turn down, a perfectly timed distraction.

JASE

Plans next week?

ME

None, why?

JASE

Vegas - chicks, booze, gambling…
Rocco and Ace are in. R U?

I read his text again and again, pondering it carefully before I respond. Rocco, Jase, and Ace are great guys on their own, but when they're together, you could find yourself in trouble. And not just run-of-the-mill trouble, but trouble with a capital T. You know the kind that always evokes the use of *what happens in Vegas, stays in Vegas.* Do I want to be trapped in Vegas with them? Acting as their glorified babysitter? I'm not sure I'm up for all the shenanigans they'll get into. However, even as unsure as I am, I still believe a distraction is necessary, and I know Vegas would provide that. I'd just have to ensure the guys don't get me into too much trouble.

ME

I'm in, but no crazy shenanigans. I
don't need Coach up my ass about
anything.

JASE

No shenanigans. I promise, man.

ME

I don't want any new silver jewelry either.

JASE

Ha! Cool. I'll add you to the flight manifest. We are doing this shit in style. Private jet, baby!

ME

See you later at the BBQ.

JASE

C U L8R

My stomach tenses. *Ugh.* It was my internal alarm system warning me of something coming. Suddenly second guessing myself, I question whether Vegas would be fun. Was I making a mistake by going? Honestly, I didn't know. With an off-limits hottie next door and my sex-starved brain coming up with multiple scenarios of how I could "accidentally" run into her, I know I need some space between us. Especially with questions of her availability plaguing my every thought. Standing wrapped only in a towel, looking at myself in the mirror, I give myself a pep talk. "Mika, you got this. It's what you need. Hang with the guys. Keep them out of trouble and maybe score some hassle-free fun."

Chapter 5

Shiloh

The playground hadn't been too busy, and the boys had fun exhausting themselves. Lian passed out in my arms about a half an hour before Samuel was ready to leave. I enjoyed the closeness of rocking him in my arms while I watched Samuel run around pretending to be a superhero, a confident, determined look plastered to his adorable face as he moved around the equipment. Shouts of "stop," "gotcha," and "hands up" filled the air. When Samuel was finally tired of jumping off equipment and play fighting invisible villains, he informed me he was ready to go. Loading Lian in his stroller, we walked home. Lian finished the rest of his nap in his crib while Samuel settled on the couch with a snack of Goldfish and the *Wild Kratts* show.

After assembling a casserole for dinner, I play mindlessly on my phone while it cooks in the oven.

Thoughts of my handsome neighbor overtake my consciousness, and my eyes flick over to his house, wondering if he's as curious about me. Desperate to know more about him, my fingers, acting on their own, perform a property search on the mysteriously sexy next-door neighbor. During my divorce from Trent, I'd learned about property searches because my lawyer was adamant about ensuring the house title changed solely into my name. Cyberstalking my neighbor is probably not the intended use of the state's website, but it provides the information in a timely manner. Unlike if I'd waited for an actual introduction. Because that would probably never happen considering how quickly he'd run away this morning.

When the property information loads, it reveals that my neighbor is Mika Popov-Stevenson. *Why does his name sound familiar? Maybe he's famous.* Another quick search informs me exactly who my neighbor is: a professional hockey player with the Chicago Steel. In fact, according to one such article, Mika isn't just a professional hockey player, he is one of the best defensemen in the league, grouping him with guys like Adam Fox and Cale Makar. Not knowing much about hockey, I trusted the articles, noting that he is quite impressive. He's quite impressive physically too.

Returning to my search, I notice the hundreds of pictures of him in the results. Excitedly, my fingers click the ones that catch my eye. Most have Mika dressed in his gear, playing hockey. *Thank you, gods of hockey.* Even tired and sweaty, he is beyond handsome. His smile is dangerous; part sin, part saint.

Flashbacks of this morning flood my mind. I'm embarrassed to admit that I excitedly watched a bead of sweat trickle down his perfectly sculpted washboard abs until it settled in the small patch of hair rising out of the waistband of his athletic shorts. *Holy shit, was it hot?* I remember how my heart beat wildly in my chest while my mind tried to contain all the lustful scenarios my body wanted to partake in.

Mika's body is insane, and I witnessed it in all its glory. I'd forever be revisiting all the mental snapshots I'd taken as he stood in front of me. During my perusal, I'd noticed that his body was cut in places I didn't even know possible. His dark brown hair was tousled and wild and so damn sexy. The day-old scruff on his face made him look rugged, and suddenly I felt the desire to go backwoods camping—something I'd never do. *I'd like to explore his backwoods.*

Mika oozed pheromones and sex appeal, and his sweat was an aphrodisiac, making my body heady with desire. I, on the other hand, was sure I'd manifested the exact opposite, repellant in every way possible. In fact, I needed a sign that read "Warning: Hot Mess Ahead." *I'd have to check for one on Etsy. Perhaps a handy DIY would be on Pinterest? Would it be cheaper to make my own or buy one ready-made?*

Thinking back to Mika, knowing I'd killed my chances, I remind myself he is definitely out of my league. Does he have a girlfriend? Adding that to my search, I fidget, nervously awaiting the results. Suspicions settle heavy in my gut, twisting and cramping it. Fear washes over me as the results load slowly. Sweat prickles my skin, and I bounce on my toes anxiously. I'm convinced I'll come across pictures of him with some leggy bombshell cradled tightly in his muscular arms. Probably a Victoria's Secret model or a Sport's Illustrated model, not someone like me, the literal girl next door.

"What?" I gasp in surprise as I glance through the hundreds of returned images. The only woman ever pictured regularly with Mika is his... mother. I'm thoroughly confused. *That can't be right. The paparazzi stalk famous people, including athletes. There has to be something.* In all the pictures I come across, I see many with breathtaking women. However, one thing I notice is that it's never the same woman. According to everything I see, Mika has never had relationships or girlfriends. Even with the pictures, I still wonder about his type. Am I it? Although in the incredibly rare possibility of that, getting involved with him would be dangerous in so many ways. As a mom, I not only have to consider myself but my two boys in everything I do. And knowing that, I know Mika is potentially trouble to not just my heart, but theirs too. Unfortunately, the more I daydream about him, the more I realize how incredibly hard it is to wipe him from my thoughts. He's invaded every facet of them, and removing him is proving to be more problematic than it should be. *Why am I holding on so tightly to this stranger? Why do I feel so connected to him?*

Ding. The oven timer reminds me I have things to do, responsibilities to focus on. There is no time for daydreams or fantasies about the delicious man next door. Just as I'm pulling the warm, bubbly casserole from the oven, I hear babbling come through the baby monitor. On my way to get him, I check on Samuel, who is looking like a king, stretched out on the couch.

"Aah-ple. Aah-ple."

Jogging up the stairs, I listen to Lian energetically sing and talk to himself. Nothing was better than my boys, and thoughts of Mika disappear as I lift Lian from his crib. We dance over to the changing table, and he continues to sing and jabber while I change his diaper.

As I deposit the dirty diaper in the diaper pail, I remind myself again I need to start potty training. Thankfully, it's summer break, so I won't have to worry about school yet. Knowing from my experience with Samuel, potty training will be a full-time job, at least for a few weeks, if I'm lucky. This fall, Lian will move into a new daycare group for kids who no longer wear diapers. Deadlines had been established, and I know I need to adhere to them. There isn't any other option. During the school year, I work as a teacher's aide at the elementary school that Samuel is starting in the fall, so daycare is necessary. Lian begins babbling about how hungry he is and that distracts me from my pre-potty-training checklist of Cheerios, M&M's, and stickers.

After dinner, I grab hoodies, diapers, wipes, and water bottles for the boys. With everything tossed in a backpack, we head to the 4Runner, hoping we can catch some of the holiday activities in town. *Happy Birthday, America.*

Wandering the streets for over an hour, we finally stop inside a local bake shop for a holiday themed dessert. The boys love their red, white, and blue, star-shaped Rice Krispies Treats, and after they've demolished them, we head home. Exhausted, I give them a joint bath to tackle all the dirt and stickiness they'd collected throughout the day. Not long after I put them to bed, I pass out too.

Chapter 6

Mika

I couldn't seem to get my neighbor out of my head, so instead of staring at her house and fantasizing about another meet up, I head over to Lucas's house early to get his take on my predicament. When I arrive, I find Lucas in his backyard, wrestling with a giant roll of plastic sheeting. A dozen brightly colored pool noodles and a pile of yard stakes lie at his feet. *This is weird.* I scratch my head, wondering what he's doing. Unable to come up with any plausible explanation that remotely makes sense, I finally ask, "Lucas, what are you doing?"

He stops wrestling with the plastic and stands up, puts his hands on his hips, and lets out a big breath before he explains in a rushed, whiny tone, "Samantha wants me to build a DIY slip 'n slide for the barbeque." I just nod at my friend, hoping I'm being supportive.

With arms waving, he gruffly explains the process

of acquiring the various supplies needed for the slip 'n slide. "Mika, I had to visit three Walmarts—*three*—to get enough pool floats. Did you hear me say three? Waalmaaarts?" Lucas drags that out, really trying to stress all the trouble he'd had to go through. I smirk, and he snarls before launching into the rest. "And then I had to go to Lowe's for the plastic sheeting and yard stakes," he says while dramatically kicking at the sheeting piled at his feet.

Watching Lucas explain everything he's done for construction of the slide is hilarious. His gestures and mannerisms are spastic and uncontrolled. In fact, I've never seen him like this. After playing hockey together for the past years, Lucas was always so calm and collected. But right now? Right now, he is the exact opposite, like a chicken with its head cut off, moving about frantically and scattered.

Trying for levity and knowing he needs something else to focus on, I make my face as serious as possible and joke, "Lucas, man, what are you *really* doing? Are you really building a slip 'n slide? Why do you need so much plastic sheeting? Tell me the truth. Did you join the Bratva as an enforcer and not tell me? Come on, man. I'm Russian. I'd totally keep that secret for you."

Lucas grunts, rolls his eyes, and shakes his head in response.

Taking it a step further, I dart my eyes around the backyard, checking to make sure we're alone. Dropping my voice to a whisper, I ask, "Does Samantha know you're a hitman for a Russian mafia? Shit, I haven't seen her yet! You didn't kill her, did you? That's not for her body, is it? Tell me. How deep are you in?"

My stern composure doesn't last when I look and see shock and horror stretched across his face. His panicked reaction is hilarious and I can't contain my laughter any longer. Lucas glares at me, only making me laugh harder.

"Har. Har. You are so funny, Mika. I didn't know you could make a joke, seeing that you're always so serious," Lucas mocks. I knowingly smile, his ribbing making me feel happier than I have in a long time. It's not that I'm grumpy or anything, I'm just quiet and reserved, choosing to stick to myself rather than engage in the drama surrounding some of my teammates. However, despite my normal quiet, reserved demeanor, something about my interaction with my neighbor this morning had left me feeling energized, optimistic, and happy. Just thinking about her makes me smile.

Lucas side-eyes me, then questions, "Are you smiling, Mika?" Before I can answer, he follows it up with another question. "Why?"

Reaching up to my mouth, my fingers follow the upturn of my lips, confirming his observation. Checking the yard again to make sure we are, in fact, alone, I quietly respond with a head nod. Lucas's eyes go wide, bugging out as if he's genuinely surprised. It's not just my smile, but my confirmation of it. His eyes focus in on me, and I know he's looking for more information, so I tell him. "Yes, I am smiling. I met someone."

Lucas steps over the plastic sheeting and comes closer to me. His voice remains quiet as he verifies what I just said. "You met someone?"

"Yes. Well... kind of."

"What are you saying? You kind of met someone? How exactly do you do that?"

"Lucas, man, it isn't a big deal. Yes. I met someone, but I'm not even sure she's available. What I am sure of is she's gorgeous."

With a confused look, he asks, "Why do you think she isn't available?"

"She's my neighbor, and she has kids," I inform him while rubbing my hand through my hair. "I mean, I couldn't believe anyone would leave her, but I've never seen a guy at her place," I further explain, still trying to understand it myself. All afternoon, I racked my brain, trying to recall if I'd ever seen a guy next door, and I always came up with the same answer: no.

Lucas nods his understanding, knowing why I'd be leery. Like me, he was raised by a single mother, and until last year when he met Samantha, he too, was a forever bachelor. Samantha, the coolest woman I've ever met, changed that for him, and now they're engaged.

Just like Lucas, my bachelor status had to do with my father. I never wanted to be like him. When he'd first learned of me, he wasn't willing to commit to us and he broke my mom's heart. Unwilling to put myself in the same position, I'd never gotten involved with any woman past a one-night stand. At least, that had always been my plan. That was until this morning, when I met my neighbor and when unexplainable sparks ignited between us. Now, I wanted more. With her. But I don't know if that's possible.

Not having a father growing up, people might've assumed that I had a terrible childhood, but I didn't. My mama, Katrya, had done an incredible job. She had moved from Russia when she was nineteen to work as a housekeeper, and the company she was with placed her with a wealthy family in Boston. Shortly after arriving, she'd caught the eye of one of the family's sons. He was twenty-one and back for his summer break from college. Unbeknownst to her, he wanted to have a little uncomplicated fun with the help. Throughout the summer, he pursued her relentlessly, wearing her down with his smooth words, gifts, and exciting romantic gestures.

Once she'd finally slept with him the week before he was scheduled to go back to school, he was no longer interested and ghosted her. By the next week, her world crashed down around her. The night after he'd left, he told my mama that there was nothing between them. He left her brokenhearted. Unknown, their one night together resulted in me.

When she discovered her pregnancy weeks later, she courageously told her employer, my grandparents, and they begged for her silence until they could speak to their son. When they eventually confronted my father a few months later, in person, during his Christmas break, he first denied it. Eventually, when his parents held his substantial inheritance over his head, he admitted the truth.

In an attempt to keep everything quiet, the family paid for my mother's healthcare and all the costs associated with my birth. Once I was born, they moved us off their property and set us up in a small ranch style home on the opposite side of town. They paid a generous monthly stipend to Mama so she'd stay quiet about the identity of my father. They also helped her find employment elsewhere so they wouldn't have a daily reminder of their son's mistake.

They thought I was a mistake, and growing up, that's what I'd always believed too. Because of that, and never wanting to repeat it, I'd never gotten into any relationship. I was terrified I'd make a mistake, resulting in an unplanned child. My plan, instead, was to be a bachelor forever. Having only one-night stands was my way of ensuring I didn't repeat history. No child ever deserved to feel like they weren't wanted. I knew that if I had a child, I couldn't just walk away like my father had. I would stay involved, even if I didn't have feelings for the mother. And I never wanted to face that situation, so I played it safe.

So, considering my past, my neighbor's situation confused me. Where was the boys' father? Was she all alone? I wasn't sure, but I was spinning aimlessly, wondering what to do next.

Lucas finally breaks me from my tortured thoughts when he says, "That's tough, man. I get why that would be hard for you. What do you want to do about it?"

Unsure how to answer, I shrug and then rock back and forth on my feet, something I'd done since childhood when confronted with a problem I couldn't solve quickly. Lucas reaches out and grabs my shoulder, halting my movement and forcing me to look at him. His worried expression acknowledges the troubled feelings warring within me. Then he says, "You know, Mika, you don't have to decide right now. Give yourself a moment to think about it and you'll figure out what's right for you."

At his words, I nod, relieved that I don't need an answer or plan immediately. Noticing my body relaxing, I roll my shoulders, shake out my arms, and chance a half smile at him. Lucas smiles back, leans down, and picks up the plastic sheeting at his feet before asking, "How about you help me set up this slip 'n slide before everyone gets here?"

Together, we get to work setting up the impressive DIY slide and the rest of the backyard for the most epic 4th of July party the Steel organization has ever seen.

Hours later, Lucas and Samantha's party is packed with teammates, spouses, partners, coaches, trainers, and our new owner, Trey McConnell. The entire party is amazing. Not only is the food incredible—my favorite being the double-patty, thick-stripped bacon burger—but the giant slip 'n slide turned out to be killer, especially when we added dish soap to it. I flew down it like Chevy Chase on the greased-up bowl in *National Lampoon's Christmas Vacation.*

When it gets dark, Samantha drops patriotically themed colored LED lights into the pool and things really get wild. Thankfully, the party is adults only because some of my teammates get a little crazy, losing clothes and becoming lewder and louder. By this time, most of the coaches and trainers have left. In fact, the only non-player remaining from the Steel team is Trey. His father, Timothy, the previous owner, had a heart attack and died the season before last, and Trey took over immediately. Most of us players haven't had much interaction with him, but coach says he's decent, just inexperienced. Seeing him alone, I figure this is my shot to shoot the shit with him, get a feel for the guy who signs my paycheck. *He doesn't look as tightly wound as he does at the arena.* "Mr. McConnell. It's good to see you here," I offer while extending my hand for a shake.

Shaking my hand firmly, I notice he looks to be a few years younger than me. I think I heard he was twenty-seven. "Thanks, Mika. I wanted a chance to get to know you guys outside the arena. I find it a bit stuffy there."

Is this guy for real? "Yeah?" Side-eyeing him, I

don't really mean to sound skeptical, but why does he want to get to know us? His father didn't. In fact, I can only recall a handful of extremely brief encounters I had with him. As long as we are doing our jobs, winning games and making the team successful, why would he care?

Taking a swig of the beer he's holding, he nods. "It's well documented how many games I've missed over the years. So, when I took over, I'd been labeled unsupportive of the Steel." *Where is he going with this?* Looking around the party, waiting to see if he'll continue, my eyes land on some of the newer guys like Ace and Rocco. They're in the pool goofing off with a few ladies. Two are familiar, Jasmine, Rocco's best friend since practically birth, and her good friend Nicole, who Jasmine seems to drag to most functions Rocco invites her to. After a moment of silence, I turn back to Trey and notice he's intently staring at Nicole. *I wonder if they know each other. If not, it looks like he'd like to.*

"Ahem." I clear my throat, hoping Trey will continue with what he was saying. Pointing to the group, I ask, "Have you met Ace and Rocco, yet?" He shakes his head and turns back to me with a question on his face. "How about the ladies? Do you know Nicole?" I ask, pointing out the woman he was just eye-fucking.

"Niiicooole." Trey drags out her name softly, like he's trying it on for size. *Interesting.* Trey looks at me and shakes his head. "No, I don't know her." Pausing for a moment, as if he's trying to recall what we'd been discussing, he then says, "What I'd said earlier about being unsupportive is false. The Chicago Steel has been my team since before my father bought it. I was away at college until a few years ago and unable to attend many games. After my father died, I was needed back here to take over. Thankfully, I'd already finished my degree, double majoring in both business and sports management."

Impressive. Guess he really is qualified, albeit a tad green. "Wow. Double major, that's impressive." Trying to make eye contact like momma always taught me, I see Trey again wishfully looking at Nicole. If he were an emoji, he'd for sure have heart eyes.

Looking back at me, Trey smiles. "I had always hoped one day I'd get the team. I just didn't assume it would be so soon or like this."

"Man, I'm sorry about your father. I should have said that earlier. I didn't know him well, but he was always fair to me."

Rolling his shoulders, he replies, "Thanks, Mika. I appreciate that. My father, the great Timothy McConnell, left some big shoes to fill, but I'm excited about the opportunity ahead of me. I've already learned I'm not him, nor will I do things the same way he did. Hopefully, you all will give me a chance to prove I want the best for the team and its players." *Coach was right. Trey seems like a good guy.*

"You want to grab lunch this week? I'm hoping to get to know the team outside of their files and stats," he asks me.

"Sounds good. I'm headed to Vegas next week with some of the guys. How about I call you when I'm back?"

"That's great. It's been nice talking to you. I'm going to go meet some of the other guys. After all, that's why I'm here, right?" He nervously laughs. *Why?*

"How about I help you out?" Walking to the edge of the pool, I holler out to my boys. "Ace and Rocco, come over and meet Trey, and bring Jasmine and Nicole with you." Smirking, I turn back to Trey and see his eyes go wide before he mouths, *"thank you."* After I introduce them, I pull away from the group and slip into the hot tub.

Not long after, Jase finds me relaxing and thrusts a red, white, and blue Jell-O shot into my hand. While slurping it down, he excitedly nudges me. "Can you believe it? Next week we will be doing this in Vegas, surrounded by hot, available chicks." I let out a half-hearted laugh, knowing going to Vegas with the guys is probably a mistake. Trying to make myself feel better, I justify it won't be as bad as I imagine. Plus, my being there might be helpful. I'll be able to temper them, set a good example of how to have fun responsibly. Right? *I hope anyway.*

It's been a long ass day, and I'm partied out, but I need to see Christian before I leave. Heading out of the pool house where I'd gone to change out of my pink flamingo swim shorts, I run into Lucas and ask if he's seen his soon-to-be brother-in-law. He shakes his head and points me to the grill. Walking away, I hear Lucas grumble something about stupid fucking s'mores, and I laugh.

Christian, decked out in a flirty floral apron, is definitely manning the grill, and sure enough, he's assembled a DIY s'more station. Before saying anything, I curiously observe him. Sensing me, he spins around, notices the confused look on my face, and lets out a boisterous laugh. Tipping my head to the s'more monstrosity cooking, I silently question him. Then there's that apron, but I'm not touching that with a ten-foot pole. *Confident fucker.*

"It's the 4th of July, and it's sacrilegious not to have s'mores today. Since Lucas and Samantha don't have a firepit in this huge-ass backyard, I came up with a suitable solution: grilled s'mores," he explains, as if it makes complete sense. Looking over at the grill, I see a deep foil pan stuffed full of graham cracker pieces, chocolate chunks, and extra-large marshmallows. I lick my lips. *It looks delicious and smells amazing.*

"Bro, I know you're intently watching your s'more concoction, but I just wanted to touch base before I headed out."

"Yeah, sure thing. Let's go over there where it's a little quieter," he says before he hands a large wooden spoon to a beautiful woman standing next to him.

"Monica, babe, can you watch our s'mores creation while I chat with Mika really quick?" Then he winks. *Such a flirt.* Despite the only light in the backyard being from an excessive number of twinkle lights and the floating pool lights, it's hard to miss the pink flush in her cheeks. Her attraction to him is even more apparent when she laughs. Standing there and watching their interaction, I can't help but wonder what the deal is between them. They seem more than friendly. But ever since I've known Christian, he's remained committed to bachelorhood. However, right now, seeing this, I'm questioning things. That or he's an amazing player.

"Christian, when can we meet up to discuss my upcoming contract negotiations?" I'm hoping sooner than later because I'd like to get it wrapped up. Plus, with my summer free, endorsement work would be easier.

"Are we just reviewing your old contract, or do I need to do some extra homework before we meet up?"

"Well, you know that my agent was old and I'm looking to have a younger representative who's willing to go to bat for me. Maybe secure me some endorsement deals. Lucas told me you are a master negotiator."

Christian grins at me, accepting my challenge. "How does this week look for you?"

I shake my head no. "Some of the guys and I are going to Vegas this week. How about the next week?"

"We can make that happen. Vegas?" His eyebrows raise in question, asking who I'm going with.

Laughing, I answer, "Jase, Rocco, and Ace."

Christian rolls his eyes and cautions, "Behave."

"Thanks, Dad," I grumble.

Although Christian isn't a professional athlete, he runs in the same social circles and knows what we're like. His warning tells me he doesn't want a scandalous new client. Saluting him, I promising to be on my best behavior. We fist bump before he heads back over to Monica. When he gets there, he wraps his arms around her, whispering in her ear. She squeals and squirms while he laughs. *There's a story there, I know it.*

Just as I'm about to leave the backyard, I spot Jase, Rocco, and Ace lined up on the side of the pool. Knowing they're crazy, especially when fueled by alcohol, I stop and watch, waiting to see what they're up to. Within seconds, I get my answer. Channeling the precision of a synchronized swim team, the guys flip perfectly into the center of the pool. A massive wave crests and splashes out of every corner of the pool, soaking anyone unlucky enough to be in the unofficial splash zone. Rubbing my head, I mutter to myself, "These guys are nuts, and next week I'm going to Vegas with them." *What have I gotten myself into?* Here's hoping I don't get roped into doing something stupid, like tattooing a rainbow unicorn on my ass.

Shaking my head, I walk out of the backyard, then I hear a high-pitched squeal. "Jasmine, what did you do to my shorts?" Rocco's voice is loud. Instead of a manly tone like you expect, the sound he emits is high and pitchy, much like a teenage girl who sucked too much helium.

Racing back into the backyard, I have to see what happened. There before me is Jasmine, laughing hysterically. She's bent over, grabbing her waist as Rocco angrily quasi-stalks over to her, tightly grasping his rapidly dissolving swim trunks. It's. Fucking. Hilarious. Without a doubt, the best practical joke I've ever seen. When they're standing toe-to-toe, Rocco drops the remaining pieces of the shorts, effectively disrobing himself, grabs Jasmine, and throws her over his shoulder. Unashamed, he sprints back to the pool, launching them both in.

Moments later, when they both emerge from the deep end, they're in hysterics. He's laughing and she's screaming. Looking to the side, I see Trey and Nicole engaged in a cozy conversation that is filled with subtle flirting between them. Not knowing how it'll turn out, but having been amused, I head out of the backyard and over to my new truck. It's been a long day and my ass is tired.

Driving back to my house, I notice how much quieter it is than the party. If my mind were up for thinking, and it's not, it'd be swimming with thoughts of her—the one I still don't know how to handle. As the miles pass by, I tell myself I'll deal with it when I get back from Vegas.

Chapter 7

Mika

Vegas was just what I'd expected. The boys and I had some fun, drank too much, and spent an excessive amount of money at the tables. However, we avoided any unnecessary jail time and crazy publicity, so all in all, it's a win in my book. The unease I'd felt before we left had been unwarranted. In fact, the only time I felt like an odd man out was at the end of the evenings. Unlike my teammates, I'd return to my room alone. Sure, I had multiple offers of company from an assortment of ladies, but not one tempted me. I couldn't seem to get my petite blonde neighbor out of my head. Honestly, it was making me crazy and cranky. The guys even mentioned it several times during our trip. Although, now that I'm home, I'm not feeling any better. I still haven't decided what I'm going to do about her. Perhaps that's why she's always on my mind?

* * *

When I get back from Vegas, I meet up with Christian like we planned, and start my transfer to Fox Sporting. Thankfully, it's pretty seamless, and by August I have new representation. Christian is already securing endorsements, one specifically with a newer vodka company. I know, funny, right? The Russian guy endorsing vodka. Cliché, much? I guess Christian thought he would capitalize on my heritage. Joke's on him. I've never been to the motherland, but I'm not about to turn down money for supporting something that is actually top notch. I've tasted it and I am totally on board with supporting it.

* * *

When training camp hits a few weeks later, I find myself busy with ice time, workouts, and dry land training. In fact, I'd argue I've been spending more time at the Steel arena than anywhere else.

Even though it's been over a month since we'd met, I've had a few sightings of my gorgeous neighbor, and I've noticed two things: there is never a man with her, and I'm still infatuated. Thinking too hard about that could get me into serious trouble because, right now, I need to concentrate on my upcoming season, not the hot AF vixen who shares a property line with me.

Trying to keep focused, I attempt to busy myself

during the weekends with things that take me away from home... and from her—my ultimate temptation. Despite my best efforts, I occasionally find myself outside in my yard, pretending to work. "You are pathetic!" I mutter to myself as I rake up the few leaves in my yard, pushing them around, hoping if I'm out there long enough, I'll get a chance to see her.

Since our run-in on the 4th of July, I haven't been able to get her off my mind. Everything I've tried to distract myself with has proved worthless. I've even agreed to attend the sixth birthday party for a teammate's son. When Cooper asked me to come, he explained that the theme of the party was hockey, and all I could think was, *how original.* Initially, I declined, saying I was busy washing my hair or something, but then he informed me I had to come because I was his son's favorite player. With a heaping dose of guilt, Coop informed me it would be shitty of me not to stop by. I agreed, telling him I'd be there. It's not like I had anything else to do. Going to a kids' party could be fun, right?

Chapter 8

Shiloh

I can hardly believe it's the middle of August. I need to get ready to head back to school. This year, Samuel and I will finally be at the same school. My job as a teacher's aide is for a second-grade teacher, and my son will be a kindergartener. This has been a summer of big changes, the biggest being that Samuel decided he wanted to be called Sam, and although it was an adjustment, I've done my best to accommodate his new request for independence.

During the summer break, we made trips to nearby parks or stayed home and played in the sprinkler. We filled many hours with chalk drawing, blowing bubbles, and eating our weight in popsicles. It was an incredibly busy summer, but we enjoyed it and had the sun-kissed skin to prove it. In fact, Sam practiced his counting skills on the freckles that had popped out all over my face.

Our messiest challenge of the summer was potty-training Lian. The first few days were especially hairy, with accidents and tears galore—not always Lian's. Nevertheless, we were persistent, and Lian loved trying to aim at the Cheerios bobbing in the toilet, squealing when he hit his target. Unfortunately, seeing that he was only two, my walls, floor, and I were hit with better accuracy than the round-shaped breakfast cereal floating in the porcelain bowl. M&M's as a reward for pooping in the potty was simply brilliant. I wish I knew who to thank for that gem of wisdom; they deserved an enormous basket of treats. Of all the things to learn during potty training, Lian caught on quickly and mastered that in no time. Thankfully, because of that, I didn't experience any of the horror stories I'd heard from other moms. Their stories of poop-smeared walls, abandoned diapers, and floating logs during bath time all made me cringe and gag.

Another reward suggestion was stickers. The happy, sticky reward became public enemy number one on day two when I discovered Lian had affixed them to everything he came across; cabinets, televisions, doors, his brother. Sam was such a trooper during that time, demonstrating unimaginable patience for a five-year-old. Time and time again, I was impressed when Sam praised his brother for all he accomplished, instead of chiding him for the accidents he had.

With fall rapidly approaching, I know I need to get Sam into an organized sport or activity to help him with his excess energy. Otherwise, he might drive his teacher crazy. After searching the community for kid-friendly activities, it took weeks for him to try several of the town's offerings. One weekend, he took part in a free trial for karate but realized quickly he wasn't into it. Another weekend, he tried basketball, but we learned he was too small to be successful at that. Music lessons were a hard no, as I didn't want to invite migraines into my life. And I'd just about given up hope when I saw ice skating lessons advertised on the information board of our grocery store. Sam seemed leery at first, and I wondered if it might be a good fit.

The weekend before school starts, we go to the ice rink, just the two of us. Monica agreed to watch Lian for me in case I could convince Sam to give it a shot.

As soon as Sam walks up to the rink and sees everyone skating, he's hooked and can't wait to try it. I chat with the employee who organizes lessons and she gives us a pair of skates to try. We shuffle over to a well-worn carpeted bench. Trying to be careful with the blades, I attempt to put Sam's skates on without hurting myself. I'm not very experienced with skating, so I'm nervous about how we'll even start. One thing I remind myself of as I lace his skates is that if Sam falls, it probably won't hurt too badly since he doesn't have too far to fall.

Just as I finish lacing his skates, a man behind me clears his throat. Thinking I'm in the way, I push my stuff to the side and apologize as I move closer to my son.

"Excuse me," a deep, dreamy, masculine voice says, sending shivers down my spine.

"Am I still in the way?" I whisper innocently over my shoulder, still looking bizarrely at the skate I've been struggling to tie.

"No, you aren't in the way at all. But I'm guessing you've never tied skates before because you aren't tying them tight enough and your son could get hurt," the voice answers confidently.

The man steps to my side, and his gigantic frame comes into view. Still hunkered over Sam's skates, I rotate my head toward him, and my eyes eat up his muscular body like a starved person at an all-you-can-eat buffet. *Hello.* When I finally reach his face, a breathy "oh" escapes my lips. Losing my balance, I fall back on my butt. He smiles widely at me. Embarrassed, I feel my cheeks grow hot. *Super!* I just made a complete fool of myself in front of... my... my gorgeous neighbor. The same one I've been trying to excise from my brain since our brief run-in months before. Let's hope he doesn't recognize me.

"Here we go," Mika, the hot neighbor I cyber stalked after I met him, says as he reaches down and pulls me up. His strong hands caress my arms as he effortlessly lifts me, carefully setting me beside him. His size dwarfs me, making me feel small and dainty, kind of like a Polly Pocket, that child's toy. As I look up into his dreamy brown eyes, I notice they're extremely focused on me. The attention making me giddy, my body pulses with desire. Still holding on to my biceps, his touch electrifies me, sending bursts of excitement rushing through my entire being.

He jolts me back to the present when he speaks again. "Mind if I retie them? Skates are kind of critical to my job, and I've been tying them since I was five," he says before his gaze travels over to Sam, who's still seated on the bench, kicking his feet back and forth, waiting patiently.

"Please," is all I can squeak out before I lower myself next to Sam on the bench. Still mortified, I watch as Mika squats down in front of Sam. Instantly, I'm drawn to his muscular thighs, which are pushing the confines of his jeans. Trying not to be too obvious, I focus on my hands resting in my lap. I intertwine my fingers so I don't fidget and look even more awkward than I already have.

"Hey, bud. Mind if I help you?" Mika asks Sam before reaching for the skates. Sam nods before Mika unlaces the ill-tied laces. Using precision, in mere moments, he's expertly retied them. Once finished, he pulls Sam's pant legs over the skates before he shifts his focus back to me.

"First time skating?" he asks.

I shyly nod. "That obvious?"

Mika laughs and then gives me a sexy grin that makes my heart flutter. "Just remember, with skates, you need to tie them tight and wear good socks that will not only keep his feet warm but give a snug fit." We stare at each other without more words being exchanged. The electricity between us is unreal. It's like I've never experienced before.

Excitedly moving next to me on the bench, Sam kicks his skates back and forth, eager to try them out. "Thank you so much," I gush to my hot neighbor as I stand up, helping Sam to his feet. Being young, it doesn't take long for Sam to get his balance, while I'm still feeling off-kilter from my exchange with my amazingly handsome neighbor. I'm not ready to leave the comfort of my running shoes, so I elect not to join Sam in wearing skates. It would be tempting fate if I strapped sharp blades to my feet. Chaos or unintended injury would definitely result. Sam tries his first steps tentatively, and although he wobbles, he recovers quickly, and in no time he's comfortably walking around on the thick rubber floor. When he's ready to try skating, he looks to Mika, and in a little voice says, "Thank you for helping me and my mom."

"Anytime, buddy," Mika answers before giving him a fist bump.

Ready to go, Sam puts his tiny hand in mine and pulls me toward the ice. Holding up my hand, I give a little wave to Mika. As I do it, I'm reminded of the one he'd given me from his doorstep months ago, the day we first met. Our eyes lock and I mouth, *"thank you"* to him, and he smiles. *Be still my heart.*

Getting onto the ice is harder than it looks. Sam and I watch several people before we even attempt it. Our first lap around the rink is painfully slow as we stick near the wall in case extra support is necessary. When we finally complete an entire lap, I feel amazing. *Victory!* An enormous smile spreads across Sam's little face, making me feel incredible, like we've conquered something monumental. Apparently, Sam loves skating, and I know lessons will definitely be in our future. If he enjoys this so much, I wonder if he'll become interested in hockey.

Just thinking of hockey reminds me of Mika, and I look over to the bench we'd abandoned, wondering if he'll still be there watching us. He isn't, and my heart drops. "Stupid girl," I mutter to myself. Why would he stay to make sure we're fine? We aren't special. I bet he didn't even recognize me. There was no way he'd even remember that we've already met. Over the past months, I've relived that brief interaction a handful of times. I'd also perused the internet, searching for recent pictures and information on him. That's not creepy, right? Maybe I have a bit of a problem; a minor crush, if you will. Apparently, though, today needed to happen so I could recognize that this thing between us is entirely one-sided and I need to move on.

Halfway through our second lap, a deep voice calls out from behind us, "Nice going, bud. You look like a natural on those skates." Mika skates past us, looking completely at ease, and my heart feels like it's going to explode out of my chest. *He's here, he's here.* Heat crawls over my body. Suddenly, I'm feeling overheated and needy. Even though Mika's only a few feet away, the heat radiating between us could melt ice caps in the Arctic. When Sam hears Mika's compliment, he squeezes my hand and points to Mika, the already present smile stretching wider across his adorable face. I feel another tug on my hand as Sam tries to skate faster, hoping to catch up to this man who is slowly becoming his new hero. *Thump, thump.* My heart is galloping in my chest.

Seeing my son happy fills me with joy, and I glance over at Mika, who's skating backward effortlessly. His eyes are locked on me. He moves with such confidence and grace, almost like he's dancing, and I have to admit I find it sexy as hell. The shift of his trim hips, the flex in his leg muscles, the chiseled lines of his mouth, his focused eyes that are unwavering as he intently stares at me.

"H-how are you doing that?" I stutter as I motioned to his skating.

"It's easy, you'll see." Then he smiles, and it's equal parts adorable and dangerous. I suspect many women have fallen victim to his charms, and that alone should make me leery, but it doesn't. His deep brown eyes not only scream sexy but genuine, and I find myself wanting to trust him. Is he saying that he'll still be around when I learn to skate? *Not likely.* This, right here and now, is a onetime occurrence. That, I can guarantee. After he's done helping today, he'll forget about us entirely. I'm sure of it. Famous people don't remember nobodies.

Mika must have been at the rink for some other event and saw us struggling. In fact, he probably felt bad for a single mom and offered to help. He was just being a nice guy. He wasn't looking for a relationship, and honestly, neither was I. However, if one skated into my life, I might be open to it, especially if it were with the right guy.

Sam tugs at my hand again, pulling me from my thoughts, and points to Mika. "I want to skate like him."

Before I can even explain how much time he'd have to put in, Mika swoops in. "It takes time and practice to learn to skate, buddy. But I know, if you want it bad enough, you can do it." Sam nods excitedly, accepting Mika's word as law.

Is this guy for real? He literally just said the perfect thing to my son. Full hero worship is in effect as Sam grins up at Mika. He has stars brightly shining in his little blue eyes. *I'm in trouble.*

We finish the second lap faster than the first, and Mika moves to skate alongside me. Our hands brush, and the touch sends tingles up my arm. My fingers tentatively reach out, wanting to hold his hand, but at the last second, I pull them back. Being this close to him makes me feel uneasy. Can he see how nervous he makes me? I'm sweating even though we're in an ice rink. How is that possible?

"Could I take Sam for a lap or two? Maybe give him a small taste of speed?" Mika asks as he gazes at me with tender eyes. His expression suggests he understands his question's a big ask. *No, you cannot.* Despite the undeniable attraction to Mika, and the good vibes I'm getting from him, my hackles still rise. Hurrying over to the wall, I pull Sam with me. With a confused look on his handsome face, Mika follows us. He stops short of the boards, faces me, and kicks one skate behind the other before resting his hand on the wall. Already annoyed, it further bothers me that he looks so comfortable on the ice, like it's his job. *Wait, it literally is his job.* "Urgh," I mumble to myself. I'm doing everything I can to stay upright and he looks like a freaking model. *Stupid, sexy, cocky hockey player.*

Pointing my finger in his chest, I say in my best momma bear growl, "You are a stranger, and I'm not letting you take my son anywhere." I pull Sam tighter into my side, protecting him.

Mika understands my warning immediately and takes an obvious step backward before he responds. "You're right. I shouldn't have asked that. I thought you'd recognize me and that you'd feel comfortable. That was my mistake. I'm really sorry."

I shake my head back and forth, indignation bubbling up within me, causing me to spew out my next words. "Recognize you? So, because you're some famous, hot-shot professional athlete, I should automatically assume you are a good guy and you won't hurt my son?"

Standing defensively, I stare him down. Even as I try to make myself bigger by crossing my arms, puffing out my chest, and scowling, I question if I really think he's a bad guy. But, when it comes down to it, I don't. Even though our time has been limited, I haven't gotten the creeper vibe from him. I'd only sensed an incredibly hot chemistry between us. Maybe he's just a nice guy and his offer to help Sam was entirely innocent? Was that possible? I really don't know. What I know is that as a single mom, I'm the only one to protect my boys. I can't afford to give just anyone the benefit of the doubt. They had to earn my trust before they could spend time alone with my kids.

Angered, I step back, my eyes darting around, looking for the exit. I'm more than ready to leave. Signing Sam up for skating lessons will have to wait for another day because, right now, it's time for us to go. Honestly, we were here longer than I expected, because I wasn't sure Sam would catch on so quickly.

Mika reaches out and grabs my arm, stilling me before I can escape. His grip is tentative, like he doesn't want to hurt me, but he doesn't want me to go. Anxious words tumble from his delicious lips. "Wait. I wasn't implying that you should feel comfortable with me because I'm slightly famous. We're neighbors, aren't we? Didn't I meet you a few months ago? Or do I have you confused with someone else?"

Mika scratches his head as if he's genuinely baffled. "Maybe I'm wrong... but don't you have two boys?"

Startled by his recognition, I freeze. *Holy shit.* Mika, the insanely hot man standing in front of me, the one I've dreamed of for months, remembers me and my boys. Replaying his earlier words, he's offering to help my son learn to skate. But months earlier, after hearing the boys in the car, he'd jetted off like he was Usain Bolt running the 100-meter dash. Back then, I'd just assumed he wasn't into kids. *What changed?*

Nodding my head, I reply, "Y-yes. You're right. We are neighbors and I do have two sons. My girlfriend Monica has my youngest because he's only two and not ready for skating." Mika nods.

"Your girlfriend is watching him? What about your husband? Or boyfriend?" Registering his questions, I'm again distracted by just how attractive he is. The casual sweep of his dark brown hair, the melt-in-your-mouth, not-in-your-hand milk chocolate brown eyes; lips that are dreamy, soft, plump and inviting. All that, an insanely well-muscled body, and he's nice too. *Freaking unicorn.*

"Yes, my girlfriend. I don't have a husband or boyfriend. It's just me and my boys," I reply clearly, wondering where his questions are going.

"Interesting." Mika smirks. *What does that mean?* My heart somersaults.

He clears his throat. "Well, now that the air is clear, I'm officially introducing myself. My name is Mika Popov-Stevenson. I'm your next-door neighbor and the assistant-captain of the Chicago Steel, though from the hot-shot professional athlete, I think you already figured that out." He extends his hand to me, smirks, and puffs out his chest. My eyes widen with wonder. *Wow.* My fingers involuntarily twitch, desperately wanting to trace over all the ridges I know that have been covered by his sexy, long-sleeve, gray Henley. Months ago, when we'd first met, his naked chest had blindsided me. *"Unforgettable,"* I mouth to myself. There's no denying it. He's in phenomenal shape.

I extend my hand to him, all the while hoping it isn't too sweaty. "I'm Shiloh Erickson and this is my son, Samuel, or Sam. My younger son is Lian. It's good to 'officially' meet you," I say with a timid smile.

Mirroring it, Mika remains silent. Panicking, I feel like I need to fill the silence. "I guess now I could come knocking if I needed to borrow some sugar?" I nervously laugh. *Why did I just say that? I'm such a moron.* It'd been way too long since I flirted, and obviously, I'm failing at it, miserably.

Mika laughs awkwardly. "Well, I guess you could, but I'd be more likely to have eggs than sugar."

I just stare, afraid to open my mouth again. Mika further explains, "I mean, you'd be welcome to whatever I have. I just don't have many sweets in the house because of the strict diet I follow."

"Oh!" I say, surprised by his answer. "I guess that makes sense. The strict diet thing. I mean, you are a professional athlete and you're in amazing shape. Sugar would be smart to avoid if you want to keep those incredible abs, right?" *Shiloh, stop talking.*

Mika snickers, raises his eyebrows, then smirks at me. My eyes follow as he trails his hands down his abs, winking when he hits the top of his jeans. Did my panties just disintegrate?

"So, Shiloh... you think I'm in amazing shape and I have incredible abs? Have you checked me out?" he cockily inquires as his smirk morphs into a sexy grin. *Kill me, please.* Mortified, there is no good way to answer him.

My cheeks grow warm, and I'm confident they've turned a lovely shade of red. The rink suddenly feels a thousand degrees hotter. "Umm... well... b-being a professional athlete, following a strict diet, and what you looked like when we first met months ago, I'm just assuming you still have a nice body." *Danger! Danger!* My brain screams at me. Shifting my feet, I wonder if it would be possible for the ice rink to crack open and swallow me whole. Could this conversation be any more embarrassing? I just admitted that I'd totally checked Mika out and that I liked what I'd seen. What a rookie move. I truly suck at flirting.

He responds playfully, "Sure, we'll go with that." The growl of his voice sends shivers through my body.

How did we get here?

Clearing his throat and the air, he asks, "Since we aren't strangers anymore, can I please take Sam around the rink a few times? I think he'd like to go faster than a tortoise." Mika laughs and gives me another knee-weakening smile. All I can do is smile back. I'm sure I look ridiculous, probably like a love-struck teen fawning over her heartthrob.

Looking down at Sam, I see his eyes are filled with hope. *I can't possibly say no.* "Okay, you can take him for a few laps. I'll be over there at the registration desk signing him up for lessons." Then, because I'm still hesitant, I ask, "Are you sure you've got this?"

He gives Sam a fist bump and then looks deep into my eyes. "Shiloh. I've got this. We got this. Don't we, Sam?" Mika's confidence is unwavering and it steadies my nerves. Releasing Mika's intense gaze, I turn my attention to Sam, who's nodding and smiling at me excitedly. Releasing Sam's tiny hand, I give it to Mika. They waste no time skating away. My heart clenches, reminding me that a part of me is leaving. Slowly, I turn toward the boards, looking for the nearest exit, but before I step off the ice, I find Mika and Sam; their smiles and laughter assure me they're having a great time. My heart flips excitedly.

Signing Sam up for lessons is fast and simple, and after I'm done, I'm eager to see the progress Sam has made. It's incredible to watch as Mika helps Sam turn his skate-waddling into walking and then gliding.

When he's mastered that, Mika turns backward, facing Sam, and holds both of my son's hands in his much larger ones. As they move around the rink, I witness Sam's confidence grow, and my heart expands in my chest. Together, they move with precision and grace. It is absolutely beautiful to watch. I'm in total awe.

Standing there watching their interaction, I realize this is what's been missing in my boys' lives. A strong male presence. One who wants to teach them things and be there for them. I'm not saying Mika is that presence. But right now, I'm incredibly aware of how important it is. As the boys have gotten older, I understand that I don't know anything about being a guy. And that fact will become even more apparent as the boys get older. I'm confident I can teach Sam and Lian manners, how to treat people. But for certain things, I'm definitely lacking a male perspective. Some things I know I could look up online, like how to tie a tie or what the best razor was for when they start shaving, but I have no clue about how it feels to be a guy. Just knowing that one day I'll have to have "the talk" with them fills me with dread. It isn't the conversation about babies or even contraception, it's how on earth I would describe what it feels like to have an erection or wet dream. The responsibility of it all is daunting, and it's especially hard not to think about when I'm watching my son blossom under the attention

Mika is giving him. Attention he obviously desperately needs and craves, especially the older he gets.

Being a teacher's aide in elementary school, you'd think I'd be tuned in to how a child's behavior and development is affected by both female and male influences, but with my boys, I've apparently put blinders on, ignoring the necessary male contribution, because it was never available. Now that I'm aware of this missing piece of their development, what am I going to do about it? Who could I ask to step into that role? *A problem for another day, focus on the present. Perhaps the man in front of you.*

In my minor cyberstalking after we'd first met, my search revealed that Mika didn't do long-term relationships or relationships in general. Plus, if he did ever decide to date, he'd probably avoid a single mom. Since our coupling is improbable, I need to stop hoping what's between us is more than Mika just being a nice guy. Fantasies involving him are dangerous to my heart, and the best thing would be to push them away before they take root and ruin me. As I stand there watching, I promise myself that after today I won't think about Mika as anything but our neighbor. *That's believable, right?*

After Mika and Sam have skated a couple laps, I wave them over. Moving toward me quickly, both are wearing the most amazing smiles, and I find myself delighted. You'd never know that only hours ago, Mika and Sam were complete strangers. Their playful banter suggests they are now buddies. Their dialogue is both effortless and comfortable. A few inches from the boards, Mika lets go of Sam's hand and allows him to skate the remaining distance to me on his own. *Go, Sam, go.* Sam does it without help and I clap and squeal my excitement. He's learning to skate and only after a short time with Mika's help. Sam runs into the wall in front of me and lets out a dramatic groan. Apparently, stopping is something he still has to master.

"Momma, did you see? Did you? I skated all by myself." He beams with confidence, and I nod excitedly as Mika skates up behind him. A proud, radiant smile, which is one hundred percent real, stretches all the way to his high cheekbones. And in an instant, I know Mika would easily destroy me if I ever gave him the chance.

"I saw you, Sam. You were a rockstar out there. I bet in no time you'll be flying around the rink. Good thing I signed you up for lessons, because before long, you'll probably show Mika up." I probably didn't need to include that last part, because in reality he'd probably never have another chance to skate with Mika, but I wanted him to be proud of himself and of what he accomplished.

"You think?" he excitedly questions in his tender voice. I nod. Sam then turns to Mika and sticks his hand out like a gentleman seeking a handshake, telling him, "Thank you for helping me."

Mika, apparently shocked by the gesture, takes Sam's hand and returns a firm handshake. "You're welcome, bud. But you did it, and you were a natural." Tears well up in my eyes at his kind sentiments, and I remain silent because I can't express how much I appreciate the help and encouragement Mika has given Sam today. Hopefully, Sam's upcoming lessons will be with someone who is as kind as Mika has been. *One can wish. I guess if I were truly wishing, it would be that Mika would be the one to teach Sam.*

I glance from Mika over to Sam and grin at my son's expression. Cue full hero worship. My son has found a real-life idol, which makes me both happy and sad. On one hand, I'm happy that Sam had such a positive male interaction, but I'm sad at the thought that it was probably an anomaly. Needing to squash the uncomfortable feeling that thought settles in my chest, I tell Sam, "We need to get going and pick up Lian at Monica's." Disappointment shrouds his face, the perma-smile he'd been sporting all afternoon instantly falling from his chapped lips.

"Five more laps, Momma?" he begs in his squeaky, little voice.

I level my mom stare at him and firmly answer, "Two more, but only if Mika has the time. I doubt he wanted to spend his entire day at the rink." I soften my look and notice Sam staring at Mika with his best puppy dog eyes, pleading.

Mika winks at me, then smiles at Sam. "There's nothing I'd rather do. Let's go, bud." Before I can give any further instructions, they're off. Five laps later, they return, laughing. On their last lap, Mika challenged Sam to a race and he'd let Sam win. *Swoon. This man.* It was adorable to watch my son fanboy. And if I had to admit, I'm also quite taken with Mika.

Sam throws his hands high in the air and shouts, "I won!" Then he looks from me to Mika for confirmation.

"You did. So, what does the winner get? We never decided on the stakes," Mika asks, then patiently waits for my son's response.

Sam thinks for a moment and then confidently replies, "Well, when I beat Momma, I get a special treat like ice cream. Right, Momma?" Sam's eyes whip to me for confirmation.

I nod, but then caution, "That's right. That's *our* deal, but Mika doesn't owe you anything. He spent hours with you today already, teaching you to skate. I think that was payment enough, don't you?" I look to Mika, hoping he'll understand I'm giving him a free pass if he wants it. *Please don't take it.*

However, when I turn back to Sam, I see his shoulders are slumped and there's a sad frown on his adorable face. His puppy dog eyes are spot on and I try to muffle a laugh when Mika replies, "I really don't mind. How about we go grab an ice cream cone? My treat. I'll get one for you too, Shiloh." The way Mika says my name makes my body shudder. And then he winks. *Lord, have mercy, this man.* Send help. I may not survive this. Or at least my panties won't. Not if he keeps winking.

Chapter 9

Mika

This afternoon was unexpected, but it had been the best one I'd had in a long time.

After appearing and helping at the birthday party for Cooper's son, I'd walked around the rink and spotted someone who looked familiar: my uber-hot neighbor.

All afternoon, I felt drawn to Shiloh. Our chemistry was off the charts, and Sam was an incredible little dude. The hours we spent together flew by and I wasn't ready to say goodbye, so when Sam asked about the reward for winning our race, I jumped at the opportunity to spend more time with them.

* * *

Growing up, I'd always wanted a brother and a father, but neither had happened. As a kid, when wishing for a father, I wanted a male influence in my life to teach me the things that my mama couldn't. However, until junior high, I hadn't been lucky enough to find one. Then Mr. Bagley, my social studies teacher, entered my life and changed it for the better. Mr. Bagley had given our class an assignment where we were required to dress up and present to our peers. I'd shown up to class on my assigned presentation day, unable to tie the tie my mama had purchased for me at the thrift store. Mr. Bagley, a father of three boys, took pity on me and showed me how. From that day on, he made me his mission. During lunch, he taught me things a father would.

His kindness is something I will never forget and I'll forever be grateful for.

Even when I'd moved on to high school, he remained a constant influence in my life. Not only was his instruction appreciated, his advice and willingness to listen were irreplaceable. His presence had been invaluable, and I'd forever miss him. Mr. Bagley had died of an arteriovenous malformation (AVM) during my second year in the league. Unfortunately, it had been discovered only after it had ruptured, sending him to the emergency room and then into the ICU. It was heartbreaking. Hearing his eldest son Jacob's tear-soaked wail on the other end of the line telling me the most important man in my life never regained consciousness after arriving in the ER, broke me. Years later, Mrs. Judith, his wife and second mother to me, was still struggling with the loss of her soulmate. Just months before his death, they'd celebrated their twenty-fifth wedding anniversary. Theirs had been the only happy marriage I'd ever seen up close. The love they shared seemed rare and unattainable, only for the deserving. And it was something I desperately wanted, even if I wasn't willing to admit that out loud.

On nights that I'd been at their house for dinner, while their boys were playing video games, I'd often watch Mr. and Mrs. Bagley wash dishes together. During that sacred time, I'd seen them laugh, flirt, and help each other, all while taking care of their family. Mr. Bagley's death was a complete shock and had rocked my world. It had been too painful, and although I'd made it back for his funeral, I hadn't visited Judith or their boys since.

Knowing I never wanted to hurt as badly as I did when he died, I'd become an expert at separating myself from my feelings, not allowing myself to get attached to anyone. Until now. Something about being around my neighbor and her son changed things. Determined to figure out why, I stand up and make my way to the rink door.

Skating onto the ice to join them, I feel riddled with anticipation and shaky from nerves. It's worse than when I'd asked Hannah to senior prom._One afternoon in late April of that year, I visited Mr. Bagley to hang out, and prom came up, and this situation reminds me of that conversation.

"Mika, isn't prom in a few weeks? Are you going?"

Pulling off my baseball cap, I ran my hand through my hair and muttered, "I don't have a date, so I'm probably not going. I don't know."

Looking at me, he squinted his eyes, questioning, "Is there someone you want to ask?"

"Maybe." I admitted while I paced around his garage, my body filled with nervous energy.

"Maybe?" Mr. Bagley asked.

Stopping, I looked at him. "Then I guess the answer is yes. Over the last few weeks, I've wanted to ask a girl I've liked all year. But every time I think I'm ready to do it, I chicken out, afraid she'll say no."

"Son, I understand. Women can be impossible to read, to know what they are thinking. What I've learned is the best way to find out is simply just to ask."

Pushing out a deep breath, I asked, "but what if she says no? I'd be so embarrassed."

Mr. Bagley nodded his head. "Yes, I suppose you might be. But if she says yes, you have a date for your senior prom. What's the harm in asking? If you don't you'll always wonder."

Everything about this afternoon has been unexpectedly perfect, even our minor tiff. The entire exchange we'd had provided me the opportunity to learn more about both Shiloh and Sam. Sure, Shiloh is undeniably beautiful, but I now recognized there is so much more to her. And I'm unbelievably impressed. Not only is she kind and considerate, she is also a fierce protector. That alone is incredibly attractive. In one afternoon, this siren has drawn me into her lair and tempted me without even realizing. She is one-hundred percent real and I pray for the opportunity to get to know her better. After spending some one-on-one time with Sam, I suspect he and his mom are similar. The things I'm most impressed with about him are his independence, hard work, and maturity. For his age, the way he behaves speaks volumes not just of him, but of the job Shiloh has done in raising him. He is the coolest kid I've ever met. And meeting Lian is something I am definitely looking forward to.

Chapter 10

Shiloh

I hadn't expected Mika to spend any more time with us, seeing as how we already monopolized pretty much his entire day. But when he offered ice cream to celebrate Sam's win, I couldn't say no. It wasn't like I was looking for an excuse to spend more time with my hunky hockey player neighbor. *Right, keep telling yourself that.*

"Are you sure?" I half-heartedly ask him before we leave the arena, hoping his offer of ice cream is real.

He smiles and nods at me. "Yep. I'm looking forward to this. I know Sprinkles 'N Scoops is near our neighborhood. Does that work? Do you need to get Lian first?" *How considerate is he?*

Sam tugs at my hand, again wearing mopey eyes. "Do we have to get Lian first?"

I hush him before answering. "Let me text Monica and see if she minds watching him longer."

ME

Hi. Hope Lian is behaving himself. Would it be possible for you to watch him for a bit longer? Sam and I were invited on an ice cream date by a HOT professional hockey player.

MONICA

WHAT??? How HOT are we talking? On a scale of ten, where does he fall?

ME

Off the charts. He's a solid fifteen.

MONICA

(Fanning myself gif) Take all the time you need. Lian and I are doing great. We'll see you whenever you get here.

ME

Thank you so much! I'll text you when we're on our way.

Turning back to them, I school my giddiness and grin. "Sprinkles 'N Scoops sounds fabulous, and Monica can watch Lian for a little longer. We'll meet you there."

It's a short drive to the ice cream shop, and within ten minutes, we're standing in line pondering our options.

Mika squats down, lowers his voice and says, "Sam our big winner. What are you getting?"

"Rainbow sherbet. It's my favorite," Sam answers.

Rubbing his chin reflectively Mika replies, "I don't think I've ever had it. If it's as good as you say it is, I may have to change my order." A loud *hmph* falls from my mouth. I can't see this mountain of a man eating the colored sugar concoction my son has just recommended. Mika's gorgeous head whips up, looking at me. *"What?"* He mouths. Tilting my head sideways, I give him a questioning look.

Unaware of the silent conversation Mika and I are having, Sam tugs on my hand. "What are you having, Momma?"

Still staring at Mika, I answer, "A single scoop of Dutch chocolate. It's my favorite."

Sam sticks out his tongue. "that's so boring. You should pick something fun, like me."

Mika laughs, and the deep melodic sound warms my body, making me want to unzip my winter coat.

"Okay, folks. What are we getting today?" the pimply teenage employee of Sprinkles 'N Scoops asks.

Mika steps up to the counter. "We'll have two scoops of rainbow sherbet in a bowl for our big champ here. A single scoop of Dutch chocolate in a cone for the lady."

"What type of cone? Waffle or cake?" the employee asks.

Mika turns to me and whispers, "Shiloh, waffle or cake?" His eyes are heated.

Suddenly parched, I lick my lips and his eyes go wide.

"Cone type?" the teen asks again.

"Shiloh," Mika says.

"Cake. I'll have the cake cone, please." Mika has me locked in his stare, and the energy coming off him is packed with pheromones, luring me in.

"Sir. Sir. Sir!" the teen says, sounding annoyed the last time.

"Momma. Your cone. It's melting," Sam informs me, breaking me from the spell Mika has me under.

"Oops." I chuckle while grabbing my cone and some napkins.

"What can I get you?" the teen asks Mika.

In a deep, sinfully sexy voice, Mika answers, "A banana split with vanilla, rainbow sherbet, and Dutch chocolate ice cream."

After scooping the ice cream, the teen asks, "What toppings do you want?"

"Fudge, whipped cream, peanuts, and cherries, please.

"While the sundae is being assembled, I poke Mika. "Interesting selection."

He smiles at me. "Yeah?"

"It's funny. I don't think I've had a banana split since I was a child."

Considering that, he leans into me. "A banana split is kind of the perfect dessert for an athlete. It includes dairy, fruit, and protein." Of course it is. Mika is adorable. Apparently, he's still in touch with his inner child.

Mika pays for our treats and then ushers us to an outside table. The flower-adorned, rusted metal table teeters off balance, but it'd been warmed by the afternoon sun, inviting us in. Setting my ice cream on the table, I drag over another of the heavy chairs and join them. Indulging in the perfectly sweet and creamy dessert, I savor the continued warmth of the fall afternoon.

Just being a silent observer to Mika and Sam's conversation while I enjoy my decadent treat proves to be very informative. The interaction between them is friendly and funny. After learning about all Sam's likes and dislikes, Mika asks about Lian, and Sam's sweet response almost brings me to tears. "Lian is the best!"

Sam loves his brother, but watching him now, that affection is coming close to how he feels toward Mika. It isn't hard to miss, even after a short time together, that Sam definitely looks up to Mika. Even better is that Mika seems genuinely interested, hanging on Sam's every word and actively responding.

When it feels like the conversation is wrapping up, I remind myself we need to get going. As I turn to Sam to tell him, I notice he's been looking at Mika with fascination and adoration. Mika notices too, and the smile he gives back to my son makes my heart feel lighter than it has in years. The rapport these two are building is amazing, and I wish I could guarantee it would last, but I don't know if that's possible. After all, we're just neighbors.

Before I can say anything, Sam shocks me, asking, "Momma, can Mika come over for dinner some night?"

I begin to shake my head. Ice cream was one thing, but dinner *in our house* is another. Panic sets in at the request. Sam isn't asking for a playmate to come over. He's asking for my ridiculously hot neighbor, who, over the course of a few hours, I've developed a major crush on, to come over.

"Please, please, please," Sam pleads. I look from his longing eyes over to Mika's face to gauge his reaction. Instead of a panic-stricken expression, I see unabashed happiness, and I'm confused. Why would a gorgeous professional hockey player want to have dinner at my house with my two young boys? Dinner would be a recipe for chaos, right? Uncertain, I finally answer Sam, nodding my approval, and Sam lets out a hoot.

Turning to Mika, I say, "You're welcome to come for dinner if you'd like. No pressure, I promise." Honestly, I don't know what he'll say.

Mika sits back in the chair he absolutely dwarfs with his size and thinks for a moment. With each second that ticks by, the more nervous I become. I really don't want him to say yes just because he feels pressured by my five-year-old. Meanwhile, Sam looks back and forth between us, trying to wait patiently for an answer. Just as I'm about to tell Mika to forget it, he turns to Sam and answers, "I'd love to come to dinner at your house. But, Sam, I'm nervous. Do you think Lian will like me?" Sam nods his head frantically before he jumps from his chair and dances like he's competing on a reality dance show, thrusting his hips, flailing his arms, and popping his butt. Meanwhile, my heart is freaking out in my chest, pounding out some beat I've never heard before. Its speed makes me feel lightheaded. Once Sam settles down, Mika and I discuss details and exchange numbers. Letting an inner squeal go and doing a mental fist pump, I try to keep it cool. I have a professional athlete's number, and he's coming to dinner at my house. Holy shit. *Shit. What am I going to serve?*

"Thanks again for the ice cream, Mika. We really need to get over to pick up Lian so I can get the boys dinner and to bed at a normal hour."

Mika stands up from his chair, gathers the trash, and throws it away. When he returns to us, he looks at me and asks, "Can I either call or text you this week?"

I blush at his question. Just the idea of Mika calling me has my stomach fluttering as if a million butterflies are trying to get loose. "Yeah, either is great," I answer, trying to sound calm, despite feeling like a tightly wound ball of overly excited nerves.

Mika smiles and then gives Sam a fist bump before he heads off toward his truck. Sam and I stand there and watch as Mika waves before he drives off. *What a great day it's been!*

Chapter 11

Mika

Just from the time we spent together today, I really like Shiloh and completely understand she's a package deal. If Lian is as cool as Sam, I know I'll be a complete goner for this little family. However, I question if they'll want me.

Our ice cream date is amazing. Sam is quick to share his favorite things with me. While I disagree with him about superheroes—Hulk is far superior to all others, because he, of course, smashes things, and being a defenseman on a professional hockey team, having to do the same thing for my job, Hulk seems like the obvious choice to support—I can see why Iron Man would be his choice.

Sam, Shiloh, and I get along great. Our interactions are natural and comfortable. The only thing that would add to it is to have Lian with us. I also wish Shiloh would talk more, but with a Chatty Cathy for a son, I understand that isn't always possible. Or maybe Sam is just like that because I'm new to him and he has so much to tell me. I don't want to make unfair assumptions about his personality because I know how terrible those can be.

When I'd first started playing in the league for the Steel, people made comments about the fact I was Russian and I always looked angry. Truth was, I wasn't angry at all. I was just quiet and reserved, choosing carefully who to let into my life. The "angry stare," as teammates had referred to it, had proven useful over the years. When I unleashed it on the ice, lifting my lip and snarling, players got the fuck out of my way, occasionally giving me an opportunity to score. I mean, I wasn't setting any records like Ray Bourque, but occasionally it happened and usually it was because of my ability to pretend I was angry. The intimidation factor was a real thing in professional sports, and I'd learned I could use it to help my team win games.

When we're about done with our ice cream, my new best friend, Sam, asks his mom if I could come to dinner. Just seeing his excitement has my heart soaring. I immediately want to say yes when Shiloh nods her approval, but I don't want to give the wrong impression. I know this is a big ask of her. A single mom opening up her home, her life, to me. I don't consider myself a stranger so much anymore, but I can empathize with her initial hesitation. My momma hadn't brought any men into my life, and when I'd asked her about it as a child, she answered that she'd never met anyone special enough. Considering that, I ponder my answer. Shiloh probably has the same concern. So, then, am I special? I really hope so, because I think they are. Even as I accept the invitation, my nerves are frazzled. *What does this mean?* After I say my goodbyes, I find myself smiling on the way to my truck. This dinner is the beginning of something, I can feel it, and I will not screw it up.

Chapter 12

Shiloh

After our ice cream date, we head to Monica's. While Sam and I walk up to her building, I feel light and dreamy, obviously still riding the high from spending the last few hours with Mika. I'm smiling like a fool, which will be a dead giveaway to Monica. There'll be no question. I'm happy. After knocking, my friend answers, and tucked between her legs is Lian, playing peek-a-boo. "Momma!" he screams, and I can't help but laugh. What a character, always so happy and cheerful.

Squatting down, I ask him, "Did you have a good time with Auntie Mo?" Lian nods, his messy blonde curls shaking as he peeks farther out, reaching his arms to me. His tiny hands, dyed blue, make it appear that he'd been transforming into a Smurf before my arrival. Confused, I look at her for an explanation, and she just giggles. Monica, a super artistic teacher, is well equipped to watch Lian. She'd kept him entertained, for sure, and apparently, they'd done some colorful arts and crafts.

Seeing my worried face, Monica says, "Don't worry, Mom. It's non-toxic and washable."

Less worried, I laugh. "Of course it is. I should've known better than to doubt you."

Monica welcomes us into her apartment so she can pack up Lian's backpack, and the boys run to the couch and crawl up on it to watch *Paw Patrol*. Following Monica into her bedroom where Lian had taken his afternoon nap, I wonder how bad her inquisition will be.

As soon as we're past the doorframe, I start talking. "Thank you so much for watching Lian this afternoon. Sam loved skating so much that I even signed him up for lessons."

Monica stops packing Lian's backpack and side-eyes me, silently demanding more. I know she's hinting at Mika and his role in the day, but I play coy. Flashing her my most poised expression, I pretend I don't understand what her look means. Exasperated, her hands fly to her hips, her eyebrows raise, and her lips dip into a scowl. *Yikes, that's terrifying. Glad I'm not her student.* After a few moments under her focused gaze, I break and my confession falls from my lips.

"So... I met Mika Popov-Stevenson today. You

know, the professional hockey player? I was trying to tie Sam's skates, and he pointed out that I'd done it incorrectly. Being helpful, Mika relaced and tied the skates and then he helped with the basics of skating." *And he was amazing.*

Looking at Monica for a reaction, I see a dopey grin covering her gorgeous face. I smirk. She loves a good meet cute, so I continue, "At one point, they did laps together and even had a race. It was adorable. After just a few hours together, Sam already idolizes Mika, and I was right. He is my next-door neighbor." *He's so close, I can almost reach out and touch him. Yes, please.*

Monica remains quiet, nodding like a bobblehead at everything I share. When I finish, her mouth drops open, emitting a high-pitched squeal. "Hold up... wait... does that mean Mika was your ice cream date? Or did you run into another hot professional hockey player while at the rink?" she saucily asks, waggles her eyebrows for effect.

"Mika was our date," I gush, a love-struck smile spreading across my face. *How can I already be so smitten? This isn't normal.*

Monica smiles back and then waggles her eyebrows again. "Anything else happen?"

I look at her, confused. "Anything else? Like what? It's not like he licked ice cream off me. We were with Sam, for heaven's sake. Plus, I'm sure he's not interested in me. Hello, I'm a single mom of two and he's, well... him."

"Pfft. Shiloh, he'd be dumb not to be interested in you. You are amazing! You are beautiful, caring, kind, loving, a fantastic mom, and a wonderful friend. Plus, if you're fantasizing about him licking ice cream off you, you must be fun in the sack, right? Me, personally, I wouldn't know, though, since I don't fancy the ladies."

My shoulders raise with my laughter and then drop dramatically. There's no point in hiding it. I am a mess of emotions. It's been so long since I've wanted attention from a man, my brain is finding it difficult to gauge exactly how I feel. One minute I'm giddy with excitement. The next I'm almost paralyzed with anxiety and fear. It feels like there is something there, but I don't quite trust my instincts. "I appreciate your comments, Monica, but let's face it, guys like him don't go for girls like me. It's not like he accepted Sam's dinner invitation because of me. He's just a nice guy and we're neighbors. Nothing more." *I wish there was more to it.*

Monica rushes over to me, her hands flying to my arms, setting me still. "You invited him over to dinner?" Startled by her aggressive hold, I just shake my head.

"But you said Sam invited him, right?" she clarifies. I nod yes.

"He's *Sam's* dinner guest. See, it means nothing," I say, reminding us both. *Maybe this time it'll sink in and I won't get my hopes up.*

Monica looks at me, disbelieving. "Sure. If that's what you say."

I brush off her suspicious comment and look over at her bedside clock. *It's six o'clock already?* Needing to get the boys fed, bathed, and to bed before it gets too late, I turn to my friend.

"Thanks again for watching Lian. I need to get them home before they stage a riot. It's too close to dinnertime and you know they get insane when they're hungry."

Monica hands over Lian's bag and says, "Little monsters. Just wait until they're teens. My brothers could eat. I always had to dish up quickly at dinner to make sure I got enough." Having met her large, well-built, handsome brothers, I understand exactly what she's saying. We both laugh and head back to the living room so the boys and I can head out. Another episode of *Paw Patrol* comes on and both boys mumble the theme song. *Okay, who am I kidding? I sing too, it's catchy.*

Monica shuts off the TV and the boys shuffle to the door, where I help Lian put on his shoes. Once we've made sure they're on the correct feet, we leave, hugging auntie before we go. It warms my heart to know they love her so much.

After demolishing our dinner of spaghetti, and giving the boys a joint bath—I know I'm pushing my luck with that, but tonight I'm feeling daring—we celebrate the fact that everyone survived, with cookies and some milk before brushing teeth and heading to bed for stories and snuggles.

All in all, the evening goes relatively smoothly. Once they're both tucked in and I turned their nightlight on and I step out into the peaceful silence of the hallway.

Then it hits me all at once. I'm exhausted, but I still have so much to do before I go to bed. Returning to the kitchen, I finish some last chores before grabbing the unfolded laundry from the dryer. Thankfully, since we were gone most of the day, toys aren't scattered everywhere and needing to be picked up. *Small miracles.*

Returning to my room with an overfull laundry basket, my plan is to rewatch a few episodes of *Bridgerton* while I fold. It's easy to get lost in Daphne and Simon's story, and before I know it, the clothes are folded and I'm looking at the opening credits for the third episode. Knowing I should sleep when the boys do, I turn off the show before I'm tempted to binge any more episodes.

I quickly get ready for bed, pulling on a basic cotton nightshirt and brushing my teeth before falling into my bed. "Ahhh, that feels so good." I moan as I sink into the Tempur-Pedic mattress. The softness of the t-shirt sheets and warmth of the down comforter make this my favorite place to unwind. As I drift off to sleep, I skim over all the highlights of the day. The smiles, laughs, and excitement. It really was a great day, and I'm certain it wouldn't have been so enjoyable if it weren't for one exceptionally handsome professional hockey player. Although I'm nervous, I'm really looking forward to dinner this week.

Chapter 13

Mika

Later this week I'm going over to Shiloh's for dinner, and I'm beyond jumpy. Is it a date? Or not? Does she like me? What is happening between us? All week long, Shiloh and I texted back and forth, and it was only making my attraction for her grow. The messages started out pretty generic with things like *how is your day?* Then they escalated to gifs we found hilarious after one night when it was late and instead of telling me she was going to bed, she typed out the word *yawn*. So, of course, I sent a gif of a cat yawning, because who doesn't love cat gifs?

The next morning as I was drinking my protein shake before heading to the arena, I opened our text thread and the gif she'd sent had me spitting my shake everywhere. It was of a bunch of cats that were catching a ride on a Swiffer being pushed around a house. It was hilarious. The only downside was I now had to change my shirt and clean my kitchen. From then on, our conversations were more comfortable and fun, even flirty at times. With each exchange, my desire to know her more grew. What was starting as a friendship made me hopeful for more.

Today, I see her and the boys in their front yard and I so badly want to go out. But I don't want to make things uncomfortable. Instead, I decide to go for a run. As I'm heading out, I hear my name being squealed. Turning quickly, I see Sam waving excitedly at me. Jogging over, I notice another little boy who looks a lot like Sam, but with curly hair. *Lian.*

Shiloh approaches with a smile. "Hey, Mika. How are you?" Pushing my shades into my hair, our eyes connect and my heart pounds in my chest. *Man, she is beautiful.*

After clearing my throat, I reply, "I'm good. I was heading out for a run when my main man called out."

Turning to Sam, I ask, "How are you, Sam?"

Sam gives me a million-dollar smile. "I'm good."

Squatting down next to him, I point to Lian and whisper from the side of my mouth, "Is this Lian?"

Sam laughs and nods his head. "Of course this is Lian. You're silly, Mika."

Looking over at Shiloh, who's smiling, I wink. Then I stick my fist out to Lian to see if he'll bump it. He tries but loses his balance and falls back on his butt, giggling. Unsure if I can laugh at that, I look at Shiloh and see she's shaking her head and laughing. Good, she isn't mad. Not having been around a lot of kids, I don't want to appear insensitive. When Lian gets back to his feet, Sam makes the introductions. "Mika, this is my best little brother. Lian, this is Mika. He lives next door, plays hockey, and taught me to skate." Excited about something I'm not privy to, Lian squeals and claps his hands. All I can surmise is toddlers are weird. So I just smile.

When Shiloh steps closer, I swear the air around us changes, and it feels like a bolt of electricity runs through my body. "Are we still on for dinner?" she asked shyly.

"Yes. Looking forward to it." As soon as the words leave my lips, Sam starts dancing. Before long, Lian joins in and it's the best thing I've ever witnessed. *Such unrestrained joy and excitement.*

My watch dings, reminding me I need to get moving. "Shiloh, I have to head out. Is there anything I can bring to dinner? Dessert maybe?"

Sam interjects before his mom can say anything. "Can we do banana splits like at the ice cream shop?"

Looking to Shiloh, she nods and I copy it. "Okay, it's a deal. But you have to tell me what to bring."

After providing me with a very detailed list, they let me go for my run.

* * *

Despite it being fall, the middle of the day is still hot and muggy. Sweat pours off me as I finish my last mile, which makes me resemble a wet dog. Walking to cool down, I focus on my breathing. When I climb the hill by my house, my quads burn, demanding that I stop the torture I'm inflicting upon them.

Reaching my street, I'm glad to see that Shiloh and her boys aren't in their front yard anymore. Still wanting to make a good impression, and being slightly vain, I don't want to remind Shiloh of what I look like after a long run. I'm trying to convince her to date me, so I want to maintain a certain appearance. *And a big, messy, sweaty beast isn't it.*

When I make it into the house, it's so quiet and lonely. Once I clean up, I call Lucas to see if he has dinner plans or wants to hang out.

"Hey, Lucas. What have you got going on tonight?"

"Samantha and I are ordering in and then watching a movie. You want to join us," he offers.

"Thanks, that'd be great," I reply.

"Perfect. We'll see you soon."

Having dinner at Lucas and Samantha's house is always entertaining. Samantha doesn't know much about hockey, or any sport, and sometimes her lack of knowledge entertains our simple minds. Despite our good-natured teasing, all the guys on the team adore her. She has a knack for giving advice, and tonight I'm desperately in need of some.

Months ago, at their 4th of July barbeque, Lucas

told me I needed to be confident in my decision to pursue Shiloh. Because she was a single mother, she and the boys were a package deal, and that fact needed to remain in the forefront of my mind. If we began dating, I wouldn't just need to consider her needs but the boys' too. Lucas's advice was sound, and I agreed with it fully. And now that I'm interested in pursuing her, I need to know exactly from a woman's perspective how to do that successfully.

Tonight, with Lucas and Samantha, dinner is simple: deep-dish pizza. Even though I've lived in Chicago for years, I'm not as crazy about it as everyone else. Sure, it's hot, cheesy, and flavorful, but if I could choose, I'd pick a steak and loaded baked potato any day.

Before we even choose a movie, Samantha settles on the couch, turns toward me, and starts in with her interrogation. "So, Mika... Lucas said you're having dinner with a woman this week. Who. Is. She?" She drags out her question. Before I can answer, she adds, "Would I approve?" Her sly smirk tells me she knows more than she's saying. *Should I be scared?*

Apprehensively, I shake my head. "Yes. I'm having dinner with a woman this week, and before your mind leads to anything sexual, her two sons will also be there. And to answer your other question, yes, you would definitely approve. Probably even agree that she's too good for me."

Surprised by my answer, Samantha's hand flies up

to her mouth and her eyes grow wide. "What? Wait? Kids? Is this the woman you mentioned on the 4th of July?"

I glance at Lucas and glare. My eyes relay the question, *Bro, how does Samantha know about Shiloh?* Lucas's hands shoot up like he's preparing to defend himself, but before he can speak, Samantha pushes her arms in front of him and answers, "No, Mika, he didn't tell me. I was coming into the backyard for something before everyone got to the party and overheard you."

Feeling guilty for being mad at Lucas, I mutter, "sorry," and he lifts his chin in response, telling me we're good.

I blow out a breath, knowing if I don't answer her soon, she'll think up even more questions I don't want to answer. "Yes, she's the one I spoke of at the party. I ran into her and her oldest son at the ice rink when I was there for Connor's son's birthday party."

Lucas sits forward, suddenly interested in the details I have yet to share with him. In fact, he doesn't even know I'm having dinner with Shiloh. I'd just left him in the dark, or else the questions he's dying to ask right now would have already been answered. "Does she know Connor? Is her son friends with his? Why was she there? Did she recognize you?" Lucas rattles off his questions rapidly, looking for the gossip.

You'd never know it, but my teammates are worse than a pack of teen girls when it comes to gossip. They fixate on juicy tidbits and half-truths. Unless it involves them, because if it does, gossiping is absolutely deplorable.

Knowing a titillating story is all he's after, so I roll my eyes, then shake my head. "No, it was a complete coincidence. I was there for the birthday party, and she was introducing her son to skating. On my way out, I saw her struggling with her son's skates and I couldn't walk by without saying something. To my pleasant surprise, it was her, my foxy neighbor."

Samantha jumps back into the conversation. "I'm confused. You went from retying a pair of skates to a dinner invitation with a single mom? Man, you are smooth. The single guys on the team should take lessons from you!" Amused with her witty repartee, she laughs, and so do I.

Lucas groans and says, "Don't feed his ego."

I scoff at that. I am the least egotistical guy on the team, and Lucas knows that.

I scratch at my head, not sure how much to tell them. "Yes, I retied her son's skates, and after they'd gone onto the ice, I had the strangest sensation. It was like something was drawing me to them, compelling me to help. Wanting to make his first time on skates a success, I grabbed my back-up skates from my truck and joined them."

Lucas and Samantha are my captive audience as I tell them all about my day with Shiloh. "At first, I just skated with them, but then, after a brief misunder-standing, which we resolved quickly, Shiloh let me take her son on a few faster laps around the rink. While together, we worked on basic skills. Sam, Shiloh's son, is incredible. He's a fast learner, and in just a few hours, he was mostly skating independently."

Samantha squeaks at the mention of Sam's name. When it looks like she's shaking from trying to hold something in, Lucas reaches over and pats her thigh lovingly, knowing exactly what's happening. They exchange a look, and I swear a whole nonverbal conversation takes place. Samantha then turns her focus back to me. "First off, the kid has a great name, but I also have two questions. What was the misunderstanding? And hours?"

Shyly smiling, I remember the time I spent with them. Honestly, I hadn't ever spent that much time with a woman without it being about sex. Of course, I would love to engage in that with Shiloh, but things between us are different. It will happen eventually. At least, I hope so.

Lucas claps his hands loudly, effectively pulling me from my reverie. "Sorry," I apologize. "I guess I could start with the simple question. Yes, I spent hours with them. I'd skated with them about an hour and a half and at the end, I'd challenged Sam to a race. When he won, maybe because I let him, I had to buy the winner ice cream. So, I did." Samantha's mouth falls open, and I have the inclination to reach over and push it closed.

"Smooth, bro," Lucas compliments, then smiles widely, like he's proud of me.

"The misunderstanding that occurred between us was... well, it was completely my fault. When I'd asked Shiloh if I could take Sam on a solo skate around the rink, she kind of went off on me." At my admission, hearing my own words, I wince. Even now, the memory of those moments haunts me. When I'd been able to take a step back and stand in her shoes, I'd completely understood Shiloh's reaction. Looking over at Samantha, I notice the worried expression on her face. She looks like she wants to ask a question, so I nod to her, letting her know it's okay to say whatever she's thinking.

"She went momma bear on you? Yikes, I bet that was extra scary, seeing that she's a single mom." Samantha's observation is spot on. Now that I've gotten to know Shiloh, obviously I'm aware of her fierce protection of her children.

The more we talk, the more excited I become over the prospect of dinner and where it might lead. Even considering all the nervous energy churning through my body, I can't wait for this dinner. Sharing a home cooked meal with her amazing boys seems destined. This woman's stirred up excitement and nerves within me, and even though it's hard to admit, I see myself falling for her already.

Smiling, I admit, "Yes, it was scary, but she was right to defend her son. After all, we were strangers. But I hope that doesn't last forever." Lucas smirks at me, reading between the lines. Even though we haven't been friends all that long, we seamlessly communicate nonverbally, and he knows I intend to get to know Shiloh in multiple ways. If she'll have me.

As if we're girlfriends, Samantha asks, "So what's your plan?"

Confused, I scratch my head. "My plan?" My head whips to Lucas and he smirks. He knows where this is headed.

"Yeah. Your plan to woo her. What is it?" she asks in a syrupy-sweet tone.

"I-I don't really have one," I confess in a stutter, sounding surprisingly unsure of myself.

Samantha gasps. "Mika... You don't have a plan? You really need one if this has any chance of working," she chastises.

Lucas stands up and grumbles, "This is going to take forever. I need a drink. Anyone want anything?" Samantha waves him off, and I look at him, begging him to save me. Seeing the worry in my eyes, he just shakes his head and chuckles before walking away. *Asshole.*

Turning away from where Lucas headed, I can't believe it. He left me alone with his woman... and she's scaring me. My palms are covered in sweat, my heart is galloping in my chest, and my breathing feels strange. *Am I going to pass out? What is Samantha going to tell me to do? Would her plan even work?*

Turning back to Samantha, nervousness rushes through my body, making me jumpy. I clench and unclench my hands before I wipe them on my jeans. My stomach, that I'd just filled with pizza, rocks and rolls. Trying to rid myself of the excess energy confined inside me, I bounce my legs repeatedly. The noise I'm making resembles a woodpecker. Samantha notices my jittery, agitated state and smiles at me. *Shit, what's she thinking?*

"Calm down. I will not force you to show up in a tux. However, I have a few recommendations that might help everything go smoother. Okay?"

Again, I wipe my sweaty hands on my jeans and nod my head. I try to force my body to relax, but it's having none of that. My posture is ramrod straight. Unable to see my face, I imagine it's contorted and covered in a scowl. Needing to calm down, I loosen my jaw and roll my neck and shoulders. Once I'm done, I feel slightly better.

"Okay, what do you suggest?" I cautiously ask.

Lucas comes back into the room, still chuckling, and hands me an ice-cold water bottle. He settles back into his seat, wearing a shit-eating grin on his smug-ass face. He pulls Samantha closer, and she goes willingly, settling into his side without even losing her train of thought.

"This—dating Shiloh—is going to differ from anything you've done in the past. Your end goal can't be getting laid. Because if it is, you need to walk away now." Samantha's tone is stern and full of warning.

Understanding her completely, I rush out. "I don't

just want a booty call. Shiloh is a package deal with Sam and Lian, and I get that. I want to get to know them all. I can't explain why I'm so drawn to her, just that I am. I don't want to hurt any of them. But I know if I don't pursue them, I'll never forgive myself."

Samantha nods her understanding. She taps her chin with her pointer finger, as if she's concocting a plan. When her eyes focus back on me, I know she's come up with something, and I'd be stupid not to admit I'm a little scared.

"You want to make a good impression when you show up for dinner? Bring Shiloh a bouquet, something simple like daisies," she states.

"Not roses? I thought every woman loved roses," I question. Having never bought flowers for any woman before, I feel completely clueless, but I remember all the ads I've seen around Valentine's Day feature roses.

Samantha sighs. "Roses, depending on their color, can convey several meanings, and most women know red means love, while yellow means friendship. But other flowers' meanings are less known. Daisies, for example, mean innocence and purity."

Looking at Lucas, he just shrugs his shoulders. Shaking my head, I ask, "How do you know all this? Does every woman? Maybe daisies aren't the right flower either."

Samantha scoffs at me, eliciting a chuckle from Lucas. *Asshole.* I glare at him and he just smiles. *Yep, he's definitely an asshole.* "I've been selecting flowers for our wedding, so I've been researching the meanings of many flowers. Likely the only reference Shiloh will have to daisies is a recollection of Meg Ryan's love for them in the movie *You've Got Mail*. Trust me. You'll be good if you show up with daisies."

Sitting forward in my seat, I rub my hands together, knowing I now have a plan. "Thanks, Samantha. I appreciate your advice." Standing up, I say, "I should probably get going. You two probably want your evening back."

Lucas also stands, ready to walk me to the door. He's ready to have his fiancée all to himself. If I were him, I'd be kicking me out too. But before we reach the door, Samantha looks over her shoulder toward us and calls out, "One more question. What are you bringing the boys?"

Thinking I have that handled, I confidently answer, "They asked for ice cream for dessert, so I'm bringing that, and all the fixings to make killer sundaes."

She smiles at me, and I think I'm all good, but then she heads toward us and my stomach drops. *What now? How did I mess that up?* Glancing at Lucas, I'm curious to see if he has any idea what she's going to say, but he looks as confused as I am. *Helpful, bruh.*

Panicked, I look at Samantha, who is approaching slowly, almost like she's dragging it out just to torture me. Prolonging my suffering.

"Mika, my advice is to get something small for each

of the boys to give to them before you give Shiloh her flowers. It'll show her you thought of her boys too." My eyes widen as the realization of getting gifts for a two- and five-year-old terrifies me. Only it's not for the reason you'd think. It doesn't terrify me because Shiloh has kids, but because I want them to like me. *What if I mess this up? This is monumental.*

Samantha's expression has turned into a frown. She must have seen the panic overtaking my body. Lucas notices too and sets his hand on my shoulder firmly, anchoring me, offering support. It's then I realize how tight I am. Whispering close to my ear, Lucas chides, "Dude, chill. You're making me edgy."

Trying to force my body to relinquish the anxiety that is again coursing through it is difficult. *Why is this date making me so anxious? I've never cared this much about impressing a woman.* Then it hits me. Dating Shiloh, a single mom, is new for me. Hell, dating is new for me. I haven't ever been in a relationship. I'd never wanted one. Until now.

Over the years, rare puck bunnies had had repeat appearances, but I was always very clear that our hookups were just that and nothing more. With Shiloh, I want something beyond that, and that terrifies me.

My shoulders tighten further, my heart thumps in my chest, and my stomach churns. Before it takes me under, Samantha calms me by placing her hand gently on my forearm. Her touch is like a balm to my anxiety, instantly making me relax. My eyes flick to her as she speaks. "Mika, you've got this. Stop overthinking things. You have nothing to worry about. Yes, she's a single mother. But you've already spent time with her and it was enjoyable. So, what's different about this? Nothing. Enjoy yourself."

I nod my head. "She was incredible, and both her boys were exceptional, and I did really enjoy spending time with them. But, this date, it feels like something bigger, and I don't want to mess things up." My head drops and hangs heavy, just like my confession. Lucas's hand, still resting on my shoulder, squeezes tight, and I force my eyes up to him. He smiles, trying to reassure me. And it works, just like on the ice after a terrible play. After all the time we've spent together over the last year, he has my back and I have his.

Samantha squeezes my arm again and reiterates, "You've got this, Mika." Knowing I have their support gives me the assurance I need. Standing taller, I tell myself the same thing. *You've got this.*

Samantha's words, *a small gift,* fly into the forefront of my mind. My knowledge of kids is minimal, but I remember some things I used to love playing with when I was small. Hot Wheels and Nerf balls were all the rage. All boys like those, right? Maybe I'll check with Connor, see what his boys are into. Feeling positive about my plan, I know what I need to do. Smiling at my friends, I realize that after the rollercoaster of feelings I've had about this date; I was finally feeling excited. The change in my mood is obvious. The air circling us feels different, almost like when a freak storm resolves instantly, leaving a peaceful blue sky in its wake. Samantha notices immediately and claps her hands together excitedly. Lucas catches on too and punches my arm.

"Thank you both. Wish me luck," I tell them before I leave. I'm so excited that I head to the store to pick out toys for Samuel and Lian.

I'm going to rock this dinner thing. If only I knew if it was a date too.

Chapter 14

Shiloh

Our date—or friendship dinner—with Mika is tonight. I call it *ours* because it won't be just Mika and me. My boys are very much included. We are a package deal, just like they'd be if Mika and I were to date. *Dating.* My mind does somersaults trying to grasp the reality of that, making me an absolute mess of emotions, differing from one minute to the next. First, I'm happy and excited, then I'm anxious and worried. At other times, if I'm entirely honest, I'm downright scared. As if the emotional chaos weren't enough, questions constantly plague my mind. What if we like him more than he likes us? Will Mika accept us all? Will things go past neighbors and friends?

Truth be told, I haven't dated at all since my divorce from Trent. Monica has tried to encourage me to get on a dating site or two, but every time I considered it, it felt wrong and I never signed up. Sure, I missed companionship, but I'm not sure I'd ever had it. Who knows if what I'm desiring is even realistic? With Trent, maybe we had it when we were first together, but I don't really know. The more I autopsied that relationship, the more insight I found into what mistakes I don't want to repeat. If I start dating again, I know I need certain things. I need to be heard and respected, appreciated and thanked, valued and seen. And above all that, I want friendship, passion, trust, and love. Huge list, right? Maybe I've read too many romance books and my list is a silly fantasy, but for right now, it's all I have. After the divorce, I promised myself that I'd never again settle for something less than what I deserved. In fact, I'd rather be alone forever than feel like I did with my ex. I also refuse to have my boys witness their mom in a dysfunctional relationship. I'm determined to raise them to respect, cherish, thank, care, empower, and adore women. Everything I want in a partner.

"Momma, when is Mika coming over?" Sam asks for the hundredth time today.

Yesterday, I caught him and Lian talking about it, and it was absolutely adorable to hear what they'd said and the hero worship they'd already manifested. Walking into the living room, I saw Sam and Lian playing with superheroes together and when I heard Mika's name; I stopped to listen.

"Lian, Mika is coming over for dinner tomorrow.

Remember, he's my friend and he taught me to skate." The tone Sam used was so matter-of-fact, making him sound so mature. It's completely opposite of toddler garble and it made me smile.

"Hulk, smash," Lian explained loudly as he smashed against his brother's Iron Man figurine.

Sam scowled at him. "Lian, Hulk couldn't smash Iron Man if he was flying away."

Not really caring what Sam said, Lian proudly held Hulk up and chanted, "Hulk smash. Hulk smash. Hulk smash."

Exasperated, Sam yelled, "Lian stop. Hulk can't smash if he can't reach him." Then he stood and held the figurine high above his brother's head, way out of reach.

Entering the room finally, I saw Sam was red-faced and annoyed, and Lian couldn't have cared less. "What's the trouble, Sam?"

"Momma, can you please tell Lian that Hulk can't smash things that are in the air?" he exasperatedly replied.

I gave him a tender look and pulled him to my side. "Sam, Lian is only two. He doesn't understand those things or why you're yelling at him."

"But he makes me so mad when he plays like that. Those aren't the rules," Sam informed me.

Keeping a laugh in, I nodded my understanding. "I know that can be frustrating, Sam, but remember, he's still small. He doesn't understand playing as you do."

Just as I was about to suggest he play with something else, Lian pointed up to him and asked, "Sam, play?" So sweet.

Sam grumbled but sat back down with his brother and began to play. Before long, they were both giggling.

They are my heart.

I hope Mika is ready for this. For us.

Before I can relax into the pleasant feeling of that, my anxiety is stirred. Mika doesn't have much experience with kids. Is he going to realize that my boys can be a handful? Will that be too much for him? Thinking about that, I guess it'd be better for him to figure that out sooner rather than later. We don't want to get too attached to Mika if he doesn't stay around long. Because if I were betting, I suspect Sam is already halfway in love with our handsome neighbor. In fact, I suspect it wouldn't take long for Lian to fall either. Really, I'm the holdout, because in reality, I have to be. Someone has to ask the practical questions and keep everyone safe, right? It's not like we could throw caution to the wind and hope for the best. That isn't how the world works, and I'm not interested in teaching Sam or Lian that way of living. I need to practice caution with Mika because he is far too tempting. He's kind, thoughtful, and beyond sexy, and if he reveals he has any other positive traits, I'm in some serious trouble and he'll be even more difficult to resist.

An impatient tugging on my pant leg brings me back to the conversation. *Hello, Lian.* Like a typical toddler, he shakes while he waits as patiently as possible for my answer to his brother's question. Patting his wild blonde curls, I tell him, "Mika is coming over for dinner tonight. That's after lunch and your nap. He'll be here in a few hours." Both boys squeal and run from the kitchen to the adjoining living room, where they'd scattered toys everywhere, making it a danger zone. Hopefully, they'll help me pick it all up after lunch and before Lian's nap and then I can do a quick wipe-down before Mika gets here. With my young men, no matter how tidy I am, sticky, dirty fingers kiss every surface, leaving grimy smudges in their path. And to someone unfamiliar with that, it could be very off-putting for them, and I want to make a good impression.

The rest of our morning goes smoothly as we visit the nearby park. The boys work off some of their excess energy while I keep busy not worrying about our dinner guest. Watching Lian's little body toddle over to the equipment is captivating.

Lian recently discovered he loves the slide, and our park has a toddler-sized one that he can use with minimal help from his brother. All morning, Sam is such a big helper, assisting Lian as he lowers himself onto the slide before he encourages him to scoot his butt forward. I'm always at the bottom of the slide, ready to catch my smiling, drooling baby, who giggles with delight every time he slides down. After he gets Lian situated, Samuel remains at the top of the slide, standing guard while beaming with pride. Just knowing he has his brother's back makes my heart soar. It's. Absolutely. The. Best. Feeling.

Once he's finished helping Lian, Samuel tackles other playground equipment. The other day, he learned how to get onto the swings by himself. He used to only swing on his belly, but last week I showed him how he could pull himself up onto the swing. Once he understood, he had it, knowing to hold tight and pump his legs. Pretty soon, there'd been no stopping him. His first time doing it independently, he didn't get too high, which disappointed him. But I'd reminded him it'd come with time and practice. Really, I wasn't ready for him to grow up, but through it all, I was proud he'd figured it out on his own.

After the playground, we eat a quick lunch and pick up the toy graveyard from the living room. Lian naps while Sam watches *Paw Patrol: The Movie.* With Sam distracted, I rush through the house, cleaning what I can. About a half hour before Mika's due to come over, I jog upstairs, baby monitor in tow, and pull on a flirty summer dress. Eyeballing my hair and makeup, I remain natural, because then I'm the real me, and if Mika doesn't like that, it's fine. *Or at least that's what I tell myself.*

Chapter 15

Mika

Pacing my living room ten minutes before I'm due over at Shiloh's for dinner is my pathetic attempt to calm my nerves. I'm half tempted to drop to the floor and pump out push-ups, but I don't want to get all sweaty.

Making sure my flowers for Shiloh and gifts for the boys are by the front door, I recheck my appearance again in my bathroom mirror. While making sure my hair is just right, I tell myself, "You're ridiculous. You took way too long to select what you're wearing, and your hair is fine." Being like this isn't normal for me, but this afternoon, I'd primped like a beauty pageant contestant. All afternoon, I focused on looking my best. *What the hell is wrong with me?*

I conduct one last breath and armpit check before I head to my kitchen to grab all the ingredients for the amazing dessert I'm bringing. Sure, Sam and Lian had given me a very detailed list of ingredients they deemed necessary for creating the perfect ice cream sundaes, but I'd thrown in a few other things I felt they hadn't considered. With my new freezer tote—who knew that was a thing—stuffed full of ice cream, hot fudge, butterscotch, whipped cream, sprinkles, peanuts, bananas, and maraschino cherries, I make my way to my front hallway. Grabbing the flowers and toys, I head out. Going on a date to my next-door neighbor's house is incredibly convenient. After locking my house, I just walk up Shiloh's driveway. The entire way, my heart jackhammers in my chest. My breathing becomes shakier the closer I get, making me feel slightly lightheaded. My nerves are beyond frayed and my palms are sweaty as I adjust my hold on everything I'm carrying, hoping I don't drop anything or crush it. Before I reach their porch, the front door flies open. "Mika," Sam and Lian squeal as they rush me.

"Hey, guys," I say as they barrel into me, hitting me right at groin level. *Ouch.* Next time I'll remember that. My breath catches as I take in their wide, cheerful smiles. *Those are for me?* Both boys are jumping excitedly in front of me. Seconds later, Shiloh steps out of the house, hollering after them, and my brain stalls. *Gorgeous.* Never have I ever seen anything so beautiful.

"Sam, Lian, slow down. Let Mika into the house before you bombard him." Her eyes twinkle and a soft smile dusts her lips. Lips that I want to reach out and touch, trace with my finger, taste, and savor. Knowing now isn't the time, I flex my fingers around the flowers, gifts, and freezer tote, reminding myself this is our first date and I need to take it slow.

Shiloh gathers the boys and marches them back to the house. Still standing in her driveway, I savor the image before me. Watching her hips swish back and forth makes me feel like a teenage boy whose body has been overrun with hormones.

When she reaches the porch, she turns and glances at me over her shoulder. *Gorgeous.* The setting sun makes her appear angelic, forming a halo around her head. She's dressed in a flirty, lacy floral dress that hugs her tanned skin in exquisite ways. Her shoulder-length blonde hair is in relaxed curls that dance along her collarbones. She's shoeless, revealing magenta painted toes that match the tiny flowers on her outfit. Shiloh's incredibly sexy, and I can't help but stare at her. Our eyes lock, and it renders me useless, completely taken by this vision before me.

"Coming?" Shiloh asks quietly as she motions toward the house.

Nodding like an idiot, I force my feet forward. Within moments, I'm at her back, and the heat radiating off her warms me. A vanilla and citrus scent floats past my nose, and my mouth waters. Licking my lips, I tighten my grasp on the items in my hands as I follow her into her house. Kicking off my shoes at the door, I remain close to her as she shuts the door behind me.

Sam and Lian come running back into the entryway, both jumping excitedly. *So much energy.*

"What do you have?" Sam asks, pointing at my hands. Shiloh hushes him and reminds him his question isn't polite. Setting the bag on the floor, I lower to one knee and look at the boys, who are wearing goofy grins, and I can't help but mirror one back.

Although I'm incredibly nervous, I try to keep my voice steady as I say, "I brought you boys a little something. Is that okay?" They nod their heads frantically, but I'm not really asking them. I flick my eyes to Shiloh and make sure she's fine with it. She graces me with a kind smile, and I'm relieved. Reaching into the bag, I pull out a Nerf football for Sam and a Hot Wheels car for Lian. Both boys yell excitedly and run at me, throwing their arms around me and hugging me. Bracing myself as best I can, their little bodies wrap around me while they say "thank you" repeatedly. Laughing, I glance over at Shiloh, who has her hands clasped at her chest. *What's she thinking?*

Within moments, the boys have already abandoned me and moved on to playing with their new toys in another room. Looking up, I see Shiloh watching me. *Breathtakingly beautiful.* Just the way she's looking at me makes me feel invincible.

When I stand back up, I approach her slowly and hold out the enormous bouquet of daisies. Taking them, she closes her eyes, buries her nose in the flowers, inhales deeply, and sighs.

When her eyes flutter open, a single tear escapes down her cheek. Wiping it away with the back of her hand, she says, "Mika, these are beautiful. Thank you so much."

"I'm glad you like them. I hope it was okay I got the boys a little something too."

Shiloh stares into my eyes before she answers, "It was so thoughtful of you. Dinner is almost ready." When she starts off down the hallway, I follow her like an obedient puppy. The most tantalizing smell of roasted tomatoes, garlic, and oregano wafts through the air. My stomach growls loudly, embarrassing me. Shiloh laughs.

"Sounds like someone is hungry. I sure hope you like lasagna. It's the boys' favorite, and they insisted I make it for tonight." Pulling a salad from the fridge, she places it on the table, which is already set. Shiloh has me put the daisy bouquet in a vase and set it on the table next to a basket of warm, sliced bread.

The oven timer goes off, and Shiloh pulls dinner out, and it looks amazing.

"Boys, go wash your hands, please," she calls out.

After a few minutes, the boys rush back into the kitchen and climb into their chairs. Wanting to stay out of the way, I sit in one of the empty chairs while Shiloh brings the lasagna to the table. She serves each of the boys first, cutting theirs into more manageable bites.

While it cools, she places a piece of bread on their plates to keep them entertained.

Shiloh serves me next, handing me a plate loaded with a giant piece of ooey, gooey, cheesy lasagna that I can't wait to try. Impatiently, I cut off a corner and lift it to my lips, but as I move it closer, heat pours off it, stopping me. Burning my lips is not a good idea, especially if I plan to use them later. Setting my fork back down, I snag a piece of bread and enjoy the warmth it still holds. The first bite of it is soft and flavorful. When the lasagna is cool enough, I take a large bite. The flavors burst in my mouth, giving my tastebuds a show. Hands down, it's one of the best things I've ever eaten. "Mmmm." The contented moan slips past my lips, causing the boys to giggle.

"What?" I ask, genuinely confused.

"You made a funny noise, Mika," Sam informs me through laughter.

Lian busily tries to replicate it, but it's more awkward than accurate. I laugh, and when I peer over at Shiloh, her cheeks are flushed. Her almond-shaped eyes are bright and responsive. She'd been thinking about moaning, for sure, but it didn't have anything to do with food. *I wonder how long it's been since someone made her moan.* Just thinking about that makes my heart rate increase, my pants grow tighter, and the air in the room feels hot against my skin. Forcing a distraction, I take a large drink of my cold water, alleviating some of my discomfort. As I sit there, it's insane to think of how responsive I am from just thinking of touching Shiloh. Hell, at this point, I'd probably blow my load if I even got the chance to kiss her. *Embarrassing much?* It would certainly be a first for me, but with her, it could totally happen. She's already tested all my self-control, and we haven't even touched.

"M... oow."

"Lian, are you a cat?" Sam asks. Lian shakes his head and tries again.

"Ohhh." Pleased with that one, he tries another.

"Ahhh," he squawks out, sounding like a startled parrot.

Soon, a cacophony of odd moaning sounds in different pitches and lengths fills the surrounding space. Being a guy who still finds crude humor hilarious, I try to muffle my laugh.

"Boys... boys." Shiloh tries to get their attention.

"Mmmm," Lian belts out, and Sam snickers. *Nailed it.*

"Sam, Lian. Really? You need to stop."

Just as Lian is about to try another sound, Shiloh issues a warning. "Enough of that or no one gets dessert." Like magic, the dining room is silent. Guess we all want ice cream sundaes.

"Now, how about you boys tell Mika your favorite thing to do at the playground?" Shiloh redirects the boys to a new and less risqué topic.

"I love the swings. When you go high, it feels like

you're flying. And I don't need pushes like the little kids," Sam proudly tells him.

"That's great, Sam. I think the swings were one of my favorites, too. Lian, what's your favorite thing at the playground?" I ask.

"Slides," Lian declares with a bright smile.

What? Concern fills my mind. "You... you slide down those huge slides?"

"No, Mika. Lian rides the baby slides. But I can do the big ones," Sam informs me. Nodding my understanding, I'm less shocked than moments ago. Apparently, there are different sized slides nowadays.

Sam turns to me. "When you were younger, what did you play on at the playground?"

"Well, when I was in elementary school, I used all the equipment, but as I got bigger, I played tag, foursquare, and tetherball. And I played hockey almost daily."

"I'm too small to play those other games, but I see the big kids playing them. I'm going to start skating lessons soon, so maybe I'll play hockey like you," Sam says.

"You could definitely play hockey. You look like a natural on those skates," I encourage him. "How about you, Lian? Do you want to skate and play hockey?"

Lian just looks at me, hits his fork on his plate and says, "Hockey." That kid. Who knows what he'll do. But whatever it'll be, he will certainly do it with flair.

"Mika, when you were little did your momma and

dad come to your hockey games to watch you play?" Sam questions.

Unsure what to say, as Shiloh and I haven't talked about our pasts, I sit back in my chair, thinking before I answer. "Yes, and no. My mama was a single mom and she couldn't always make my games, even though she tried her best. I've never met my dad."

"I don't know my dad, either," Sam declares. "And I don't want to." I nod my understanding. I know exactly what Sam is saying.

I guess it's pretty obvious Shiloh and I need to have a private conversation, especially if this, us, is turning into something. *I hope it is.*

Telling Shiloh about my dad and his parents will be tough for me, I'm still angry and hurt by their actions. When I was first drafted into the NHL by the Steel, my sperm donor's parents—my biological grandparents—tried to reach out via their lawyers. But from the stories I'd heard from my mother, it was only for appearance's sake. If they wanted a relationship with me, they wouldn't have waited until I was all grown up and a professional athlete. So, in response, I'd chosen to ignore their correspondence, and they eventually gave up.

The rest of dinner goes well. Following the meal, while Shiloh busies herself in the kitchen, the boys drag me out to the living room and continue to pepper me with questions.

"Mika, who's your favorite hockey team?"

"That's easy, Sam. The Chicago Steel, of course."
Smiling at him, I ask, "Who's yours?"

Sam laughs. "You're silly. You are my favorite
player and the Steel is my favorite team."

"Thanks, Sam." I ruffle his hair, then turn to Lian.
"Lian, I know Sam's favorite superhero is Iron Man,
but who is yours?"

"Hulk smash," he declares as he pounds his chubby
toddler fists together.

Laughing, I reply, "Mine too, buddy."

The entire time we chat, Lian sits in my lap while
Sam sits nearby. Not having been around a lot of kids,
I'm not exactly sure what to expect of them. They
constantly surprise me. My exposure has always been
limited to parties or organized events where parents
closely monitored their kids' behavior. But after
spending hours with Sam and Lian, I could admit that
these are some of the coolest kids I've ever met.
Spending time with them is enjoyable.

Time together passes quickly, filled with laughter,
tickling, and talking. Shiloh calls us into the kitchen to
assemble our sundaes, and all three of us waste little
time getting to her. Sam arrives first and pulls out a
step stool to aid him in reaching the counter. He's so
big and independent. Wanting a better vantage point,
Lian tugs on my leg and I pick him up easily.

"Everything looks good. What are you going to
have on your ice cream, Lian?" I ask while I ponder

what I want. If I'm splurging tonight, I'm making it worth my while.

Pointing excitedly, Lian selects vanilla ice cream, whipped cream, and sprinkles. Thank goodness Shiloh is here to interpret or who knows what we would end up with.

Sam, still waiting patiently on his stool, eyes the toppings. "Which one looks good?" I ask.

Without hesitation, he declares, "Hot fudge." *Classic. I can respect that.*

I like all the toppings. So, despite my rigorous training schedule and diet, or the fact I don't partake in it too often, I decide tonight I'll indulge. Once Shiloh and I have fixed our sundaes, we all head outside to the backyard where she's spread out an old quilt.

After demolishing our desserts, the boys run around the backyard, whooping and hollering. Sitting still and taking everything in, I decide the evening has been perfect.

"Thanks for having me over for dinner tonight. That was the best lasagna I've ever had."

Shiloh laughs. "I'm glad you enjoyed it."

"I did. It's been a long time since I've had a home cooked meal."

"You're kidding, right?"

Shaking my head, I admit, "If I'm lucky enough to score a dinner invite to one of my married teammate's houses, I'm gold, but most of us are single and definitely not skilled in the kitchen. And it's been way too long since I visited my mama."

"Where's home, Mika?" Shiloh asks.

"I'm from Boston. My mom immigrated to the States from Russia when she was nineteen and ended up there working as a housekeeper."

"And she still lives there?"

Nodding, I reply, "Yes, she does. How about your parents?"

Shiloh looks away and then quietly says, "They died when I was little. My grandparents raised me in this house. We—my ex-husband, Sam, and I—moved in after my grandmother's passing a few years ago."

Sad that she's endured so much loss, I quietly say, "I'm so sorry for all your losses, Shiloh." We both sit there lost in our own thoughts. Mine, of course, are about her ex-husband. Nervous, I stutter when I ask my next question. "Y-you said, ex-husband?"

Hanging her head, she let out a deep breath. "My ex-husband, Trent, and I began the process of divorce not long after we moved in. I was pregnant with Lian and he decided he didn't want to be a part of our lives. And the boys and I have been much happier since. I don't talk about him much because the boys don't need to hear me bad-mouthing their dad, but he wasn't a good guy. We don't have any contact with him and haven't since he walked out the day I told him I was pregnant."

My fists tighten, and I wish that Trent guy were

here so I could teach him a lesson or two. What an asshole. Beside me is a stunning woman who, from everything I've seen, is an outstanding mom. Why the fuck would you walk away from this? I know I wouldn't. Being here with Shiloh stirs up so many thoughts and feelings. I definitely like this woman, and I want the chance to get to know her better.

I nudge her with my shoulder. "Thank you for sharing all that with me. I can't imagine it's been easy. From all I've seen, you are incredible." Shiloh rewards me with a smile that I'd do anything to get again.

Just as I'm gathering my courage to share my past with her, our bubble of conversation is popped. I hear something that stops my heart. It's a resounding thud, followed by frightened whimpering and soft crying. Quickly, I look around, feeling panicky, and then my eyes find Lian crumpled in a ball at the base of a tree. Springing into action, I make a beeline for the tree and look him over before I move him. Not being a trained medic, I want to be sure that I don't harm my little buddy.

"Lian, are you okay?" I ask him as I kneel next to him. His eyes are wet, and a grimace stretches across his adorable little face. I rush my hands over him, checking for bumps, bruises, and visible bleeding. He appears all right other than the tree litter sticking out of his curls and a smudge of dirt smeared across his cheek.

Sam hurries over to us and peers down at his little brother with concern. "You okay, Lian? Did you run into the tree?" The little man below us sniffles and nods his head, acknowledging what happened. Apparently, while running, he hadn't been paying attention and had run right into the only tree in the backyard, knocking the wind out of himself.

I pick him up and cradle him in my arms. Just as I'm standing back up, Shiloh rushes over to see if Lian is okay. Just seeing his mom, his little chin quivers. But then he gathers his strength and says to her, "I'm okay, Momma. I'm tough and strong like Mika. See?" Then he flexes his arms, making me laugh and turning his mom's frown to a smile. Relieved he's okay, I set him down. We fist bump, and he runs off to join Sam, who is now on the other side of the yard, poking something with a stick. Boys sure make life interesting.

Shiloh and I walk back over to the blanket, and I see her smile fade into a look of concern. *Had I mishandled the situation? Was she upset with me?* Needing to know we're okay, I risk reaching out and touching her. She smiles and moves closer. Not being a parent, I assume she's worried about Lian getting hurt, so I lean over and whisper into her ear, "He's fine, Shiloh. Just boys being boys."

When we reach the blanket, we sit down and Shiloh relaxes against me. My protective instincts flare, and I vow to protect her. That feeling is new and intense, and I like it. Is it excessive? Yes, probably so. But Shiloh brought that out in me. From the first moment we met, I wanted to be near her, providing for her and caring for her. Now that she's by my side, everything seems right with the world. Wanting to convey my desire for her, I nuzzle my nose into her hair and inhale deeply. On her head, I place a soft kiss and she makes the most breathtaking sound—a wistful sigh.

An hour passes and it seems the boys' sugar high has worn off, and instead of looking like battling super-heroes, they are channeling sloths. It's probably time for bed.

Grabbing the sundae dishes, I head into the kitchen to clean them up while Shiloh herds the boys into the house. When they walk me to the door to say goodnight, I drop into a squat in front of the boys. "Sam, Lian. Thank you so much for inviting me to dinner. I had the best time. Hopefully, we can do this again, real soon." Both boys nod furiously, and I chance a glance at Shiloh, who is wearing a brilliant smile. The boys and I fist bump before I head out. Before I'm off the deck, I turn and mouth to Shiloh, *"I'll text you later."* She nods her head. At the same time, her gorgeous smile gets wider and her blue eyes twinkle. As I walk away, all three of them wave at me. Before I reach my door, a thought strikes me. That could be my life; they could be mine. And instead of feeling panic or fear over that, my body is filled with overwhelming excitement.

Chapter 16

Mika

After I arrive home, I try to wait a respectable amount of time before I send Shiloh a text. Who am I kidding? I pace my house for an hour, hoping that by then she'll have gotten the boys to bed and will be free to talk.

> **ME**
>
> Thanks again for dinner. I hope we can do that again.

> **SHILOH**
>
> I'm really glad you came. I agree, we need to do it again.

> **ME**
>
> Since we agree… What are you doing tomorrow night?

A few minutes pass. I watch the screen as three

dots appear, then disappear, then appear, then disappear.

ME

No pressure. I was just wondering if we could share dessert after the boys go to bed. Have a conversation.

SHILOH

Okay, that sounds good. We could play twenty questions. A sort of get-to-know-you.

ME

I'm totally in. What time do you want me there and what is your favorite dessert?

SHILOH

The boys go to bed by eight. My favorite dessert is ice cream, and there's plenty left over from tonight.

ME

See you then. I can't wait.

SHILOH

Me too. Good night, Mika.

ME

Night. Sweet dreams.

* * *

Last night, our dinner hadn't been a date. However, tonight I'm heading over for dessert. Shiloh had mentioned twenty questions, which I've never played before. This ought to be interesting.

After Shiloh puts the boys down, she texts me and then meets me on her front porch. Dressed in another cotton dress, she takes my breath away. "You look beautiful, Shiloh."

A faint blush appears on her cheeks as she smiles and says, "Thank you." We tiptoe into the house like teenagers sneaking in after a night out. Careful not to bump anything, we make our way to the kitchen. "I thought we could make our sundaes and then head out back like last night."

"Sounds perfect," I tell her as I let my eyes rove over her, forcing myself not to openly gawk. She is stunning. Trying to be respectful, I do my best to restrain myself from touching her.

Her dress is short, highlighting her well-toned, sinfully tanned legs. It's flirty and fun, and the neckline dips low, putting her cleavage on full display. Shiloh's breasts are small, just right for her body, and certainly not anything to complain about. In fact, her petite frame makes her perfect for tucking into my side. Almost as if her curves complement mine.

Heading outside, Shiloh grabs the quilt we'd used last night and leads me over to a patch of grass that seems hidden from any prying neighbors. Once we've settled, I notice she has some sort of walkie talkie with her. "What's that?"

She laughs. "I have a baby monitor in the boys' room in case they need me. It's hardly used anymore, but since we aren't in the house, I feel more comfortable having it."

"Are they light sleepers? If we laugh, will that wake them up?"

"Heavens no. Both boys sleep like rocks. Usually once they're out, that's it."

Taking a bite of ice cream, I ask, "So what's this twenty questions game you mentioned? How do we play?"

"It's a get-to-know-you game where you and your date rotate asking each other questions. It is supposed to be fun, but I've never played."

"Me either. How about you go first?"

"Okay, but I'll warn you... I'm holding nothing back. Ready?" Her voice is both snarky and flirty, and I find that a deadly combination.

"Yes. Hit me," I answer.

"What's your favorite emoji and why?"

Scratching my chin, I think it over. *Are there any wrong answers? No.* So I tell her, "Definitely the poop one, and not for the reason you think."

"Really? Is it because you're a guy and you all think poop, farts, and burps are funny?" The smirk on her face is adorable, even if I have to wipe it off.

"No. Well, kind of. But the reason I like it the most is that it can convey good or bad." Shiloh looks at me like she's stunned by my answer. "Think about it. We can interpret it as funny or crappy. And yes, the pun was totally intended," I tell her before winking.

Her cheeks turn pink and the most melodic sound tumbles from her kissable lips as she laughs at me.

"What?" I shrug my shoulders in question.

"Next question, Mika. You ready?" She gives her best challenging stare, which is adorable.

"Wait. You have to answer the emoji question too," I protest.

She crosses her arms, smiles at me, and says, "My favorite emoji is the heart one because it conveys exactly that; its meaning is clear."

Well said. Although I haven't ever told a woman I loved her, I can see the importance of doing it once you feel that way. We sit in silence for a moment before she asks another question. "What's a weird, totally useless talent you have?"

"That's easy. I can pick up things with my toes. Not normal items like a sock, but weird things like a billiard ball."

"Really? You're talking about a ball you use to play pool?" Shiloh stares at me. "How do you do that, and how did you figure it out?"

"Yes, a pool ball. I figured it out in high school when I was playing pool with some buddies. One guy hadn't played before and jumped the ball off the table near me. Here's another fun fact about me: I hate socks. So I'm standing in my buddy's basement sockless and this ball rolls over to me. For some reason, I tried to pick it up with my toes and it worked."

"Wow. I wish I had a pool table so you could impress me with your skills." Her flirty tone beckons me closer. Now that our bodies are only a few inches apart, my body hums with excitement and anticipation of what's coming. I'm not expecting anything, but a kiss would be welcome.

Dropping my voice, I ask, "What's your hidden talent, Shiloh?"

Pointing at my half-eaten ice cream sundae, she says, "Gonna eat your cherry?"

Picking it up, I ask, "This?" She nods and I hand it to her, curious. She slowly places it in between her front teeth and tugs the stem out before she sucks it into her mouth and eats it.

Although watching that was sexy as hell, I wouldn't call it a hidden talent. "That was your talent?" I question.

"Nope." She emphasizes the pop of the p. "This is." She puts the stem in her mouth and closes it. Transfixed, I watch as her jaw moves back and forth. A few seconds pass and she opens her mouth and presents her tongue with a perfectly tied cherry stem on it.

A breathy "wow" is all I can say. I've heard people could do that, but I've never seen it. And, of course, now I'm transfixed on her magical mouth. *What else can she do?*

"How about we turn up the heat a bit? You okay

with that, Mika?" Still tracing the lines of her lips with my gaze, I nod my agreement.

"Have you ever used a dating app?" Shiloh's question is quiet, as if she's not sure she wants to ask the question. Maybe she doesn't want to know the answer. Either way, I'm answering her, because I want to know her answer too.

"No, I've never been on a dating app. I've never had a need because I've never been intentionally looking for a relationship." *Shit. Did that sound as harsh to her as it did to me?* Until meeting her, I'd never met any woman I wanted to pursue, and I didn't want the hassle of a dating app to act as a screener to my happiness when I didn't really know what I wanted. But looking at her now... she's it. She's what I want.

"Oh... okay. I guess that makes sense. I guess if you don't know what you want, a dating app would just be a waste of time. I haven't been on them either. My bestie, Monica, tried to encourage me to give them a shot after my divorce, but it never felt right. Plus, I wasn't really looking for anything permanent either. With my boys, I have to consider who I allow into our lives, you know? Maybe you don't. Geez, now I'm rambling."

Reaching my hand over to hers to settle her, I interlock our fingers. A rush of endorphins shoots through my body, lighting me up. "I understand completely. You know, Shiloh, if I had been on a dating app, I definitely would have swiped right on you." Just confessing that has my stomach tensing, eager for her reply.

Chapter 17

Shiloh

When Mika threw out the idea of coming over for a dessert date after the boys had gone to bed, I was suspicious. Was he just trying to get me alone? We hadn't talked about us. Is there an us? Hell if I know. I'm not about to demand an answer. However, when he hints that he would have pursued me, it makes me realize he's actually interested in me. Sure, I can't gauge how much, but it certainly intrigues me.

"Mika, although I would have been intimidated, I would have swiped right for you too." Admitting that feels amazing. But I hadn't been lying. I understand we don't seem to match. He is a single, wealthy professional athlete and I'm a college dropout, divorcée, and single mom. But despite all that, we connect so easily and our chemistry is off the charts.

Looking down, I notice my sundae has become a

sloppy mess. Taking Mika's bowl of ice cream soup, I set both bowls on the patio next to me. I shift my body to better face Mika for conversation. And no sooner do I do that, Mika is pulling me forward and placing a heated kiss on my lips. He tastes like chocolate and caramel, decadent and sinful. Pushing my hands into his hair, I tug at the ends and he rewards me with a throaty growl that sends my insides quivering. Needing air, I pull back and Mika traces the lines of my lips with his tongue before he bites my lower lip. *I'm not sure this man could get any sexier.*

Mika pulls my body over and suddenly I'm straddling him. He places a tender kiss on my nose, encouraging me to look up. When our eyes lock, he confesses, "You are beautiful, Shiloh. And I'd like to see where this goes." My heart thumps wildly in my chest. *Is this for real?* Blinking a few times, I make sure I'm not actually dreaming. *I'm not.*

Placing my hands on the side of Mika's face, I pull him closer and kiss him. What starts as chaste turns heated quickly. Mika wraps a hand around each of my hips, anchoring me to him. Feeling the heat between our bodies does strange things to me. Only, I'm not alone in that. Mika hardens below me. He lifts me up and readjusts himself, and my eyes go wide when I see how large he is. "Oh... w-wow." I gasp as I glance down at his crotch. Outlined in all its glory, straining against his jeans, is his cock, hardened like steel. Eager for what's next.

"That's what you do to me, Shiloh. You are the sexiest woman I've ever known." When he lowers me down and our centers meet, that becomes a lost thought. My hips act on their own and grind into him, building a pressure within my body that's vaguely familiar. Before I had the boys, I'd taken care of my own pleasure. Trent had never lasted long enough to do the job, or he just didn't care to make sure I was satisfied. After the boys, I'd been too tired. But now, my body reacts to the bursts of excitement, the pulls of pleasure, the build-up to something big, and I'm more than ready for it.

Before I lose all control, I press my thighs tightly against him to center myself. Instead of doing that, it creates a provocative pressure that causes Mika's hips to involuntarily flex up and into my center. *Direct hit. Hang on, girl, you are on your way to O-Town.*

I'm rubbing up against his very swollen cock, and Mika runs his hands from my hips to the hem of my dress. He pushes it up my thighs, and that's when I really start to grind against him. The heat between us is intoxicating, making me wild with need.

"Shiloh." A deep moan tumbles from Mika's lust-drunk lips as he pulls away.

Before going any further, Mika stops to check in with me. His eyes communicate everything; he wants to know if I'm okay with what we're doing. *Yes, I am.* Nodding my agreement; I continue my rapid pace of grinding and thrusting against him like I'm a cat in heat, using his leg like a rubbing post. "So, so close, Mika."

When he finally reaches under my skirt and finds my panties, he discovers they are soaked. He slips a finger under my thong and rubs circles on my sensitive clit. "Please don't stop. Feels. Too. Good," I moan in a throaty voice I don't recognize. Before I know it, I'm unraveling. Quaking and shaking in Mika's lap as he holds me tight to his chest. My back arches at the peak, and I'm panting like I just completed a marathon. I don't care that we are in my backyard because what we just did was mind-blowing.

When my body finally settles, he lifts me up and gently lays me back. Opening my legs wide, he crawls between them. When our pelvises are pressed flush together, he rubs his cock against my sensitive clit, causing a shiver to ripple through my body. "Shiloh, you feel so damn good." With him looking down at me, I suddenly feel incredibly vulnerable, like he can read my thoughts. Not being prepared for that, I reach up and pull his lips to me, kissing him with such ferocity it should scare me, but it doesn't.

What starts as a slow, innocent, tender kiss morphs into a deep, tongue-twisting, thrusting, and twirling feverish kiss in no time, turning me to putty. Grinding his hips forward into me, I wrap my legs around his waist, locking us together. Our bodies rub mercilessly against each other while chasing a high we're both pursuing.

I climax again and arch my back off the blanket, pushing Mika's whole body into the air. Our bodies return to the quilt and he sits up quickly. When the lust haze has cleared from my eyes, I sit up and stare at him, silently questioning. Mika reaches for my hand, then kisses my knuckles. "Shiloh, sweetheart, I need to go home." *What? Why?*

"You're leaving? Did I do something wrong?" I ask in a quiet, worried tone.

Shaking his head, he answers me, "No, you didn't do anything wrong. I really like you, and I'm trying to behave. This—what's happening between us—isn't a booty-call, one-night stand, quick-fuck scenario for me. I want something more, and tonight I'm choosing to be that man for you."

His confession is perfect. I nod my agreement and stand up. Lacing our fingers together, we walk hand in hand to the front door. Turning to me, he gives me another gentle kiss and then heads out.

Chapter 18

Mika

The week following our dinner and dessert date is busy for Shiloh and the boys. She goes back to work, Sam starts kindergarten, and Lian returns to daycare. Every time we talk or text, Shiloh is running some errand to get her back-to-school list accomplished; haircuts, clothes shopping, doctor's appointments, shots, dental cleanings, and school supplies. How she keeps it all straight baffles me. Other than a quick greeting on the first day of school when I brought her coffee, I haven't seen them all week, and I miss them. *Crazy, right?*

Tonight, when I know the boys have gone to bed, I call her.

"Hey, beautiful. How are you?"

"It's been a long week," she replies, sounding weary.

"Can I see you tonight?" I ask.

"I don't know, Mika." She's exhausted, I know. My hope is that her desire to see me will outweigh any argument occupying any space in her head.

"I won't stay long, I promise. I just need to see you. We can sit out on your porch and talk."

"Hmm... I suppose we could do that. But just for a little bit. I need my beauty sleep," she teases.

"Great. I'll be right over," I say, then add before I hang up, "Wait... beauty sleep? Unnecessary, you're already gorgeous."

I slip on my Crocs and head over to her house, eager to see her.

As she steps out her front door, Shiloh is wearing a matching cotton tank top and short set. She looks ethereal, and my brain stutters, making me stop in place. Standing on her porch, shoeless, with her hair tied up in a messy bun, I realize something. She is my greatest temptation.

Closing the space between us, I take in her now-familiar scent of vanilla and citrus and feel my body respond. My shoulders relax, my mouth waters, and my cock twitches. Shiloh is overwhelming all of my senses, pushing me into very unfamiliar territory, and I'm finding I crave it. The only question is, how am I going to react? Will I be a gentleman and remain respectful or a caveman and take what I want? The verdict is still out.

Shiloh sees my indecision on how to initiate things, so she grabs my hand and leads me over to a wicker couch, and I follow. When we sit down, I pull her legs across my lap, taking a foot in my hand and giving her a foot massage. I notice the longer I rub and manipulate her tired feet, the more relaxed she becomes. Her body sags across the couch, melting into the faded cushions. It's amazing to watch.

Once I'm confident she's relaxed, I trail my fingertips up and down her smooth-as-silk legs, not going any higher than the hem of her shorts. It isn't that I don't want to explore higher—I do. I so do—especially when I notice her breathing hitch every time I get closer to her center. But I want to be respectful and show her I'm not here just to fill a need or scratch an itch. Already she's become more than that to me. Shiloh lights my body up in ways I didn't even know possible. Absolutely everything she does arouses and intrigues me, leaving me panting for more.

"Shiloh, what's got you so wound up?"

When she pushes out a breath, I feel more tension fall away. "The kids can be a handful. Especially the first weeks back at school after the summer break. It's like some of them forget how to do basic things like wait their turn or raise their hand."

Huffing a laugh, I say, "I know grown adults who still struggle with those things. Not sure what that means, but I hope your students catch on quicker than they have."

With her eyes still closed, Shiloh smirks at me. "Me too."

A minute of silence passes and then she adds, "It's hard to believe it's only been a week, and I'm already exhausted."

I can't even imagine. It seems like the tiredness she's referring to differs from what I feel after a long workout or tough game. It's not just physical, it's emotional too. "Anything else happen this week?"

Again, she smirks. Then she opens her gorgeous blue eyes and looks at me before answering in a sultry tone, "I had a really sexy professional hockey player bring me a coffee on Monday." She teases me with a wink. *This woman.*

Two can play this game. "You don't say? Is there someone I need to beat up?"

She represses a laugh and shakes her head no. "I can handle him. He gives really great foot rubs. I'm considering keeping him around for a bit, but thanks for the offer."

During our conversation, I discover Shiloh is even more incredible than I already believed. Even though I'm really trying to listen, I'm finding it challenging. Between the feel of her silky soft skin, the whiffs of her body spray, and the relaxed moans she keeps making as I massage her feet, it seems she's making everything hard. Hard to listen, hard to concentrate, and hard as steel in my shorts. As I sit there on her porch, caressing her skin, I remind myself to focus on her words rather than the determined throbbing in my lap.

"Mika. Mika. How was your week?" My body goes

rigid as I realize she's been calling me and I'd yet to answer.

"Yeah. Sorry. My week was... average. I skated every day and visited the weight room. Nothing out of the ordinary or particularly difficult." Shiloh needs a little fun, so I ask, "What are you doing tomorrow night? Can I bring over dinner? Maybe take one thing off your plate."

Giving me a sleepy smile, she answers, "You don't have to do that. I don't mean to complain. I truly love my job and the kids. It really isn't that bad. Sometimes it just makes me tired."

"Shiloh, I want to do something for you. I want to take care of you and the boys. Please let me do this. Plus, if I bring dinner, it's a guaranteed way to spend time with you all."

Shiloh removes her legs from my lap and stands up. Side-eyeing her, I'm confused by what she's doing. But when she climbs up onto my lap and brings her lips to mine, everything makes sense. She tastes better than I remember from the week before, and I easily fall under her spell.

My hands run down her sides and trace over to her butt, where I squeeze hard before I pull her tight into me, eliciting a sensual moan from her. *Holy fuck, that's sexy as hell.* I pop open my eyes and watch her continue to unravel. With our bodies pressed tightly against each other, I could swear I've died and gone to heaven. Kissing Shiloh is like nothing I've ever experienced. It engages all five of my senses, lighting up sections of my brain that normally remain dormant except for when I'm playing hockey. Kissing her is like a pure shot of adrenaline.

Reminding myself that we're on her front porch, I force myself to behave when all I want to do is stand up with her still wrapped around me, push inside the house, go upstairs to her bedroom, close the door, and take my time getting to know every part of her. However, there are some things to consider with that plan. We've only had one quasi-date, her boys are asleep inside, and I don't have any condoms on me. So, for the second time in under a week, I purposefully give myself blue balls. Even though pulling back from our kiss feels like ripping my own arm off, it must be done. "Shiloh... babe." The pain of separating tears through my body and makes my stomach churn and my skin prickle. When her eyes flutter open, I remove my hands from her butt, place them around her face, and lower her eyes to me. Rasping, I say, "Shiloh, it's time to call it a night. Otherwise, I'll go caveman on you and push far past any boundaries we've yet to set. Maybe tomorrow after dinner, after the boys have gone to bed, we can talk about that and discuss what we want. What do you think?"

Instead of hurt spreading across her face as I expected, her eyes are clear, her mouth upturned, and her brow is relaxed. "You sure about bringing dinner, Mika?"

Bringing her in for a tight hug, I nod against her. "I can definitely bring dinner. Do the boys like pizza? Do you?"

Shiloh giggles into my chest. *Dumb question.*

Pushing off my chest so she can see me, Shiloh replies, "Yes, we like pizza. The boys love cheese, and I'll eat anything as long as it doesn't have anchovies or banana peppers on it." Her cute nose squishes up, and it's adorable, even tempting me to bop it. But like the civilized man I am, I resist.

Having Shiloh climb off my lap feels wrong. Immediately, I miss her closeness, but I'm glad that I'll see her tomorrow, when we'll get more one-on-one time. Plus, we're planning to add some definition to our relationship. *No more constant guessing for me.*

Standing up and wrapping her in my arms, I'm once again struck by how petite she really is. Kissing the top of her head, then her lips, I mumble "goodnight" across them before I turn toward my house and walk home. *Tomorrow can't come quickly enough.*

Chapter 19

Shiloh

True to his word, Mika knocks on our door at six with pizza in hand. I didn't tell the boys he was coming over and when they see him, I almost go deaf from the whoops and hollers that come out of my guys. And the smile that Mika wears speaks volumes to my heart. It's completely genuine and full of excitement. He looks almost as excited as Sam and Lian.

"Mika, Mika, Mika," both boys squeal as they wrap themselves around his legs to hug him.

"Hey, guys. I brought dinner. Hope you don't mind pizza," Mika says, his deep voice filling our entryway.

Excitedly, the boys chant "pizza, pizza, pizza." Then Sam asks, "What kind did you bring?"

Mika looks at me, smirks, and answers, "Your mom said you love anchovies."

Sam looks concerned as he turns to me. "Momma, what is an anch-o-vey?"

Making a squished-up, disgusted face, I stick out my tongue. "It's a stinky fish that has no place on a pizza."

Lian laughs and Sam puts his hands on his hips. Then he whisper-asks, "Do I have to eat it? I know Mika is a guest, but I don't like fish on my pizza." Looking up at Mika, his massive body is shaking from the laughter he's holding in.

"Sam, I think Mika is pulling your leg."

Sam looks down at his leg and shakes his head no. Then he looks at me, confused.

Laughing, I say, "I think Mika is teasing you. He was trying to trick you."

Understanding, Sam smiles and turns his focus back to Mika. "Mika," is all he says. Mika lets out a whoosh of air along with a deep chuckle that registers warmth deep in my belly, filling it full of comfort and love.

"Sam, your mom is right. There is no fish on your pizza, only cheese and sauce. Your mom and I have a few more toppings."

After stuffing ourselves full of pizza while watching the boys' favorite movie, *Cars*, I get them in their jammies before they rush downstairs with a book. They're hoping Mika will read it to them before they go to bed. I didn't intend to assimilate him into our bedtime routine, but the boys insisted, and if I'm being honest, it just feels right. Maybe it's too soon, but are there set timelines everyone has to follow in the progression of a relationship? *I don't know.*

Running into the living room, decked out in matching jammies, the boys fly at the couch Mika's settled on. Lian, who's managed to carry the book downstairs, walks straight up to Mika, thrusts it at him and orders, "You read." Not even waiting for an answer, he uses Mika's leg as leverage to pull himself up on the couch, plopping down right next to him. Mika's eyes flick to me, but instead of worry, I see they're filled with happiness.

"Can I?" he mouths to me. Shocked, I nod, and Sam and I join them on the couch. *Be still my heart.*

Marching the boys upstairs after multiple good-night hugs is a challenge. But Mika rescues me when he calls out, "Can we maybe go to the park tomorrow?"

Lian and Sam both shout "yes," and I quickly remind them, "You need to get enough rest so you can keep up with Mika tomorrow at the park." Desperate for sleep, they climb into their beds with no further hassle. "Night, boys. Sleep well. I love you," I tell them as I flick their light and close their door.

Heading downstairs to have the relationship talk should make me nervous, but it doesn't. I really like Mika, and I'm hoping he feels the same. I rarely imagined myself dating after my divorce, mostly because I couldn't picture anyone being as comfortable with my kids as me. However, Mika is amazing with them and I know it isn't an act. He's completely genuine and real with us.

When I reach the last step, my stomach feels like it's filled with butterflies taking flight. Instead of it being nervous energy, it's excited and hopeful. When I reach the couch, Mika turns to me. "Shiloh, your boys are incredible. I don't have much experience with kids, but they are some of the coolest people I have ever met." My heart beats out an unsteady rhythm in my chest. *Is he for real?*

Lowering myself next to him, I smile. "Thanks, I think they're pretty great too."

Mika laughs, and again the sound registers deep, stirring up a whole plethora of emotions. He reaches for my hand and intertwines our fingers. "Not only are your kids cool, but I really like their mom. She's incredible."

His words act like a balm to my tattered heart. "I think you're pretty incredible too, Mika." Suddenly, the air around us shifts, almost as if speaking those confessions into existence changes the magnetism. Off-kilter, I ask, "Now what?"

Mika squeezes the hand he's holding and speaks five simple words. "We give it a try."

"Okay," I answer, knowing we will have to have more discussion about that later, but now, I'm just going to enjoy the moment where Mika and I decided we want something more.

* * *

The past few months have been busy, but good. School and the students have finally settled into a schedule that feels amazing. Sam is adjusting to kindergarten beautifully, and Lian is thriving in his new big kid's group at daycare. Mika's hockey season is in full swing, and he's traveling so often that we do our best to make the time he's here memorable, with trips to the zoo, parks, and museums.

It's been a hellacious week and a disastrous start to the weekend. But late Saturday night, Mika arrived back in town, and first thing Sunday morning, he becomes my official knight in shining armor.

On Monday morning, I'd been running late when I spilled coffee all down the front of me after dropping Lian at daycare. Thankfully, I had some spare clothes in my 4Runner, so I didn't have to drive home, making me even more behind. On Tuesday, I'd got us out the door on time, but one of my tires looked a little flat. Past lessons from Grandpa to the rescue, I got a portable air compressor hooked up so I could pump my tire. While waiting for it to fill with air, I called the mobile tire service, and the tire gods must have been smiling on me because I could make arrangements for them to come check my tire while I was working. Five hundred and fifty dollars later, I had a new tire and a bent nail to help cushion the blow to my wallet. Wednesday started with an explosion, or that's what it felt like when Sam woke me up at two thirty in the morning with a weak sounding "Momma." Then he puked all over me. The next days were a blur of laundry, sanitizing everything, and so many cartoons. I kept Lian home in case he came down with the twenty-four-hour bug, but we were lucky and avoided it. Sam was finally feeling well enough by Friday afternoon that he could stomach some chicken noodle soup. On Saturday, he was still wimpy, so we stayed near the house. When Mika arrived back in town late Saturday night, he texted me he'd be over early on Sunday to help with whatever I needed to accomplish before Monday. *My hero.*

Like a true knight in shining armor, at seven Sunday morning Mika knocks on our front door, holding an extra-large size blended mocha, glazed donuts for the boys, and a bouquet of wildflowers. "Hey, beautiful," is all he has to say in his deep, sexy voice to get me feeling on top of the world. That voice of his does funny things to my insides and makes me want things I never thought possible. After he hugs the boys, we all walk into the kitchen, where he ushers them to their chairs before grabbing plates for their donuts. As Sam and Lian bite into their sugary breakfast, Mika pulls me into a hug. Rubbing my back and whispering in my ear how much he missed me is just what I needed. Pulling back with tears in my eyes, I whisper, "Thank you, Mika. Thank you so much."

Mika responds perfectly by placing a tender kiss on

my lips and asking the boys, "How are those donuts?" With full mouths, you can barely make out the garbled "mmms" of their agreement.

Handing me my coffee, he says, "Now that the boys are fed and you're caffeinated, what's on the agenda for today? I'm ready for anything."

Oh, he's in for a real treat with what I have planned.

Chapter 20

Mika

When I told Shiloh I was ready for anything, I hadn't expected her to laugh. *That sounds ominous. What is she thinking?* Taking a large drink of the iced beverage before she answers nearly kills me. "Mika, we need to go to the grocery store, and since we haven't left the house in days, I want to go to a park so the boys can run a bit." *That doesn't sound so bad.* Slapping my hands together, I say, "Let's go."

On the drive to the store after everyone's dressed, I feel Shiloh staring at me. "What?" I ask.

"Oh... it's... nothing," she answers in a sweet voice, but I don't miss her pause.

Turning my head to her, I ask again, "What?"

Out of the corner of my eye, I see her fidget with her hands. "Um... Have you ever been shopping with kids before?"

"No. Why?" I question. *What am I missing?*

"It's an experience sometimes, and I want to warn you," she says in a hesitant voice that makes me instantly edgy.

"Warn me about what? Should I be worried? Aren't we just going to get groceries? How hard can that be?" My questions come out panicked.

Before she can answer, a little voice from the back seat pipes in. "Sometimes we get into trouble at the store." Really? What can a two- and-five-year-old get into at the grocery store? Aren't they usually strapped in the cart? My head whips to the right like I'm possessed and controlled by demonic spirits. I know my eyes are demanding answers as I stare her down. "Shiloh, what is Sam talking about?"

A nervous laugh falls from her lips. "Remember the day we met?"

I nod my head, even though I'm not following her train of thought.

"That morning I had taken the boys to the store to get the basics and they hadn't had a race car cart," she explains.

"And?" I question, needing the rest of the story.

"Well, when they don't have the race car cart, Sam walks alongside me and is sort of... well... he's kind of..." Her voice trails off.

"He's what, Shiloh?"

"I'm free!" Sam declares from behind me.

Lian squeals and yells, "Fwee!."

Shiloh just shifts in her seat. *Why does she look so worried?*

"Okay. So, we need to make sure we find a race car cart. That sounds simple enough," I say out loud so that everyone knows the plan as we drive into the parking lot.

"Otherwise, it'll be chaos." I hear Shiloh whisper to herself when she gets out of the truck. *Nah, we got this.*

As we approach the store, the boys race up to the carts, desperately searching for *the* cart. But to our disappointment, there isn't the sacred race cart one, and after Shiloh secures Lian in the seat of a regular cart, I stick my hand out for Sam to hold. Hopefully, by doing this, it will keep our excursion chaos free.

Grocery shopping with kids is different; they want everything that's terrible for them and they can sing you all the jingles to whatever is hot at the moment.

"Sam, you're not supposed to climb on the shelves," Shiloh says in a calm voice, then more forcefully, "Sam. Samuel, this isn't the playground. You need to get down. Now."

"Paygwnd. Paygwnd," Lian chants and claps his chubby hands together. If it didn't look like steam was about to pour out of Shiloh's ears, I'd definitely be laughing, but she looks upset, and I'm not about to make it worse.

After a few minutes in the cereal aisle, I'm sure Sam is channeling Spiderman, and removing him from the situation so Shiloh can finish her shopping looks like a good option.

"Hey, Spidey, I mean, Sam. Want to get out of here so your mom can finish shopping?" I offer.

Sam's eyes go wide and he excitedly nods. Jumping off the lowest shelf, he lands perfectly before he runs to me and snatches my hand. *What a character!*

As he and I walk out of the store, I tell myself that next time Shiloh needs to go to the store, I'll offer to watch the boys at the house so she can shop in peace.

Chapter 21

Shiloh

Since Mika and I started dating, we've spent a lot of time together. When he's out of town for an away series, we try to watch his games and when he's home; we do our best to utilize the time we have. After he got a taste of shopping with kids, Mika now tries his best to be available to watch the boys when I need to grocery shop. To this busy single mom, those few hours every so often are truly magical. Mika encourages me to take my time and enjoy the time away. I definitely do, and I think the boys enjoy the break from me. With Mika, they're getting uninterrupted time with their hero. It's a win-win. *What could be better?*

As the days click by, I find myself falling deeper and deeper for Mika. He is everything I ever wanted in a man, partner, and father to my boys, and it's hard to not picture him in those roles permanently. I know we haven't been together long and no one's perfect, but he's pretty damn close.

After putting the boys to bed, Mika and I snuggle together on the couch, talking.

"When do you leave again?" I ask, confused. His travel schedule is insane and tough to follow.

"I fly out the day after tomorrow," he answers while holding me tight.

"Yeah!" I cheer while snuggling in deeper into his chest. You'd think with all his muscles it wouldn't be comfortable, but it surprisingly is. And it's warm too. Almost perfect for sleeping. "Ahhh," I yawn into his chest.

"Shiloh, I think you're tired and it's time for bed." Mika's deep voice speaks against my head. Knowing that he'll go home, I shake my head because I'm not ready to let him go. Rubbing my back, he gently says, "I'll see you tomorrow."

Still buried in his chest, I whisper, "Why don't you stay?" Mika instantly goes rigid. Nervous, I pull back slightly to see his wide brown eyes staring at me.

"Did you just invite me to sleep over?"

Shyly, I nod.

"Shiloh?" The question in his tone is confusing. I don't know how to interpret what he's asking. Does he want to stay or doesn't he? My thoughts spin out of control. As if he can see the whirling chaos in my head, Mika places his hand on the side of my face. His eyes lock with mine. "Hey, beautiful. I do want to sleep over, but I think we need to talk about some things first."

What does he want to talk about? Haven't we talked about everything already? I've shared everything with Mika. Or so I thought. But his next five words prove I left something major out.

"Tell me about your ex."

I guess it's time. It isn't that I was withholding the information from him about Trent. I just don't like to remember him and how he'd treated me. How I'd let him treat me. There aren't a lot of things I regret, but giving Trent permission time and time again to treat me poorly for years is one of them.

"Okay. What do you want to know?"

He places a tender kiss on my lips before he answers, "The big stuff."

Where to start?

"Trent and I started dating in high school. He was older than me and went to college first. I graduated early so I could join him. After my freshman year, he proposed, and we got married. About a year later, while he was still in school finishing his degree and I was working to support us, I found out I was pregnant with Sam." I look at Mika to see if he has any questions, and he remains silent. "Once he graduated, he went to work and I stayed home. Our marriage wasn't great. He spent nights after work at the bars with friends, and I suspected some ladies, but I never had any proof. My grandpa died just after Sam was born, so

I tried to spend time with my grandma, but then when Sam was two, she passed away too."

Again, I take a break in the story to see if Mika has questions. "He cheated on you?" The rasp of his voice sends chills down my back. *Why does he sound like he wants to hurt someone?*

"Like I said, I never had proof, only suspicions. But his denial from as far back as college was always the same. He didn't cheat, he was only hanging out with friends." I can hear the grinding of Mika's teeth as he acknowledges that last part. "Shortly after Grandma died, Trent *convinced* me to move into their house that she'd left me in her will."

Tilting his head at me, he caught the emphasis I'd placed on "convinced." "How did he convince you, Shiloh?"

Wringing my hands, I continue, "Trent knew I wanted another baby, and he used that as his reasoning for wanting to move. It would be bigger, safer, more family friendly. All his points were solid, but I was missing a major thing. He didn't want a family, kids, or to be married to me." My confession weighs me down, and I'm embarrassed to admit I stayed with a man who obviously didn't want me. Mika's hands have dropped from cradling my face and now they're tightly curled into fists and his face looks murderous. Stunned, I ask, "Mika, are you okay?"

Through gritted teeth, he answers, "No, Shiloh, I am not. That fucker had everything and he cast it away like it was garbage. You, Sam, and Lian didn't deserve that."

This man. He is such a fierce protector. "You're right, we didn't, and that is why we aren't together anymore. On the day I told him I was pregnant with Lian, he was so ugly and hateful, and I swore I would do better for my boys. For myself."

"You are so strong, Shiloh. I'm sorry you had to endure that piece of shit."

I huff out a laugh. "Yeah. Except that piece of shit gave me my two best gifts, Sam and Lian. And I refuse to be upset about them. Yes, in the long run, Trent was terrible in every meaning of the word, but I have two incredible kids and a pretty amazing boyfriend. So, I'm thankful that the bumpy road I was on led me to where I am."

"Ahhh." Mika yawns. "Is that everything? The highlight reel, so to speak."

"Almost. To add more to the character assassination of my ex, he was also incredibly greedy. As part of our divorce, I agreed to give him the two million in bonds I'd inherited from my grandparents for an uncontested divorce and the relinquishing of his parental rights of both boys."

Shaking his head, he growls, "What an asshole."

That went easier than I thought. I smile at him. "I agree completely."

Pulling me in for a tight hug, he finally agrees to

my request. "If I'm sleeping over, I'm just planning to hold you, okay?"

We haven't had sex yet, since Mika is still trying to prove to me I'm more than a booty call or quick hookup. So his offer of sleeping in his arms tonight sounds absolutely perfect. Mika again proves he's everything Trent wasn't. He is a good man. Rising off the couch, I tug him with me. "Let's go to bed."

Chapter 22

Mika

Toward the end of October, Lucas and Samantha host a fall harvest party for the team. Unlike many other parties they've hosted, it's family-friendly, so Shiloh and the boys are invited too.

Introducing them to everyone is intimidating at first, but once I see how receptive my teammates are, it's phenomenal, and the boys have a great time being doted on by everyone. They swim, carve pumpkins—with help—and eat as much chili as they can.

Making it even more comfortable for Shiloh is the fact that Monica is there because of her connection to Samantha and Christian. Throughout our relationship, I'd heard of Monica, but until tonight, I hadn't realized we were talking about the same person. *Small world.*

That night, after the party, we give the boys their baths, read their favorite books, and tuck them into bed. They're worn out from the excitement of the day and fall asleep quickly.

We relax in her living room and share a pumpkin beer Josh, my team captain, recommended. Overall, it had been an excellent day. My team rallied around us, welcoming Shiloh, Sam, and Lian into the fold, like they were officially mine. As far as I'm concerned, they are. And nothing is going to prevent us from becoming a family. I just have to bide my time until Shiloh comes to the same conclusion. She's definitely more cautious than I am, which is understandable.

Wanting to end the evening on an even higher note, I decide I'm finally ready to have sex with her. From the first moment I'd seen her, I'd wanted her, but it was important for me to convey to her I want more than something physical between us.

For weeks, Shiloh has been trying to get me to fold by wearing outfits she knows I'd like or by suggestively touching me. The straw that almost broke the camel's back was when she invited me to sleep over. Even though I'd caved, I remained clothed the entire time we slept next to one another. The first night, holding her in my arms, was like a dream. It was then that I discovered it was everything I never knew I wanted. Waking up with her warm body against mine, the scent of her surrounding me, her sleepy voice, her gentle morning kisses. I craved it all. For. The. Rest. Of. My. Life. I had never considered a forever until now.

With thoughts of her constantly churning through

my mind, I know I'm ready to take the next step with her. Shiloh has my complete heart, and now I want her to have all of me. Holding back had seemed so foreign to me when we started dating months ago, but now it feels entirely intentional and right. It's almost like I'm a virgin again, saving myself just for her.

Draining the last sips of beer from the amber colored bottle, I stand up from the couch. Pulling Shiloh up, I drag her past the kitchen and toward the front door. As we get closer, I feel her grip on my hand tighten and hear a sigh fall from her lips. Reaching for the handle, I slowly lift my hand to the deadbolt and lock it. Knowing that means I'm staying over, Shiloh excitedly squeaks next to me, causing my heart rate to climb. She doesn't know what I'm planning to do next; we haven't discussed it. My only hope is that she's as ready for it as I am. In fact, I'm so geared up, I already have a steel rod in my jeans, and I pray I don't embarrass myself.

Before meeting Shiloh in July, I hadn't been with a woman in months. Still unsure what motivated that dry spell, I suspect it was boredom from the one-night stands I'd been having. Back then I'd been craving something different, something more. Now that I have that in Shiloh, I'm inexplicably nervous. Unlike when I was a teen, I've got three factors in my corner: I'm older, larger, and more focused on pleasing her. Even with those advantages, I'm still terrified I won't last long because of my self-imposed abstinence and because I've wanted her since I first met her months ago. Thankfully, if that happens, at least I'm still young and recover quickly.

Reaching her bedroom feels monumental, and I suppose it is. Shiloh's room is the perfect balance of comfortable and sensual. It reflects her perfectly. She's an uncomplicated beauty. Everything I love about her is housed in a simple package that radiates a confidence that is undeniably sexy. I'd learned early on that, out of necessity, Shiloh has never been one of those women who are concerned with name brands, latest trends, makeup, or overt sexuality. And honestly, she doesn't need any of it. To me, Shiloh, fresh faced, hair down, dressed in a tank top, yoga pants, and shoeless, is perfection—the epitome of sexy.

Closing the door behind us, I flip the lock, and Shiloh spins around, confused. In all the times I've slept over, which has been practically every night since our first sleepover, we've never locked the door, just in case one of the boys needed Shiloh. In fact, I suspect that until I began sleeping over, Shiloh had left her door cracked in case Sam or Lian called out. But tonight, with questioning eyes, Shiloh hesitates.

Normally, we'd both brush our teeth, and while Shiloh was in the bathroom changing into her pajamas, I'd pull on a pair of athletic shorts I kept in her top drawer, then we'd crawl into bed and make out like horny teenagers. Over the past several weeks, we've progressed to extremely heavy petting, but we've never crossed the line into actually having sex of any kind, even though I'm pretty sure we're both eager for it.

Standing toe-to-toe, I lift her gaze to me by placing my finger under her chin and pushing up. When her blue eyes meet mine, I smile. "I didn't mean to startle you when I locked the door. I just know I'm finally ready to take this relationship further, and I don't want Sam or Lian to come in and see what I'm going to do to you. Is that okay?" *Please say yes.*

When she finally understands what I'm saying, her eyes grow wide and they burn bright, letting me know she's excited. Instead of answering with words, she nods her head. Needing no further discussion, I swoop down and pick her up and carry her over to the bed, where I gently lay her down. I strip off my shirt and crawl over her, trapping her between my arms. Lowering my head to hers, I want to know if she's alright with my plan. "Shiloh, I've tried so hard to be a gentleman, not wanting you to feel pressured into doing anything you weren't ready for. I wanted to prove to you that this—what's between us—isn't about sex, it's about wanting more." She places her hand on my cheek and nods her understanding. And that's all the encouragement I need to keep going.

"I don't know when it happened, but sometime since we met, I've fallen completely in love with you." Before I can say anything else, she pulls my lips down to hers and kisses me passionately. Her hands weave through my hair, occasionally tugging, spiking my desire for her. When I've reached my limit, I drag my lips from hers, pull her hands from behind my neck and place them above her head, instructing her with a growled "Stay." Her giggle causes me to smirk as I wonder how she'd do with other commands in the bedroom. *I can't wait to explore more later.*

Slowly, I peel her cotton nightgown above her head, revealing flirty magenta panties and two beautifully naked breasts that I've longed to taste. Shiloh's dusky, rose-colored nipples call to me, begging for my touch, and the thought of finally being able to lick, bite, and massage these perfect pillows makes my cock leak.

Knowing I need to slow things down before I cause myself any embarrassment, I lower myself, trailing light kisses down her sternum, nuzzling the side of each breast when I pass them. I continue on with my exploration by placing a trail of kisses to her belly button. Swirling my tongue around the divot makes my insides feel funny. Suddenly I'm picturing Shiloh swollen with my child, and the thought of that makes my chest quake with excitement. Before this moment, I'd never pictured having my own children, but this vision feels so real. Having Sam and Lian was the only consideration I'd made when contemplating children, but now I recognize there could be another option. *Fuck, that's thrilling.*

Wanting to feel even closer to Shiloh, needing to kiss her, I crawl back up her body, squeezing and massaging each breast along the way. When I reach her lips, I dive in like a starved man, nibbling, thrusting, swirling, sucking, licking, and savoring everything she gives me. My hands travel back to one of her breasts and I rub it tenderly, plucking and squeezing the nipple. Shiloh responds instantly, arching her back, thrusting her hips, and biting my lip. The longer I massage her breast, the more she moves beneath me, rubbing against my swollen cock.

"Ahhhh." Shiloh releases a deep, throaty moan into the air surrounding us when I pinch and tug on her nipple. Hands down, it's the best sound I've ever heard, and I want to hear it again, along with any other noises she might make.

"Let me make you feel even better," I whisper to her.

She answers with a needy, "Please, Mika."

Sliding my body back down hers, I trace my tongue past her breasts, giving each one a squeeze before I continue my way down to her hot-as-fuck magenta panties. Running my tongue along the seam makes her whimper. Her hips rise toward me as I slip my tongue under the silky fabric, teasing her with the pleasure I'm about to deliver her desperate, needy body. My cock throbs angrily in my jeans, seeking release and punishing me for the self-imposed abstinence I have made us endure for the past months. *It'll be worth it, buddy. I promise.*

Lifting my hands, I trace over the edges of her panties before I anchor my fingers in them and work them slowly down her legs, dropping them to the floor. Wrapping my hands firmly around her hip bones, I pull her to the edge of the bed. Kneeling before her, I tuck her legs over my shoulders. Blowing on her most sensitive part sends shivers cascading through her body, and a mewl falls from her pinched, pink lips. Testing my restraint, I finally dip my head to her and place a long lick along her wet folds. From the first taste of her, I'm hopelessly addicted, knowing I'll never get enough. Each time I reach her clit and wrap my lips around it and suck, Shiloh lets out an ego-boosting moan I feel deep in my bones.

When she begins to pant, I insert one finger, and her muscles squeeze me like a vise. Feeling the tightness, I know I need to prepare her or I'll never be able to fit inside before I blow. Moving in and out, I curl my finger, reaching for her G-spot. Brushing against it at my second pass, her hips shoot up reflexively, tearing my mouth away from her clit. I kiss and nuzzle her thigh, and when she relaxes, I resume licking and lapping at everything her body gives me. Inserting another finger gives me what I desire most, and Shiloh moans out, "More, please, Mika." And I oblige, thrusting into her with more force.

The signs of an orgasm overtake her petite body, and I continue, chasing her high with her, desperate to see her unravel. When her legs shake, I bite her clit and insert a third finger, causing her to nearly come off the bed. "Holy shit, do that again." Shiloh's throaty voice instructing me makes my skin hot with desire. I double my efforts and increase my speed. Moments later, I watch as a powerful quiver overtakes her body, ripping through it, leaving her shaken and spent on the bed.

Rising off the floor, I move her back toward the center of the bed. I strip off my jeans and boxer briefs, dropping them to the floor, and climb over her. Shiloh's eyes flutter open, and she reaches for me, pulling me down to her. When our lips touch, it feels like coming home. Then our hips meet, and I know being with Shiloh will be the most incredible experience of my life.

Our bodies settle against one other, matching perfectly, as if we were two halves of the same whole. Our kisses deepen and Shiloh's legs wrap around me, tucking me into her. She's done this many times before when we were fooling around, but until now, I hadn't realized how possessive it felt. She's claiming me, and damn, that feels good. I'm hers and she is mine.

Shiloh takes one hand she's threaded through my hair and trails it down my side, hitting a patch of skin that is ticklish. I squirm and pull up, ending our kiss.

"Ticklish?" Shiloh purrs at me while her hand delicately traces over the traitorous skin. Reaching down, I mean to grab her arm so I can push it above her head and resume kissing her senseless, but she has other plans, and she thrusts her hand between us. As soon as her fingers graze over my swollen cock, I feel a tingle start to dance up my spine. She's playing with fire, and if she keeps up with her tentative exploration, I'll be coming for the first time all over her and not where I want at all.

"Shiloh, babe," I growl. She giggles but keeps at it. Defeated, I do the only thing I can think of to buy myself more time. I pull away.

Shocked, she gasps and asks, "Mika, where are you going?"

Taking a second to get my body under control, I blow out a breath, reach for my jeans, and pull out the condom I brought with me. "I'm not going anywhere, babe. I just needed a moment, or our first time together wouldn't have ended the way I want."

Shiloh looks at my hard cock and the condom in my hand and her eyes shine. Then she licks her lips. *Fucking vixen.* I don't know if she was aware of doing it, but she had, and now images of her on her knees, taking me down her throat, flood my brain. Being the dick that he is, my cock twitches and Shiloh's eyes go wide. Wanting to keep him under control, I wrap my hand around him and squeeze, alleviating some of the constant throbbing. Then I rip open the condom and slide it on. Wanting her final permission, I look at Shiloh for her consent, and she smiles.

Chapter 23

Shiloh

The time has come. *Finally.*

Mika eyes me, and his brown eyes darken to almost black, appearing intense and focused, almost like an animal stalking its prey. Settling back, I let him come to me. Despite my body whirling with giddy anticipation, I manage to stay relatively still. His tight, sexy body hovers above me, and his long, hard cock drags between my legs, leaving a trail of heat in its wake. My eyes flutter but don't close, replaying the feel of our bodies coming together. As Mika lowers himself to me, I spread my legs, showing him I'm ready. Always considerate, he looks into my eyes, seeking permission, and I smile. Surrounded by a strong, sexy, and sweet hockey player, I make my first move, pulling his lips to mine and kissing him with all the love I feel for him.

Reaching between us, I run my fingers up the

length of him, memorizing the touch of his heated skin. Mika lifts his hips, and I take the opportunity to stroke his cock. He arches his back and lets out a guttural moan from deep within, showing me his pleasure. Reaching the base of him, I squeeze like I'd seen him do, and goose bumps break out all over his skin. Guiding him to my center is like taking a shot of concentrated ecstasy. Slowly, he pushes in and my body unwinds around him. When he reaches the hilt, a full shiver racks my body, and he holds me through it.

"Shiloh... you are perfect... you were made for me," he says as he rocks inside of me. It doesn't take long for another orgasm to build within me. Mika rolls us to our sides, and I slowly slide up and down his cock, squeezing him tightly as I lower back down. A deep groan falls from his lips as his eyes roll back in his head. Tipping his head forward, he sucks my breast into his mouth and it's like a direct strike to my clit.

"Yes," I moan.

Mika continues to suckle and nip at my breast, hurtling me toward a cataclysmic release that has started tearing through me. Everything tightens around Mika. "So tight. Holy fuck," he gasps out as his orgasm overtakes him.

When it's over, he pulls my exhausted body tighter to him and kisses me tenderly. We lie there, clinging to each other, knowing we've crossed into unfamiliar territory together. Not wanting to figure out what that means just yet, I slip from the bed to clean up.

After using the bathroom and pulling on my discarded nightgown, I crawl back into bed and cuddle up next to Mika, who is still perfectly naked. A stunned look is plastered on his gorgeous face, and I wonder what he's thinking. Had finally having sex been as monumental for him as it was for me? Remembrance of how good my body felt under Mika's touch lures me to sleep, and within minutes, I'm out.

The next morning, I wake up without the help of an alarm or a little person. Sitting up in bed, I notice Mika's spot is cold and empty. Happy noises creep up from downstairs. The air smells of pancakes, bacon, and coffee, and my mouth waters. Pulling my hair into a messy bun, I slip into the bathroom to pee and brush my teeth.

Giggles fill the kitchen as I descend the stairs, and my heart soars. Mika stands at the stove, dressed in only athletic shorts, making breakfast while Sam and Lian color at the table. With them unaware of my presence, I take a moment to watch the interaction between them. "Guys, what do you want? Pancakes in fun shapes or boring circles?" Mika asks, ready with batter in hand.

"Curcles!" Lian shouts, and I wonder if Mika will figure out he means circles. Before even giving him a second, Sam shouts out, "No circles, Lian! We want fun shapes, like stars." Muffling my laugh, I watch as Mika scratches his head, probably figuring out how he's going to pull that off.

Mika pours a pancake, trying to use a spatula to pull out the edges to make it resemble a star. Knowing it will never work, I step into the kitchen and over to the drawer that holds all my shape cutters. I pull my star molds out and walk them over to him. Relief washes over him when he sees what I'm holding. *"Thank you,"* he mouths before placing a kiss on my lips.

"Thanks for last night. I've never slept better," I whisper in his ear before I step away to say good morning to my little guys.

Later in the morning, before lunch, I recommend a visit to the playground. After throwing dinner in the crock pot and getting bundled up, we head out. Even though it's chilly, I know the fresh air will be good for us all.

"Brrr, it's colder out here than I thought," I tell Mika as he pushes Lian on the toddler swing.

"You think?" Mika asks. *Of course he isn't cold, he's a professional hockey player. His job guarantees he's used to this.* Sam, a few swings away, practices his pumping. In just a few months, he seems to have it nailed.

"I wish I were on a beach right now," I mumble to myself.

"What's stopping you?" Mika asks.

"Do you want a list?" I joke.

"Sure," he answers while still pushing Lian.

"Let's see... there's my job, Sam's in school now,

and the big reason... the cost. But someday I'll get there; it's on my bucket list."

Mika stops pushing Lian and walks over to me. "Go with me?"

"What? When? How?" I sputter as questions appear faster than answers.

"Shiloh, I'm serious. Lucas and Samantha are doing a destination wedding in Maui in December. You and the boys can come with me. While we aren't doing wedding stuff, we can explore the island. I've never been there and it would be fun to have some travel buddies. Especially if one of those buddies had a bikini." He adds a wink before walking back to Lian.

Lost in thought of how to respond, I hear Lian squeal. *Could we go to Maui? With Mika? Is he serious? We've only been dating for a short while. Would that be weird?*

"Momma, watch me," Sam hollers before he jumps off the swing and tumbles like he's a stuntman. I gasp.

"That was outstanding, Sam," Mika praises. "But you have to be careful you don't jump when you're too high. Otherwise, you could get hurt. Okay?"

Sam nods his head, wipes the dirt off his jeans, and jogs back over to the swing.

"Shiloh. What's going through your beautiful head?"

"Your offer sounds like a dream come true, but I'm nervous," I confess, my fears heavy on my tongue.

"Are you nervous about us?" he asks. But before I

can answer with a resounding yes, he does the unthinkable. "I get it. We just started dating. This—us—is new and untested. But I'm confident in what we're building. I know we'd have an amazing time. Trust me."

And for the first time in a long, long time, I take the leap. "Okay," I whisper.

"Okay?" Mika repeats.

I smile. "Yes, we'll go. Thank you for inviting us."

Later that day, after getting the boys to bed, Mika and I pass out, exhausted from our lack of sleep the night before. Thankfully, we remain clothed, because when Sam wakes me up early the next morning, he's surprised to find Mika in bed next to me.

The other times when Mika had slept over, we'd set an alarm, making sure that we were awake before the boys got up. Except for yesterday, when Mika had woken early and was fixing coffee in the kitchen when Sam came down looking for me. Instead of panicking, Mika had gotten Sam something to do until I woke up. When Lian made a noise, Mika had gotten him out of his crib and off to the bathroom before whisking him downstairs to join Sam while he made breakfast. They'd let me sleep in.

But this morning, when Sam was hungry and asking for breakfast, he didn't find me downstairs, so he came to my room. Awoken by Sam and still foggy from sleep, I fumble over my explanation of why Mika was here. Coming to my rescue, Mika drops to his knees next to the bed and gives Sam a good morning hug. Then he asks him, "Sam, who is your favorite person in the entire world?" I'm not sure where this is going, but I figure Mika knows, and I trust him because he's really great with my boys. They absolutely love him.

"Lian," Sam proudly tells Mika. It's a proud momma moment, and I smile.

"How do you show him how much you care about him?" Mika asks. Sam stands there for a moment, thinking about his answer.

Finally, he says, "I play with him. Hug him and tell him I love him." Nodding, Mika acknowledges his well-thought-out answer.

"Those are great ways, Sam. You know what?"

"What?" Sam replies with big, expressive eyes.

Mika points up to me and says, "You know your mom? She's my favorite person in the entire world, and I love her. Last night I wanted to be near her. Is it okay that I stayed over?"

Sam looks up at me with an expression I can't place. It's excitement mixed with hesitancy. Even though I'm not surprised by Mika's confession of love, I have no idea what Sam could be thinking.

"Sam," I say, and his eyes flick from Mika to me. "Is what Mika said okay?" Sam takes a moment before he nods yes.

Questions still linger in his eyes and I ask again, "Are you sure?"

Sam turns to look back at Mika and questions,

"You love my momma?" His tiny voice tugs at my heart.

Mika looks at Sam, then at me, and smiles. When his gaze returns to Sam, he's still smiling. "I do, Sam. But you know what else?" Sam shakes his head. Mika leans in closer. "I love you and Lian too." Sam jumps at him, his little arms thrown wide as he wraps himself around the man I love.

"I love you too, Mika," Sam's little voice squeaks out.

Tears stream down my face. I sink to the floor and wrap my arms around both of them. Catching Mika's eyes, I mouth, *"I love you so much."*

Life couldn't get any better than this.

Chapter 24

Mika

Leaving to go to New York is tough. It isn't the first trip away since Shiloh and I started seeing each other, but for some reason, I have an uneasy feeling about this one. Chalking it up to nerves, I pack my bag, say my goodbyes, and board the team flight.

When we land, some of my teammates are pumped, especially Lucas. Before he'd come to the Steel organization, he'd played his entire NHL career in New York, and he was ready to see his old teammates and friends, Miles and Jack.

While they make plans to catch up, I grab my bag and board the team bus to the hotel. Once in my room, resting before a scheduled practice, I notice the uneasy, anxious feelings have transformed into feelings of dread. What is going on? Is something about to happen? To me? Someone I love? Worried, I call Shiloh to make sure she and the boys are okay.

"Mika. Did you get to New York?"

Pacing my room, I say, "I did. But I just wanted to make sure you and the boys are good."

"We are. We hate it when you leave, but it's your job, and we know you'll be back in a few days."

Dread still hangs heavy, but I'm glad they're fine. "I will. Miss you already."

Shiloh sighs sweetly. "Miss you too. I love you and so do the boys."

"Love you all too. Maybe we can FaceTime tomorrow?" My voice fills with hope.

"Looking forward to it. Have a good game, Mika."

Three days away from them will suck, but it's only temporary. "Thanks. Bye."

Knowing they're fine gives comforts me enough to get through our light practice.

On game days, we always have the same schedule. Light practice, protein-packed lunch, and an afternoon nap. After six years in the NHL, eighty-two games each season, the pregame schedules were fully ingrained. But today? Today is different. Even after I'd done everything required of me, I still feel restless and edgy. Maybe I just need to play to work out all this pent-up energy? Perhaps it's left over from the last time we played New York. The rivalry between our teams gained immediate traction when Lucas left and joined the Steel. Leaving their organization was a decision he made to secure the future he wanted. Most everyone supported that, but there were a few outliers who seemed to take his leaving personally. In fact, some had come right out and bashed him across social media before we'd even arrived in town. Honestly, it all baffles me. From talking to Lucas, he was going to transfer or play one more year before he retired. Either way, he was going to Chicago and they'd lose him. I'm not sure why some are holding on to this so tightly.

Right when I skate onto the ice for warm-ups before the game, I can sense a difference permeating the air, like it's feeding off the feelings I'd been experiencing earlier, making it completely unnerving. Usually, when my skates touch the ice, I instantly feel a calmness wash over me. But tonight, tension radiates off the surface, making me uncomfortable.

Within the first period, both teams have received a record number of penalty minutes for checking and tripping. A negative energy hangs low over the arena, and I fear everything will come to a head at some point. Maybe that's why I've been so edgy all day. Maybe my body was aware of all the tension before my brain was. I don't know what's happening, but something horrible feels inevitable. Hopefully, we'll get through the game without a catastrophe occurring.

Chapter 25

Shiloh

It's been a strange week. Mika left for a series against Lucas's old team, the New York Chargers. And even though the boys are growing familiar with his hockey schedule, they've been particularly clingy. And apparently, only Mika can appease them. I don't know. All I know is that not being wanted by my own kids feels pretty crappy. Especially considering that I've always been the only one they'd ever needed.

In our daily talks and texts, Mika tries to reassure me he's still like a new toy to the boys, full of energy and endless fun. He tells me his novelty will wear off eventually and I'll again take center stage in their lives. I realize we've only been dating for a few months, so what he says sounds right. But it still worries me. *What if we're getting too attached? Has everything happened too fast?*

Our relationship has been a whirlwind. We comfortably flew through the stages quickly, and after our first night together, our lives resembled a well-established couple living together.

During the week, while I'd be getting ready for work, Mika would help get the boys ready for school and daycare, and he would start on breakfast. I can't tell you how many times I walked into my kitchen to the sounds of laughter. A deep, husky laugh mixed with my boys' high-pitch giggles always made me stop and give thanks. It was a beautiful sound that not only warmed my heart but repaired so many of the deep, dusty broken cracks I'd carried for so long. Making it even better was knowing he showed up because he wanted to.

With Mika playing a two-game series against New York, he left at the beginning of the week, and recovering from the loss of help is noticeable. I hadn't realized how much I've learned to rely on him. Despite playing a lot of catch-up, I still try to keep up with his games, and last night's had been rough. I'd missed a good chunk of it because it coincided with the boys' bedtime. But after they were down, I grabbed the basket of laundry that needed folding and tuned back into the game on my laptop.

Just when I'd gotten the game reloaded, Ace went down. It was horrific to watch. And while the team doctor assessed him, the station broadcasting the game played the hit repeatedly, slowing it down to really show the damage Ace's body had sustained. As far as I could tell, Ace hadn't moved, which instantly made me sick to my stomach. Worry overtook my body, and I fisted a clean shirt I'd pulled from the basket, twisting it tightly between my hands. After what seemed like forever, a medical team with a backboard came onto the ice and they carefully placed a collar around Ace's neck. The medics eased Ace onto the board and transported him off the ice. Scared for him, I wondered what this injury would do to the team's dynamic. From what I'd seen, they were a tight-knit group who really had each other's backs. Meeting most of the guys recently, and hearing what others had said about athletes, I knew these guys wouldn't just let this slide. The hit to Ace appeared intentional, and it was anyone's guess what the fallout might be.

Before I went to bed, I assumed I might hear from Mika, but when I didn't, I figured he was still wound up from the game. I'd talk to him later, knowing he had one more game left in New York before he'd be home. After watching Ace's injury tonight, I wanted to get my hands on Mika and make sure he was okay.

The next day flew by with no major hiccups. Again, I tried to watch most of the game, but responsibilities with the boys took precedence and I missed the majority. When I'd finally switched it back on, Mika was on the bench. Not knowing much about hockey, I assumed there was a good reason for it. Mika would explain it all to me when he got back. When I'd gone to bed, I knew in the morning, I'd wake up to the large, well-built, muscular man I loved in my bed. I went to sleep feeling giddy.

However, when my alarm sounds at five o'clock, the spot next to me is empty and cold. Mika hadn't come over. My stomach drops. Did something happen? Is he okay? Did the team make it back safely? I throw off my down comforter, jump out of bed, and step over to my bedroom window. From the way our houses sit, I can see the front of his house perfectly. And what I see confuses me. Next door, in the driveway, is Mika's white GMC Sierra truck. He's home, but why hadn't he come over? I move to my charger and snatch up my phone. Maybe he texted me to let me know he wasn't coming? Three text notifications show on the screen, and I click on them, expecting one to bear his name. But none of them are from him, and it's beyond strange.

While away, Mika always stayed in contact, texting me throughout the day, talking when we could. Again, I look at the unread messages and notice all three are from Monica, and that further baffles me. *What is going on?* Glancing at the time they were sent, I see they were all sent within the last half hour. At the thought of that, I really panic. *Why did she need to get hold of me so desperately? Is she okay?* I read each message carefully to see if I can decipher the problem before I call her back.

MONICA

Are you okay? Please call me.

MONICA

He told Christian it isn't true. Call me.

MONICA

CALL ME! Babe, you have me
worried. Please.

What is she talking about? What's happening?

My hands shake as I call her. Thankfully, she's already programmed in, or else I'm not sure I'd dial correctly.

"Oh, thank goodness," Monica rushes out in a strained voice before I even speak. "Are you okay?"

I let out the shaky breath I've been holding and ask in a low trembling voice, "What is going on? What isn't true? Who told Christian what? Is this about Mika?" My confusion is clear as questions tumble from my mouth. Waiting for answers is complete agony. My stomach rolls in protest. I'm worried, nervous, and scared. Bile bubbles up my throat, leaving an awful acidic taste behind as I wait for any explanation.

"You haven't seen the articles?" she asks in a hurried tone.

Articles? What articles? I try to remember the last time I'd seen any news broadcast and came up with nothing. But feeling myself growing more agitated by the minute, my thinning band of unease snaps.

"Ugh! No, Monica, I haven't seen any news articles. I am a single mother of young children. The only things I see are children's programming. I don't have time for scouring the latest news sites to keep up with everything happening in the world. So, if anything happened recently, I don't have a clue. Literally. I do not know what you are talking about! What is going on?" I growl.

Normally, I'm not like this, but she's stirred up so much emotion in me, and now I demanded answers.

I hear a muffled side conversation and assume it's probably with Christian, her boyfriend/hookup/whatever. Not so patiently, I listen, hoping to catch a clue, and then I hear something that makes my entire body grow cold.

"She doesn't know?" asks Christian.

"Christian, this will break her heart," Monica replies sadly.

"He says it isn't true," Christian states.

"Okay. If that's so, why isn't he telling her? Why doesn't she know already?" Monica questions.

After listening to them go back and forth, I've had enough and demand, "Tell me what's going on or I'm hanging up. I heard your conversation and I know it's concerning Mika, so spill it. Now!"

Monica answers quickly, stumbling over her words. "Shit! I don't know how to tell you this. While the team was in New York for their games... Mika kind of made the papers."

I nod my head, trying to absorb what she said but

not really understanding it's importance. Mika is a professional hockey player, and making the papers isn't uncommon. However, when I replay their conversation, something registers, sitting heavy in my gut. Mika made the papers. Considering their flustered state, I know it's not for anything good, but for something that will hurt me. Dread sets in. Tears fall before I even know what's happened.

"O-okay," I say hesitantly, trying to hold in the sob desperately threatening to escape. Still needing to know, but not being sure I can handle it, I brace myself against my messy bed. Fear washes over me. What's coming next is going to destroy me. I can feel it.

"Babe, the tabloids got pictures of a woman draped all over Mika in a bar the other night," Monica quietly admits.

Nodding my head, I remain silent.

"Oh, honey, they look bad, but Christian tells me it wasn't anything. He talked to Mika and Connor and they both told him the same thing. The night before last, they'd gone to the hotel bar for a drink after their game to unwind. It was right after Ace was injured. They'd wanted a drink, and these super aggressive puck bunnies approached them. They'd tried to brush off their unwanted advances, but nothing they tried worked. The guys think it was staged. A tabloid photographer got pictures of the interactions before the guys even had time to leave the bar. But they both swear Mika left alone."

"Okay," I stoically respond.

Pain crashes through my chest as my heart shatters into a million pieces. The sharp agony that radiates throughout my body is unbearable. Through my sobs, I find it difficult to breathe. Not knowing what to say or do, I force out, "I've got to go," then hang up before she can even reply.

Unable to control it any longer, the emotional dam breaks and a loud sob rushes from my mouth. My body shakes, and I sink to the floor, suddenly weak and overcome with grief. After an unknown amount of time passes, I force myself up. On shaky legs, I look out the window, and Mika's house sits quiet, almost peaceful. The opposite of what I'm feeling. Hopelessly broken, I wonder if there is any truth to the pictures or the story. Hurt and anger lance through me. Why didn't he tell me? Why let me find out this way? Perhaps there's more truth to the story than he was willing to admit. And confessing to Christian, another playboy, rather than his girlfriend, whom he claims to love, would be easier. Maybe he finally got his opportunity to get away from the clingy single mom and her kids.

As I stand there looking out the window, I give myself a few moments to cry. But I know I need to get myself together because there is no way I'll let my boys see me like this and I have to get them up soon. Reality slams into me like a bolt of lightning. *Shit!* What am I going to tell them? They thought they'd see Mika this morning. Now I'll be forced to disappoint them and break their little hearts. How am I going to tell them Mika won't be coming around anymore? What will I say? I don't know. Grinding my molars, I take one last look at Mika's house before I drop my head and make myself move forward, shattered heart and all.

Needing to get ready for the day, I stumble into my bathroom, dazed. Moments later, while stepping into my shower, it hits me. Right now is the only time I'll get to deal with all of this alone. In the safety of these tiled walls, I know I don't have to pretend I'm strong and that nothing can hurt me. In here, I can cry, scream, agonize, and fume, and no one would ever see. In here, I'm protected.

After I'm lightheaded from crying so hard, I turn off the hot water and step out of my shower, dripping wet. While I towel off, I remind myself that I have to show the world I'm not broken. In fact, I'm fine and unfazed. Strong as ever. Even if that's a bald-faced lie and I feel like my heart has been decimated. No one will ever know. And hopefully, after some time, losing Mika won't hurt as badly.

While drying my hair, I rehearse what I'll tell the boys. While organizing that, I also decide I'm done with relationships. Well, at least until the boys aren't living at home anymore. In no time at all, my boys idolized Mika. He was like a superhero, and now, as far as I'm concerned, he's morphed into a villain. The only way to handle this is to cut him out of our lives permanently. My boys don't deserve any pain, and being around Mika would hurt too much. Just having to close the door on him is going to destroy them.

While stepping out of my bathroom with my towel tied around my chest, I remember it's Friday and casual day at school. *Thank fuck.* From my closet, I pull out my most comfortable, well-worn jeans and my school sweatshirt. After I dress, my hair goes into a messy bun and minimal makeup dusts my face, mostly to hide all the patchy blotches from crying.

Before leaving my room, I take one last look in the mirror, confirming how I feel. Destroyed. Attempting to smile is a bust. The corners of my lips don't reach high enough. Instead, they're stiff and forced. Completely fake. But really, who cares anyway? That's all I have. People can take it or leave it.

Not caring about putting any more effort into my appearance, I head out of my bedroom and into the hallway. Unlike the past few months, I hear nothing. Normally when Mika's here, there's talking, laughing, pans clanging, and life being lived. Now it's eerily silent, and just the thought of that makes my heart squeeze tight. Mika isn't home. Well, not in my home anyway, and as far as I'm concerned, he never will be again. Sadness rushes through me and I'm tossed off balance. Grabbing the railing, I brace myself from collapsing under the invisible pain that's destroying my body. Feeling the tightness in my mouth, I realize my lips are pinched together so I won't release the sob building up within me again.

Cruelty slaps me in the face when I go to wake the boys. Each one gives me a sleepy hug before excitedly asking, "Where's Mika?" I put off answering their question as I pull clothes from drawers. They disrobe, and before I know it, naked ninnies who are giggling and gyrating surround me. Laughter, although it's weak, sneaks out, and I feel a little less broken. Even through my sadness, these two boys of mine fill my life with such joy and immeasurable love.

"Bathroom," I choke out, knowing their bladders have to be full. They race to their bathroom to pee before returning to me for clothes. Sam gets dressed easily, but Lian definitely needs help. When dressed, we brush their teeth. Like normal, more of their electric blue, sparkly toothpaste ends up in globs on the edge of the sink instead of on their toothbrushes. While they head down to the kitchen for breakfast, I wipe down their sink, hoping to get the sticky paste scrubbed from the porcelain before it dries like cement.

When I enter the kitchen, Sam is helping Lian into his chair. Grabbing the cereal, bowls, and spoons, I set them on the counter before I grab the milk from the fridge. Emotionally overwhelmed, my brain feels sluggish, like I'm having to talk myself through basic tasks. Heading over to the table proves to be even more of a chore because I have to step over the boys' lovies that are lying on the floor.

Breakfast goes off without a hitch, thankfully. After the excitement of this morning and my mind operating in shutdown mode, anything could've happened. Right now, I'm thankful we avoided any hassles. The boys happily scarfed down their breakfast while I packed their lunches and continued to ignore the missing person. The boys don't ask about Mika again, seemingly he slipped from their minds. Hopefully, I'd avoid all conversations about Mika indefinitely, but I doubt I'm that lucky.

Just as I'm finishing making sandwiches, my phone signals a text. Uncertainty creeps in. Will it be Monica checking to see if I'm all right? Will it be Mika? Perhaps someone who's seen the articles? Honestly, I don't want to hear from anybody, and I'd rather just silence my phone and ignore everyone. Then it sounds a second notice, reminding me it's better to deal with the situation head-on. With shaky hands, I do just that. Flipping over my phone, I'm more nervous than I've ever been. My face, despite the scowl I know is plastered there, unlocks the screen, giving me my answer. It's Mika. Just seeing his first word, *Babe*, sends me spiraling. Tears cloud my vision, and a knot forms in my throat, making it difficult to swallow past the grief I've been trying my best to ignore.

Babe, I'm so sorry. I just spoke to Christian, and he informed me that Monica told you about the article… umm… the pictures. I didn't do anything with that woman. I know they look bad, but I promise you, I would never do that. Those pictures don't tell the entire story. Yes, she hit on me. Puck bunnies do in every town we visit, but usually they aren't so aggressive. When I figured out she wasn't taking the hint, that I wasn't interested, Connor and I left. Honest! Those pictures suggest something more, but there was nothing more. We need to talk. I know I've hurt you, and so far, I haven't handled things well. I don't know what to do to make it right. Please, Shiloh, call me. I don't want to lose you over a misunderstanding. I love you.

He kept mentioning the pictures, but I've yet to actually see them or read the article they were featured in. Honestly, I don't want to have them floating around in my mind. But now that he's brought them up, I have to see what everyone will be talking about. So, while my coffee brews, I google him and the notorious article. Shock slams into me, pulling the air from my lungs after the site loads, revealing it all. I wasn't prepared for it. The headline is salacious enough, but the pictures piggyback it perfectly.

"Mika's in the City Looking to SCORE!"

My stomach, which I thought had somewhat recovered from earlier, churns violently. There isn't just one picture, there are several, and they show a scantily-clad blonde with fake boobs pressed up against Mika. In one, the woman looks to be whispering something in his ear. In the next, she's laughing. And the final one, the icing on the cake, captures her licking her lips and giving him sex eyes. I have no words. As if the pictures weren't enough, the woman in them, who was interviewed for the article, mentions a scar he has on his upper thigh. *Who would know about that? Only someone who'd seen him naked or in his underwear.* Dropping my phone on the counter, I sprint to the half bath, feeling incredibly nauseous. Managing to hold it down, I set my forehead on the toilet seat and pray for the sick feeling to pass. The coolness of the seat seems to do the trick and settles my quaking stomach. Instead of moving, I stay there, leaning against the toilet, taking deep breaths, and willing my body to stop sweating.

A few minutes pass, and I hear little feet pad down the hallway. Then a small, warm hand rubs my back tenderly. "Momma, are you okay?" Sam's little voice, filled with worry, asks. Apparently, my sprint from the kitchen had startled him. I didn't mean to scare him, but I had. Actually, this is all Mika's fault. He harmed us. What he'd done was terrible, but is it unforgivable? Considering what he said to Christian, maybe it wasn't, but I'm not in the forgiving mood. Hurting me is one thing, but hurting my boys is inexcusable, and that's exactly what he's done by doing nothing. If only he'd come to me when he first learned about it, I suspect things would be drastically different now. But that didn't happen, so I just have to deal with what is happening now.

I blow a deep breath out, push off of the seat, and give my eldest a weak smile. "Hey, Sam. Mommy isn't feeling the best, but it'll pass. I'm okay."

My response seems to be just what he needs to hear. He hugs my legs tightly and gives me a killer smile. What a caring kid he is.

I flush the toilet and then rinse my mouth out before we walk back to the kitchen, hand in hand. Lian, none the wiser, is perfectly content crunching away at his cereal. Sam grabs his empty bowl and takes it to the sink. I finish packing up our stuff for the day, and when I reach for the phone, I cringe at the screen; the pictures are still on display. Closing the article, I switch over to my texts and respond to Mika.

ME

I have nothing to say to you other than goodbye.

We're finished. I'm done! Getting over him will be painful, but there is no way I'll subject my boys' hearts or mine any longer to him. I silence my phone, not wanting to hear if he responds or if anyone else tries to get a hold of me. Lian squawks and pounds his spoon on the table, pulling me from my thoughts. Taking that as my sign that he's done with breakfast, I clean him up and put the dishes away. When I've tidied everything up, we head out.

Being the beginning of December, it's extra chilly in the morning. So, before we walk out to my 4Runner and load up, we pull on our boots, coats, hats, and gloves. While I'm buckling up Lian, I see movement at Mika's house. His front door flies open, and within its frame stands a hulk of a man, looking frazzled. His clothes are rumpled and wrinkled, like he'd slept in them. And his normally well-styled hair is messy, sticking out in every direction. His eyes, which usually look so bright and alive, are red-rimmed, squinting, with dark bags underneath. Mika looks a mess, but I force myself not to care. After all, this is all his fault. He longingly watches as I finish getting the boys buckled in. I try to distract Lian and Sam so they won't notice him, and thankfully, they don't. Any conversation about Mika is going to be painful, but the one with the boys will definitely be the hardest. They'll never understand.

Looking in my rearview mirror as I back up, I see his shoulders slump in defeat. Again, I tell myself it doesn't matter anymore. We're over. I don't need to concern myself with him any longer. My brain tries desperately to embrace that thought, but my heart downright refuses. The message of moving on is not transmitting, and I'm doubtful it ever will. Despite what happened, I still want to run to Mika, to hit him, scream at him, cry with him, kiss and hold him. But we're done, and those things will never happen again. I need to move forward with my life. Put one foot in front of the other. Determined, I grit my teeth, strangle the steering wheel, and tell myself I have to be strong for my boys.

Driving away, I do just that. Harnessing strength I wasn't sure I had, I start down the path of moving on. Or at least I try. As the day drags on, even though I try to avoid any and all conversations about Mika, he's still a topic of conversation. When I start to feel my control slip, like I'm going to burst into tears, I excuse myself and find a quiet spot to regulate my breathing and recenter my thoughts. Off of him.

Chapter 26

Mika

Two Days Earlier

onight's game had been a complete clusterfuck. Ace, our best forward, only in his second year in the league, was intentionally checked hard from behind, sending him headfirst into the boards. Checking wasn't uncommon in hockey, but when he'd flown into the boards with such substantial force, it'd completely taken him down, and it became more than just a penalty. It became personal. The referees had to stop the game as Ace was laid out on the ice, not moving. Trainers dashed to the ice to quickly assess him. The fall had knocked out his front teeth. Losing teeth was not an unusual hockey injury. Unfortunately, the trainers were more concerned about a possible spinal cord injury because he had complained his neck hurt and his legs felt weak and immovable.

We all stood there watching, uncertain what to do.

Josh skated up next to him and kept him calm while everyone rushed around, readying him for transport. The team all huddled around him, giving words of encouragement. Before they carted Ace off the ice, he looked at us and growled, "win this." Then was rushed into the tunnel, out of the arena, and to the nearest hospital for evaluation.

Before we retook the ice, Coach informed us we were not to retaliate. We needed to win the game, and the series, based on our skills, not our fists. Each second on the ice with the player whose cheap shot had taken Ace out was painful, and I wanted to make him pay. Being a defenseman, every time he skated toward the net, my mind churned with ways I could take him down. Jeremy Kane, the asshole who'd hit Ace, had only received a five-minute major penalty. That was it, and in my opinion, that was absolute shit. Kane had been taking cheap shots the entire game, like always, and finally, after inflicting enough damage, they'd given him some ridiculous consequence. In my position, I understood protecting my net at all costs, but I didn't play dirty, and that's exactly what Kane had done. And we did just as Ace asked. Pumped up with anger and adrenaline, we won the game.

Later that night, I'd learned that when the ER staff had removed Ace's gear and tested his reflexes, he'd been slow to respond. Apparently, that's not a good sign. The doctors wanted to make sure he was fine, so they ran a CT scan. Thankfully, his scans came back clear; there was no injury to his spinal cord. Ultimately, he was fine, just majorly bruised and banged up. Coach said that Ace would likely rest for the next few weeks until doctors cleared him to play. Trainers were also able to get him a dental consult, and he had an appointment with a world-class dentist in the morning to address his missing teeth. He could totally kill it on TikTok with a video about how all he wanted for Christmas was his two front teeth. It'd go viral, for sure.

When we get back to the hotel, I nudge Connor and ask, "Drink?" Visibly vibrating with anger, like me, he nods and heads in the direction of the hotel bar. Normally we'd each retreat to our rooms for room service, but tonight is different. Tonight, my blood is still boiling and the only thing that will calm me down, other than pummeling a certain New York hockey player, is a stiff drink.

Talking to Shiloh has calmed me down in the past. But I don't think it would be fair to call her and complain right after she's finished getting the boys to bed. Shiloh is a single parent who never gets a moment to herself, and I'm not about to steal that sacred time from her with my bullshit. Honestly, I just need to vent, and Connor is a perfect sounding board. We were in the same boat, so we could grumble together. Connor's wife is also home with their kids and probably enjoying the quietness of their house after a long day. And being married as long as he has, he knows better than to bother her.

We grab a table off in the corner with a high top, hoping to have some privacy. Climbing up on my stool, I look at Connor. "That game was shit."

"What can I get you, boys?" an older waitress asks with her two-packs-a-day rasp.

"Two fingers of a ten-year-old McKenna, neat," I growl out. Normally, seeing the waitress flinch at my surliness would garner sympathy. Tonight, I don't care. I'm pissed off.

"I'll take a Heineken," Connor barks at her.

Without wasting a beat, she scurries off, probably relieved to be away from our surly attitudes.

Only when I'm finally holding my glass of perfectly aged bourbon do I start to settle. I swirl my drink, clinking the ice in my glass before I take my first swig. When I do, flavors burst on my tongue. "Ahhh," I say out loud to no one. My body hums as I savor the butterscotch undertones of the alcohol.

A few swigs later, when I've almost finished my drink, I'm feeling a bit more relaxed. That is, until I see a flash of red, like a blinking beacon, out of the corner of my eye. Turning my head slightly to place it, I don't miss the stick-figure, fake-boobed blonde strutting toward me. *Shit. I'm not in the mood for this.* She and her plastic rack do absolutely nothing for me. In fact, I feel sorry for her. Here she thinks she's going to get lucky, and I'm thinking how I can best get away. I notice a brunette in tow.

"Here we go," I mutter under my breath as I look at Connor. Noticing the same women, he just shakes his head and lets out a deep-throated laugh. "What?" I question.

With their hungry, focused stares and promising swaggers, I know I need to keep my distance. Aggressive puck bunnies were a bad thing, and these women, just moments in, have already set me on edge. Being in the NHL, they came with the territory; they were expected. Normally, they didn't bother me much. Except now I have a perfect woman at home and I'm completely disinterested in anyone but Shiloh. She's it for me. I just haven't told her yet. Hell, I just recently told her I love her. Our relationship is still so new, and I'm afraid of doing something wrong. She's like a frightened bunny, and I'm afraid of scaring her off.

"Hi boys," the blonde says, dragging out the s like it's sexy.

The brunette tries to get closer but is boxed out by Malibu Barbie. "Hi," she says in a sweet southern drawl. She sounds nice, and I'd probably respond to her if I wasn't worried about what this other woman would do. Connor just sits back and nurses his beer while enjoying the show. Apparently, they know he isn't to be messed with. Connor is the well-documented, happily married guy on the team. He always raves about how amazing his wife and kids are. There was no way these women, or any woman for that matter, would even tempt him. I'd listened to him over the years talk about marriage and fatherhood, and until I met Shiloh, I hadn't really paid attention to what he said. Now I listened intently, trying to absorb everything so I could remember for the amazing woman in my life. All he'd been talking about these years finally made sense, and I want what he has. Telling Shiloh, however, is another story. When it comes to us, she's been gun shy. Trying my best to respect that, I even held off sex until she knew I was there because of her and not just to get laid.

"Great game tonight. Saw you guys won." The blonde spouts out facts she could have gotten from any cable sports show.

"It's a shame about your friend," the brunette pipes in.

Just as I'm about to tell the women we aren't interested in conversation, the blonde tries engaging me again. She begins running her long, pointy talons up and down my arm, which sets my blood boiling. Wanting to remain the nice guy, for my image and everything, I wrap my hand around her wrist, effectively stopping her from pawing me, and growl. The woman throws her head back, letting go of one of the most obnoxious laughs I've ever heard. *Is she insane? Who in the hell cackles?* I haven't technically said anything to her.

As I slightly tighten my grip on her wrist and

firmly say "enough," she dials it up. I've seemingly just encouraged more of her crazy antics, because moments later she responds.

Lowering her overly-Botoxed, blood-red lips to my ear, she whispers, "Don't worry, baby, I like it rough."

Appalled and disgusted, I release my hold on her like she has the plague. I push myself roughly back from the table. "I'm leaving," I growl at Connor.

Needing to get away before the situation escalates, I move toward the exit. Connor quickly follows behind, knowing that if I stay there any longer, I am going to lose my shit. As we stalk out of the bar, I see the brunette's reflection in a mirror. She looks confused, while Barbie looks evil. Apparently, she is the ringleader in their circus. Hearing the rapid clicking noises in the distance, I register it as familiar, but I don't give it too much thought. I need to get away.

Connor and I make a quick getaway through the bar and into the lobby. We rush the elevators and hop on just as the women are exiting the bar. It's too close a call.

"What the hell just happened?" Connor asks as we ride back up to our floor.

Shrugging, I say, "That blonde was crazy. I think we just dodged a bullet."

"One more night and we're home," Connor reminds me. Before meeting Shiloh and the boys, I hadn't missed home. But now, I can't wait to get back to them.

I remind myself that after tomorrow night's game we'll catch a late flight back to Chicago and I'll see Shiloh and the boys. Before them, I hadn't missed anyone when I traveled.

When I finally reach my room, I notice how late it is. Needing to wash the feeling of the woman's touch off my skin, I hop into the shower before I pull on boxers and climb into bed.

When I wake up the next morning, I feel ready to take on New York and finish out the series with a sweep. Hopefully tonight Jeremy Kane will be on a much tighter leash. It's still hard to believe he wasn't given a game misconduct after the shit he pulled last night.

After an early skate and lunch, I head back to our hotel for a pre-game nap. Following an hour-long rest, a shower, and dressing in my suit, I return to the hotel lobby to meet the rest of my team before we head to the arena.

Fresh from a restful nap and feeling great as I walk through the hotel lobby, I'm on top of the world. That feeling doesn't last long, though. Large print, splashed across the front of another hotel guest's paper, rips my happiness from me. Not wanting to be rude by pulling it from her hand, I swivel around quickly, looking through the lobby for any discarded papers. When I finally spot one across the room, I jog over to it. When I read the article's title, my stomach heaves and I think I'm going to be sick all over the marble flooring.

"Mika's in the City Looking to SCORE!"

Holy shit! This is not happening. Ripping through the paper, I try to find the pictures they mentioned in the teaser. What the fuck had I done in the time I've been here to give anyone any indication I'm here to get lucky? I'm a fucking professional hockey player who's in town for one reason only: to play a series of fucking hockey games. Shiloh, the only woman I ever intend to get lucky with ever again, is at home.

When my eyes finally find their supposed proof, my stomach rolls and anger courses through my body. They spread multiple pictures throughout the article, showing me interacting with the crazy woman from the night before. *Fuck.* I couldn't deny that I had interacted with her, but the pictures don't show what truly transpired between us.

To make matters worse, the crazy woman had given an account of our supposed evening and it was full of sordid details that said I'd invited her back to my room for "a good time." She even mentioned the scar I have on my upper thigh, which I'd gotten during one of Lucas's team-building activities that involved a charity. The press had caught wind of it. It hadn't been major, but when I'd been asked about it during a press conference a few weeks later, I'd admitted to it, even giving a description. Which coincidentally matched her detailing of it in the article. The article was lies, utter horse shit.

Crumpling the paper, I storm around the lobby looking for something to swing at, and my teammates, unsure of what to do, give me a wide berth. Connor, however, doesn't. He stalks up to me, grabs the paper from my hands, unwrinkles it, and reads the printed garbage. Still needing to burn off excess anger, I step away, afraid I might take a swing at him. When Connor gets to what I'm guessing is the part about me inviting the woman to my room, his eyes go wide, a deep scowl settles across his face, and a growl fills the surrounding air. He's pissed off on my behalf.

When he's finished the article, he steps over to me, places his large hand on my shoulder, and looks into my eyes. A series of apologies, sadness, and anger come through his gaze, and I let out a deep breath. Connor knows the truth, but I wonder if it even matters. Would anyone hear our voices screaming the truth over all the others spreading lies and gossip? The longer we stand there silently staring at each other, the more I feel Shiloh slipping away. After her dick of an ex, I know she wouldn't even think twice about walking away from me if she suspected I'd done the same thing as him. This article makes me sound like a fucking cheater. I would never cheat on Shiloh. She's my world. All I want. Well, her and the boys. So, what am I going to do now? I look up at Conner, silently questioning him.

"Mika, these are lies. We both know that, and we

will set it right," he says in a firm, take-no-prisoners tone.

I shake my head. "No, man. I've lost her. Her ex cheated on her and now she'll think I did too. She'll never forgive me, even if it's total bullshit."

He pulls me into a bro hug and whispers, "She will if she loves you. And she does. Now, let's go skate out some of this aggression. We need to beat New York tonight to maintain our standing."

All I can do is nod. Not knowing what to do or say, I follow my teammates through the lobby and onto the bus. Doing the best I can, I avoid eye contact with everyone. I don't need anyone giving me pitying looks; I feel shitty enough. When I settle in my seat, I put my ear buds in and try to tune out the sound of my thoughts with a hard rock playlist.

Getting to the arena, I rely on muscle memory to get ready for the game. Dressing, stretching, and warm-ups are so ingrained in me, I do them without thinking.

We win the game, but I'm sure I'm not any help. Coach Tristan finally benches me after the second period, when he sees I'm not fully engaged. He pulls me aside on the way back to the locker room, telling me he's here for me if I need it. I appreciate it, I do, because I know it doesn't look good to have your assistant captain riding the pine. But, honestly, right now, I don't care. My heart is breaking, and that doesn't have any chance of getting better until I can look Shiloh in the eyes and know things between us are okay. Not hearing from her all day messes with me too, as I'm not sure if she knows what happened, and because of that, I'm terrified.

After the game, before we leave New York, I call Christian.

"Christian, some real shit hit the papers about me today and I need your help to fix it."

"What shit are we talking about? How bad?" Christian asks.

"The newspapers printed I was basically in the city looking for a booty call," I grumble to him.

"Well, were you?" he questions.

Trying my best to restrain my anger, I snap, "Are you fucking kidding? No, I wasn't here for a booty call. I love Shiloh, and I'm in New York for my job, to play hockey."

Christian laughs.

"This is not funny, asshole," I growl.

"I know it isn't funny. The way you said it was," he defends. "Does Shiloh know?"

Hanging my head as I board the plane, I admit, "I don't know. I'm afraid to call her. I need to talk to her in person."

"You're flying back now, right? You can tell her first thing."

"That's my plan. Hopefully she doesn't find out before then or I'm screwed and we're over," I huff out.

Christian scoffs. "Don't be so dramatic, Mika."

"Plane's about to take off. I've got to go."

"Okay. I'll call Jennifer, Fox's PR manager, to find out how to handle it."

On the flight home, I think about all that is happening. During the game, I was all up in my head, wanting to know if Shiloh had seen the papers. If anyone would know, it would be Monica, Christian's fuck buddy/friend with benefits/girlfriend, whatever they were. Even though Shiloh and I had a tough time defining ourselves, Christian and Monica are something else. In reality, they need to take the plunge and commit, make it official, but Christian is dragging his feet. *Stubborn ass.*

Christian confirms Shiloh is unaware of the article. He warns me I need to tell her, informing me that if I let her find out any other way, I'm a coward. Agreeing to what he says is the simple part. Having the right words to explain it to her, not so much. Getting the courage for the conversation takes everything out of me. I'm already expecting it will go badly.

As soon as I deplane, I jog to my truck and tear out of the airport. When I pull up to my house, I power my phone back on, then glance up at Shiloh's house to see it's dark. Assuming she still doesn't know about the article, I breathe a sigh of relief. I know there is no escaping this. Dread once again coils itself around me, dragging me further into my fear.

Instead of going to her house like had become habit when I return from road trips, I pace my living room, trying to come up with the perfect thing to say.

Wanting desperately to go pull her into my arms is crippling, but first comes apologizing for what happened and explaining that what the woman said isn't true. But it would have to wait. I don't want to wake up the boys if it all causes an argument. For now, I'll wait impatiently, watching for the first signs of life.

* * *

Knowing Shiloh's alarm will go off soon, I get ready to head over. As I'm reaching for the door handle, my cell phone rings. It's Christian, and the hesitation in his voice makes my body freeze and blood stop. "Monica saw the article this morning, and she's been calling Shiloh every fifteen minutes until she finally called back. And... their conversation... it's... it's not going well."

"Wait! What? I thought you were going to tell Monica about the article in case Shiloh saw it and called panicking. You were supposed to be my safe harbor, running interference, not making it worse. Christian, I was up all night, running scenarios and was just about to walk out the door when you called. Now I'm really screwed. What am I supposed to do?" I growl. *Shit. This isn't really happening, is it?* I'm extremely pissed Monica is telling Shiloh instead of letting me do it. Doesn't she understand what this could do to us? To Shiloh? The boys?

"Hey, man, I get it. But I told you that you'd be

smart to get in front of it and tell her right after it happened and you didn't, so that's on you," he replies in a defensive tone, one that I've never heard from him. Is he defending himself or Monica? Why hadn't he told her to wait because he knew I had a plan? Dwelling on that won't help. It won't change anything now, because now I'm truly fucked. Fucked with a flashing capital F.

Christian's right, but my ego won't be admitting that to him, ever. I stop pacing around my front room and sink into a comfortable leather recliner. Mindlessly, I rub at the arms of the chair, wondering what I'm going to do. Her knowing about the article means I have to reevaluate my approach. When I was confident Shiloh was still in the dark, I knew it would hurt when I told her, but doing so, in person, would allow me to gauge her response in real time and respond immediately. Now I was at the mercy of what she'd heard and read, and there was no way I could prepare for that.

Completely blindsided, I don't know how Shiloh will react. Throughout our relationship, we haven't even had anything close to a fight. I've never seen her angry or upset. Is she the forgiving type? Maybe she's into giving second chances. Or does she do what I fear the most—cut and run? Worry shakes me to my core because the more I think about it, the more I suspect she'll leave me.

She told me a little about her ex and what had happened between them. I'd agreed that he was a class-

A dick, and I told her I'd never let him near her or the boys again. But considering what had happened, would she differentiate between us? His behavior was intentional. They manipulated mine to look like it was something it wasn't. The situations were completely different. But I'm not confident I'll even have the chance to explain. After what transpired, I fear I'll go into the same category as Trent and be issued the status of persona non grata.

My stomach cramps, and my heart twists at the thought of losing her. It's unfathomable. Not seeing her smile, hear her laugh, kiss her lips, spoon her as we sleep, or spend time doing nothing with her and her boys, would kill me. I want to be there for everything. To be standing beside her, supporting, encouraging, and loving her through everything. Now, everything is being ripped away from me over some article filled with lies.

Bewildered, I ponder what I can do. Maybe sending a text would at least get her to talk to me? I pull my cell phone from my sweatpants and pour my heart out over text message. After I send it, I sit back in the chair, hoping not only that Shiloh receives my message, but that she responds. I need her to listen to my side of the story. I need a chance to explain and beg for her forgiveness.

While waiting for a reply, I shift anxiously in my seat, run my fingers through my hair, and grind my molars. Being patient is killing me, but what other choice do I have? It seems like an hour passes before I finally hear that familiar sound. The sound that will either give me hope or rip it away. *Ding!* The noise of it echoes eerily through my house, and I peer at her response through tired eyes, squinting at the words spread across the screen. When they finally register, any hope I'd been clinging to crashes down. Shiloh's message is direct and final. Effectively shattering my heart completely. Ten words destroy me.

SHILOH

I have nothing to say to you other than goodbye.

Goodbye? We're over? *No!* This cannot be the end of us. I won't accept it. Not caring what it will cost, I'll do whatever I have to do to make things right. Anything she asks of me. Adrenaline spikes through my weary body and I shoot up out of the chair, ready to get her back. But first, I need a plan, so I call Christian. He answers immediately.

"She ended things with me, and through a text too. What the fuck am I going to do?" I say miserably.

"Shit, man. I don't know. I don't do relationships. And this is a big reason why," he pointedly answers.

"You. You don't do relationships? Excuse me? What is it called what you're doing with Monica?" I snap sarcastically. If I'm going to feel miserable and uncomfortable, I'm going to drag someone down with me, and he seems like the perfect target. After all, he knew what was happening and he didn't step in and stop Monica.

In the background, I hear giggling, groaning, shuffling, and a door creak. It sounds like he's getting out of bed and leaving the room. Interesting. Is Monica in his bed right now? Is Christian leaving the room so she won't hear our discussion?

"What I'm doing with Monica is different. We are not in a relationship. We are more like friends with benefits," he reasons in a hushed tone.

I'm dumbfounded. Is he actually buying his own shit? He's crazy to think they're just fuck buddies. I don't know Monica well, but after a few encounters, I've learned that she isn't the type of woman who would be cool with that setup. Still pissed, I poke the bear. "Would she be cool with that title? If I asked her if you were just her friend with benefits, would she agree?"

He growls a warning. "You will not be asking her that. She knows the deal with us, and I don't want you messing it up!"

I laugh haughtily. "Oh, I see. I would mess it up? Is that right? Huh? It would have nothing to do with you and your inability to commit to someone who is fucking perfect for you? Whatever you say, man."

He huffs before saying, "What do you mean, Mika? I thought you called about *your* woman problems not to psychoanalyze mine."

I can't help the sarcastic smile spreading across my

face. "So, you're admitting you have women problems? It's about damn time. Christian, even though I don't really like your woman right now, considering the shit storm my life has become in the last forty-eight hours, even I know Monica deserves better than being temporary. She is the one for you, and you'd be the stupidest man alive to keep calling her your fuck buddy and not make her permanent before she gets sick of the shit you're selling and walks away *forever!*" I hang up before he can peddle any more of his lies.

I push up out of the chair I'd apparently settled back in during my conversation with Christian and hear noises outside Shiloh's house. A quick glance at my phone confirms that she's most likely leaving for work and to drop Lian at daycare.

Speed walking like it was an Olympic sport, I reach my front door and throw it open, hoping to see her. My eyes fall upon a sight that further crushes me. The woman I've fallen for looks as destroyed as I do. Her shoulders are slumped, and she appears exhausted despite just waking. Even though she still looks beautiful, I see her eyes are red and puffy and her cheeks are splotchy. She doesn't have her ever-present smile across my favorite feature—her incredibly kissable lips. My heart stutters and my stomach churns. A tight pressure wraps around my chest, squeezing tightly, making me feel lightheaded. Spots dance in my vision as my breathing becomes labored. Reaching out to the door frame for support, I wonder if I'm having a heart attack. Is that possible? Could you die from a broken heart?

Hanging on to my door for assistance, I long to run to her, hold her, explain everything, apologize, and promise her I'll never hurt her again. But I stop myself from even moving an inch when her eyes connect with mine, warning me off. Even though it kills me and physically hurts to do so, I remain still, respecting her wishes. I watch on helplessly as she finishes buckling Sam and Lian into their car seats before climbing into her own and driving away. Standing there, frozen in place, I watch her taillights disappear. Pain explodes in my chest. My heart feels like it's been ripped from my chest and they took it with them when they drove away.

I'm not sure how long I stand there, but when I finally hear my cell phone ringing, I snap back. Pulling it from my pocket, I don't want to answer it, but considering it's Josh, our captain, I do.

"Yeah?" I say with a sigh.

He huffs. "Christian wasn't kidding. You okay, Mika?"

Knowing Shiloh wouldn't be returning anytime soon, I turn and drag myself back inside while shaking my head. "Not even fucking close."

"How about I grab Connor and Lucas and we head over with food and drinks? Or we could go skate and shoot?" he suggests.

I appreciate the offer, but I don't want company.

"Thanks, man. I appreciate you calling, but I'm lousy company right now. I'm going to take the weekend to get my head right. I'll be ready for practice Monday and the upcoming series, but right now I want to be alone. Okay?"

"Sure, man. Take your time. But call us if you need anything, okay?" I can hear the concern in his voice, but he doesn't understand. Even though his woman is a she-devil, he still has her, and right now, I want to wallow alone. Once we hang up, I glance back at Shiloh's house to see if she changed her mind and came home. But her driveway is empty, just like my heart.

Feeling destroyed, I head up to my master bedroom. Moving slowly, I walk past my still packed luggage. When I reach the edge of my king-size bed, I strip to my boxer briefs, dropping my sweats in a heap on the floor before I crawl between the soft cotton sheets.

As I lie there, curled into a ball, reality sinks in. If I can't fix things with Shiloh, this space next to me will remain empty. Forever. There is no way I'd try to fill it with someone else. There is no replacing her. Shiloh is the only woman I'll ever be close with, the only one I'll ever consider letting into my life. The only woman I'll ever love. She is everything I've ever wanted.

Closing my eyes, I try to remember every curve of her body, the sweet noises she makes, and the expressions she has. Shiloh is beyond beautiful, and it hurts that I don't know if I'll ever have her close again. My heart aches in my chest. It feels like I've taken puck after puck to it without wearing protective gear; it's agonizing.

The idea of a future without Shiloh and the boys is bleak. We're neighbors, so I will physically see them, but that's all it would ever be. I'll never be privy to the intimate moments, thoughts, and nuisances she'd only shared with me. Losing her is tearing me apart in the worst possible way—piece by piece—and only she can fix me. But this morning, when I needed her most, when she needed me most, she chose to walk away, saying goodbye forever.

Chapter 27

Shiloh

The weekend after my breakup with Mika, Monica spent the entire weekend at my house, caring for the boys and keeping them entertained so I could hide out in my room and cry in peace. I promised myself then I would give myself those two days to get over Mika, but after that, I would move on. After all, I have two kids that need a parent who is present for them.

The following Monday, I woke early. Spending extra time on my outfit, makeup, and hair, I didn't want anyone gossiping about me or commenting about my devastated look. Instead, I planned to project strength, even if the opposite was true. That morning, I made sure I appeared perfect before I left my bedroom. Was I being fake? Yes. But I was doing what I had to, fully embracing the saying, "fake it till you make it." In fact, I made that saying my bitch. As far as anyone was concerned, I was completely unaffected by Mika and what had happened between us.

However, as the days drag by, each evening after putting the boys down for bed, I retreat to my room, where I finally allow myself to grieve what I lost, what I said goodbye to. A goodbye that still hasn't been acknowledged. Mika hasn't tried to contact me to explain what happened. He just cut his losses and walked away. The realization of that slices deep. It's one hundred times worse than the article, which Monica and some of his teammates keep reassuring me was full of lies. The entire time, their stories haven't changed, and I believe them. But Mika doesn't seem interested in addressing it. Apparently, he's moved on. Thankfully, Christmas break is only a few weeks away, and I'll get a respite during that time away from school.

The final week of school in December arrives, Monica heads to Hawaii for her best friend Samantha's wedding to Lucas. Mika will be in attendance too, and that stirs up a lot of conflicting emotions for me. On the one hand, I'm relieved he'll be gone, so I'll have a reprieve from attempting to avoid him if I take the boys outside to play. On the other, I'm jealous. Hawaii has always been on my bucket list, and we'd talked about taking the boys there so we could attend the wedding with him. Before we broke up, he'd reserved a suite, tickets, and mentioned some fun, family-orientated activities we could partake in when we weren't busy with wedding festivities. But since we aren't together anymore, I canceled the plane tickets and asked the airline to credit the miles back to Mika. It was just another time I expected to hear from him, but again, radio silence.

While they're all in paradise, the boys and I are stuck in cold, windy, dreary Chicago. Too many times I picture Mika sitting pool side, drinking a daiquiri with a few scantily clad bimbos hanging on his every word. I know I sound jealous, but I'm not. Not one bit. He can do whatever or whoever he wants. It doesn't bother me at all. *Does that sound believable? Yeah, it doesn't to me either.*

* * *

With each passing day, I know I need to get over him and move on. But it's more difficult than I expected; the pain of it all is still so raw and intense. Every time I see him or hear about him, my stomach revolts and a mini panic attack plagues me. Calming myself down afterward proves to be challenging, especially when I have a five- and two-year-old in tow, wanting to know what's wrong with me. The days trudge by.

Before long, winter morphs into spring. As the trees bud and bloom, I notice the pain that had been ever present during the harsh winter months suddenly isn't as noticeable. Maybe I'm finally getting over him and moving on?

* * *

Before I know it, Mother's Day weekend arrives. The boys bring home the crafts they made with their teachers. What treasures they are. Sam's handwritten message of *I LOVE YOU, MOMMA* and Lian's handprint flowers make me feel like the luckiest lady in the world.

That weekend, Monica and Samantha decide I need a night out and take care of all the arrangements for that to happen. They plan everything. From my outfit and hair, to where we're going, and who will watch the boys. They thought of it all.

We'll be heading into the city to a newer club, and we're all getting ready together. Samantha hired a hairstylist and makeup artist to come to my house too. She also asked her mom, Susan, to come to town to watch my boys for the night. Secretly, I think Susan is wishing for grandkids, and until that happens, spending time with my boys fills the vacancy. Over the past few months, my boys have seen her several times, and they adore her, even lovingly calling her Nana Fox.

Every time Susan came to town recently, she kindly agreed to watch the boys so the ladies and I could go to the salon or out to brunch. The plan for tonight is that Susan will take the boys for a sleepover at her hotel and I'll pick them up there the next day. Susan is hosting a brunch for us all in her suite the following morning.

So, before I get my hair and makeup done, I kiss my munchkins goodbye and they head out for what I know will be a grand adventure. Susan mentioned a giant bathtub and pizza, and I know she'll be fine. She also told me her plan includes watching a newly released movie. Hands down, she'll be giving my boys the best day of their lives. Hopefully, my evening will be as equally exciting.

Going out has never been a priority for me, and this is my first opportunity in years. I plan to drink, dance, and have fun with my best friends. I'm not sure when it happened, but after I met Samantha at her harvest party the previous fall, we spent time together and grew closer. She and Lucas are quite a pair, and the boys visit their house often. Thankfully, none of those times Mika had been in attendance. I'm not sure that either the boys or I could handle seeing him again. Or maybe that's my excuse?

After the boys leave with Susan, Samantha pops open a bottle of champagne and toasts our night. Knowing we need something in our stomachs to combat the drinking we plan to do, I quickly pull together some hors d'oeuvres from things I have in the fridge. It isn't fancy, but it'll probably save us from a dreaded hangover tomorrow.

We dress and put the final touches on our outfits and makeup before we head out. Forever a planner, Samantha arranged for one of the Fox Sporting drivers to act as our chauffeur for the evening. After snapping a million selfies, we're finally ready for our night on the town.

Slipping into the black Cadillac, Samantha has another surprise for us—a highly coveted seating for a late dinner at a new pop-up restaurant run by a Michelin Star chef. The only caveat to our dining is that we won't be told the identity of the chef. Curious by nature, we try to guess the chef's identity through all five courses of the decadent meal, but in the end, no one is correct.

When we're finished dining on the exquisite food, we head to our final destination for the night, Polaroid, a new club that Monica and Samantha have been talking about for weeks. The closer we get, the more nervous I become, making it feel like a hundred butter-flies are flapping their wings in my stomach.

Clubbing was foreign to me because, before tonight, I have never officially been "out on the town." Trent and I had married before I was twenty-one, and when I was finally of legal age, I'd been expecting Sam. And after Sam arrived, going out became even less important to me.

Now, though, with all the heartache of the past few months, I want to do something different, something impulsive, something unlike me. I desired to feel free, sexy, and uninhibited, and nothing is better than a club for achieving that. It's time for me to let loose and not answer to anyone or anything.

When we finally pull up to the curb at Polaroid,

Monica and Samantha squeal. Even though I'm a nervous wreck, it doesn't seem to hamper their excitement. I know I'll relax once we get inside and I have a few sips of liquid courage coursing through my body.

Entering the club is easier than I expected. I figured we'd have to wait in a line for a while before they gave us access, but again, Samantha comes through. She walks straight past the line of waiting patrons and up to the bouncer. Monica and I trail behind like dutiful groupies. After she gives our names, they usher us past the velvet ropes.

Samantha always carries herself with such confidence and grace. If she hadn't become one of my closest friends, I'd probably hate her. She looks like she has a perfect life, but I knew from many conversations, her image was carefully constructed and only those who really know her knew otherwise.

We hit the fully stocked bar shortly after entering the darkened club to decide our game plan. As we plot the evening, out of the corner of my eye, I notice a group of attractive guys approaching. They remind me of jungle cats stalking their prey; eyes focused, and movements smooth and calculated. I know we look fierce, but we're unavailable. Well, they are, but my heart is still trying to recover from the large Mika-sized hole he left behind.

Forgetting the guys and turning back to my drink, I take another swig of rum and Coke, enjoying the carbonation. With this drink and the couple of flutes of champagne I drank at my house, I'm happily on my way to buzzville, the inebriated state, not the town.

I don't remember the last time I had a buzz, but I'm definitely enjoying the relaxed feeling I'm experiencing. I've always been responsible with drinking, and with the boys around, I never cross the line. Even if they were in bed, I only ever had a glass or two of wine. Maybe tonight, with my friends, having a driver, and the boys at a sleepover, I could finally let loose?

When I hear Monica and Samantha's giggles over the music, it sounds flirty, which sets off warning bells. I take a final swig of my drink before half turning toward my friends, and what I see before me makes my stomach plummet. What is going on? Did I miss something? Why are they giggling like that with complete strangers?

Finally, correcting my posture and facing them fully, I shake off the booze-induced haze that clouds my vision. Reality hits me in the face. Actually, it slaps me. Slaps really fucking hard. Christian is standing next to Monica, wearing a filthy smirk on his face, whispering something into her ear. Lucas is nuzzled up against Samantha, giving her his best fuck-me eyes.

Dread fills me. The evening had shifted from girls' night to fifth-wheel awkward in about two seconds flat. Surrounded by hundreds of people dancing, I still feel incredibly alone.

Slowly, I back away from the happy couples, knowing that if the guys are here, then Mika must be too. I'm not prepared to see a woman hanging all over him. My emotions, although well camouflaged, are still so raw and explosive. Jealousy, anger, and hurt flow through me, lighting my body up like a heat conductor. Not wanting to feel it, I walk to another section of the bar and order a shot I heard could make you forget everything. An adios motherfucker.

To hell with it, I think before throwing the shot back. I close my eyes and savor the burn as it travels down my throat. I pray it will take effect quickly, because I don't want to remember anything right now. The only thing I want to do is move, because this music is making my body feel alive.

Pushing away from the bar, I look over at my friends and see they're still distracted by their men. Heading to the nearest open spot on the dance floor, I dance by myself. Not caring that I have no partner, I move my hips to the beat that pounds around me. The rhythm that fills the space is both sexy and sinful, and I raise my hands high in the air and close my eyes, finally feeling free. Bodies are everywhere, gyrating, grinding, and thrusting. And instead of caring about anything, I clear my mind and let my body embrace the rhythmic beats enveloping me, begging to take me under.

Song after song play, and I just keep moving. I'm not the best dancer, but I can hold a beat, and this DJ is playing amazing dance songs I've never heard before. They turn the lights in the club down lower, creating the illusion of almost complete darkness.

Thankfully, the dress Samantha got for me is sleeveless because it's hotter than Hades on the dance floor and I'm very much in need of ventilation. At one point, I debate going to get water at the bar, but I'm having too much fun by myself. When another new song comes across the speakers, a deep masculine voice behind me whispers in my ear. The timber of his voice registers, sending shivers across my body, instantly cooling me. His words hit me and turn my brain to mush. "Talk dirty to me," is all he rasps before he possessively wraps his large hand around my waist, tapping my hip bones just like Mika use to. *That's strange.* When the mysterious man firmly pulls me into him, I gasp. The faint scent of sandalwood and leather tickles my nose, instantly reminding me of Mika. When he settles me in front of his crotch, I can't help but feel how turned on he is. Then he juts his hips forward, grinding himself against me, and I grip his muscular forearm to keep myself upright. *Why does this feel so good?* His ministrations make my knees turn to Jell-O.

Having him so close feels right, but even in my tipsy state, that doesn't make sense. He's a stranger. I shouldn't like this, but I do. Instead of running away, like I probably should, I continue writhing in his grasp. Being here, right now, feels... it feels like coming home. And after many months of questioning everything, home is the only place I want to be.

The thought of enjoying this taboo connection

with this stranger seems ridiculous, and I not only justify it with my alcohol consumption, but with the way it makes me feel. There is no way I'm moving away from it. I don't know who's behind me, but his being there feels perfect. Like it's meant to be. Confusing me further is how familiar it all seems too. If he's a stranger, why would I feel comforted and protected?

Chapter 28

Mika

The last few months without Shiloh have been beyond miserable. For the first time in my life, I don't care about anything. Food doesn't taste good. Going out seems pointless. Hockey isn't fun. I'm in an awful place and the guys know it. Even Coach Tristan visits and tries to get me out of my funk. But nothing takes. Deep down, I appreciate all the support, encouragement, and talks, but nothing changes the situation I'm in.

Going to Hawaii for Lucas and Samantha's wedding a few weeks after Shiloh ended things hadn't proved to be very distracting either. I'd avoided all the things she and I talked about doing. The suite I'd reserved and forgot to downgrade was painfully large and mind-numbingly quiet. Avoiding it, other than for sleeping, became my primary task for those five long days I was in paradise.

I'd spent most of my time either at the beach, swimming in the ocean, or reading the latest thriller on my iPad. One morning, I'd gotten up incredibly early and biked down the volcano at sunrise. The day before the wedding, Lucas, Josh, Christian, and I had taken a surf lesson. Hanging with the guys had given me enough of a mental break that I could enjoy the groomsmen activity without Shiloh crowding my mind too much.

Samantha and Lucas's wedding was amazing and I'd enjoyed it. I knew it would have been better with Shiloh and the boys there. The unfortunate truth was they were no longer part of my life. Watching my friends exchange vows had reminded me that their happiness was something I no longer had. Their promises to each other, a stark reminder it was probably time to move on. I wanted desperately to fight for Shiloh, Sam, and Lian, but it felt like I needed to respect her wishes to walk away. After all, she'd said goodbye to me. The pain I saw on her face the morning she found out about the article was seared into my brain, and I never wanted to cause her pain like that again. Giving up feels like I'm a quitter, and I am not one. I don't want to move on, but I'm cutting my losses. Her ex hadn't given her any power, and I don't want to be like that. I don't want her to be pressured by me. She needs to make the best decision for herself and the boys. And even if it doesn't include me, I have to learn to accept it.

Feeling lonely and needing to get away from all the festivities, I'd left the wedding celebration and gone for a walk on the beach outside the venue. Setting my shoes and socks on an empty pool chair, I'd rolled up my pant legs and walked down to where the sand met the water. As the waves rolled in, they washed over my sunken feet.

Alone, I listened to the sounds of the ocean. In the distance I could still hear the noise of the after party, but that bubble I found myself in was peaceful and renewing. A breeze whipped across me, but unlike in Chicago, it had been warm and comforting, almost like a hug. As I'd stood there, staring out into the darkness, smelling salt in the air and being caressed by the wind, I'd felt okay for the first time in weeks. The pain of losing Shiloh was still raw and real and not likely to go away anytime soon, but at that point in time, I hadn't felt like there was anything I could do to make things better. At least not yet anyway.

The last day in Hawaii had gone better than the first ones. I'd taken another surf lesson and gone to a nearby town and ate fresh-cut pineapple while I'd watched a local surf competition. After flying all day, exhausted and ready to be home, I'd pulled into my driveway and saw Shiloh getting out of her SUV. I'd frozen. She hadn't seen me and I could watch her undisturbed. My heart thumped in my chest, telling me I needed to go to her, but as I'd reached for the handle of my door to do just that, my brain chimed in a reminder. *Time heals all wounds.* I didn't know who'd said it, but I hoped it was true. If I gave Shiloh enough time, then maybe I'd have another chance. I'd be patient and bide my time, even if it tore me apart.

* * *

The new year arrives in the blink of an eye, and nothing really changes. Practices are a blur, like most everything since Shiloh walked away, but when I saunter into Coach's office this week to "check-in," he insists we go to dinner.

Unlike when I have an impromptu visit to his office, the restaurant we've chosen tonight feels smothering. My chest squeezes like I'm suffocating from within. When the server takes my order, I hear the rasp in my voice. After the server leaves, Coach turns to me, giving me an understanding look and says, "Mika, it'll feel better if you just get it off your chest. Tell someone what's going on."

Not really believing what he said, I say nothing as I lean back in the booth, putting my arms behind my head, feigning innocence, attempting to convince him I'm fine.

"Really? You aren't going to say anything?" he asks.

"What? I'm fine," I scoff.

"You are something... but you are definitely not fine. You are the moodiest SOB in the NHL right now and that's saying something. If you're not hitting something, you aren't happy. Killing the gym equipment during workouts has become your modius operandi. And anyone who tries to talk to you gets their head ripped off. You, my friend... are miserable."

Coach's words hit hard. The fact they're true makes them even tougher to accept. I'm not ready to admit that to anyone. So, I just shrug my shoulders and say, "Maybe."

When my single word answer registers, he drops his shoulders in defeat. He mutters "maybe" under his breath while shaking his head in disbelief. *What did he expect? I'm not ready to talk to anyone about what's going on.*

"You know, Mika, I see a lot of myself in you, and I'm trying to help you avoid some of the pain and heartache I've had to deal with because I was too stubborn to push my ego aside. From what I know, Shiloh and her boys were good for you. When you got together, there was a change in you as both a person and a hockey player. You became unstoppable. It was like we were finally seeing the real you. Then the New York drama happened and it knocked you down. And I get it. What went down was not fair or your fault. But how you choose to deal with it is. You can step aside from your anger, ego, and hurt, and you can make things better. I once lost the love of my life because I let all those things control the outcome for me, and I've been miserable since. I don't want the same for you."

Since it's Coach, I listen to what he has to say. But

in the end, I only take part of what he says to heart; I'm not totally convinced. After all, he's a moody motherfucker too. Ever since the Steel fundraiser this past spring, he's been different. Now, instead of a hotheaded asshole, we have access to an intuitive diplomat spouting transformation and forgiveness. Honestly, the change in personality has been a mindfuck.

When our dinners arrive, we eat hurriedly, both wanting to escape the awkward discomfort we find ourselves in. When the server returns to ask if we want dessert, we're both quick to answer no. Before the bill even lands on the table, we're both reaching for cash to cover our share. When we exit the restaurant, I tell him I'll see him at practice before practically jogging away. *This night needs to be over.*

Just like Coach, some of my teammates, ones I don't care too much for, suggest a cure for my heartache. According to them, the best way to get over Shiloh is to get under another chick. But those assholes don't get it. Shiloh isn't just any woman. Yes, she's beautiful. But she is also kind, funny, giving, resourceful, sexy, honest, and playful. She is everything I want. There would be no substitutes.

After a few more weeks of grumbling, I fly to Boston to spend a weekend with my mama. While there, she notices my sad demeanor, and one night over Plov, my favorite Russian meal, she forces me to tell her. At first, as I push the hearty meat and rice dish around my bowl, I try to select the best words to explain my predicament. Noticing me floundering, Mama places her wrinkly hand on mine and whispers, "Mika, my son, you look heartbroken. What is going on?"

Nodding, I answer in a weary voice, "I am. I was dating an amazing woman months ago, and the tabloids published some fake news about me and she broke up with me without even letting me explain what happened. Instead, she closed herself off, shut me out. She's been hurt before. I *know* that, but I would *never* hurt her like that."

"Fake news?" she asks, tilting her head at me as if she either doesn't believe me or maybe doesn't understand.

Knowing my mama as well as I do, I know she doesn't doubt me, but she probably doesn't understand fully what I'm saying. So, I do my best to explain.

After hearing it all, she looks at me with eyes that are heavy with unshed tears and lets out a sigh.

"Mika, I am sorry this has happened to you. I know you wouldn't hurt a woman intentionally, but why didn't she listen? Or why didn't you fight for her? It's obvious you have strong feelings for her."

My head hangs low in defeat. "Yeah, I still have feelings for her; probably always will. But she didn't want my explanation. When I reached out to her, she said goodbye, ending things between us. What could I do?"

Mama remains quiet on the other side of the table. *Is she expecting me to figure this out on my own? Because so far, my plan of just getting over Shiloh and moving on has been shit.*

Hating the silence, I ask, "Mama, what should I do?"

Finally, I take a bite of dinner that I know is delicious but has remained untouched on my plate. And I wait as Mama contemplates her words before answering. "If you care for her so much, you fight for her. Make her listen. Only then, when you've spoken your piece, can either of you move forward. I can't promise it will be the ending you want, but until it happens, you remain stuck."

Her words are prophetic and powerful, reminding me that staying where I am won't give me any closure. Listening to my mama, I want her to tell me that everything will be fine, kind of like she did when I was a child. But she doesn't. Her advice is correct. I can't move on unless I finally confront Shiloh.

Taking another bite of the Plov, I let the flavors dance on my tongue. The comfort and familiarness of the spices, the warmth of the paprika, soothes my weary soul. Savoring bite after bite, I notice I'm feeling better than I have in weeks. Just being around my mama again is the much-needed balm to my splintered heart.

Although our visit is short, it's nice to have great food and conversation with Mama again. It had been too long since I saw her last, and I promise to come back soon. In all the years I've been playing for the Steel, she's only visited once, and I hope in the future we'll change that. Our goodbyes are difficult, as I came to her a very broken man and I'm still hurting. Her words resonated, and now I just have to wait for the opportunity to talk to Shiloh.

Another few weeks fly by and winter passes to spring. Most of it is a blur to me, but I show up when it matters. And next week, the guys and I are playing for a shot at the Stanley Cup. It's a long road to the finals. We won the cup last year, and there is talk in the league that we have a great shot at it again this year. We will see.

In commemoration of our advancement to the next stage, the guys and I are going out, or that's what they told me. However, I heard them in the locker room earlier this week when they were talking about how they're sick of my mood and this would be their last attempt to get me out of my rut. Joke's on them, because the only thing that will fix things for me, they can't deliver—Shiloh. She is all I want and need, and she hasn't made any contact with me after her quick goodbye.

Even though time has passed, I still miss her just as much as that first day. I know I won't find anyone like Shiloh again, and the thought of that makes life seem unbearably painful. Slightly depressed, I feel weighed down by my sadness. Being so close to her, but not being able to see, talk, or kiss her, makes my days miserable. I've even started avoiding my house unless it's to sleep or do laundry. I've spent far too many hours at the arena working out, skating, or watching tapes.

When I get sick of all my normal distraction techniques, I tend to invite myself over to one of the guys' houses to hang out. Even Coach receives weekly extended visits from me. He never once complains about it, but again that may be because I'm pretty sure he reconnected with someone from his past.

* * *

When my doorbell rings tonight, I consider not answering it, but I remember Mama's advice to seize the moment. Yet I sit in my recliner, thinking and waiting. Waiting for what, I don't know. If this is truly my last shot, I'll be an absolute moron not to jump at it. After a few rings, the guys knock. Then they add chanting. "Open up. Open up. Open up." *WTF?* They are so loud. Is the entire team outside my door?

I pull up my doorbell camera and am relieved to see just a few of the guys. Besides Lucas and Christian, there are Rocco and Ace, the team's resident playboys, hooting and hollering. Not understanding the plan for the night, I hesitantly let the guys in.

Rocco and Ace shove their way in. "Mika, move, we're coming in whether you like it or not," Rocco threatens. I growl at him.

Ace smacks me in the arm. "Stop being a growly bear. Tonight is the night. We're going to Polaroid, so you have exactly five minutes to turn that frown upside down and get ready to party."

I roll my eyes at them. *I'm going clubbing? How will I get Shiloh back by clubbing?*

When everyone's escaped to my kitchen, I see each guy holding a bottle of alcohol. Apparently, they decided on their way over that I'd need a few pre-drinks before we go clubbing. Normally, I'm not a big drinker, but maybe a buzz would deaden the constant pain I still feel living in my chest.

Lucas confidently strides up to my cabinet, acting like he lives with me. He pulls coffee cups from my open kitchen shelves. I guffaw and say, "Make yourself at home, Lucas. Nice shot glasses, asshole."

He smirks, laughs, and starts pouring shots from the bottle he's holding. When he finally has all the drinks poured, he hands them out before lifting his to make a toast. "If you'll excuse me, please... Tonight's poor decisions will not be making themselves." He thrusts his plain white ceramic mug into the air and the others follow. I slowly join in, questioning whether a night out will make a difference. I don't know. Maybe the guys are right. I need to move on, and tonight could be the first step.

Slamming back my large shot, I register that it's whiskey. The burn is immediate, and so is the warmth spreading through my body. "To bad decisions," I say.

Hopefully, I won't make too many of those, but I still motion for another shot. Slamming that back, too, I set my mug on the counter, slap my hands together, and shout, "Let's go!" All the guys look at me, stunned, and then rush for the door.

Once we breach my front door, my eyes land on a decked-out black SUV with a suited driver standing by. Like giddy teenagers, we race outside. The driver steps forward and pulls the door open. We clamber for seats, pushing each other out of the way. Messing with my guys like that is the best I've felt in weeks. Thank you, whiskey. Feeling relaxed and energized, I'm excited about what's coming. Tonight, I'm ready to let go. To be ready and open to whatever happens.

After I climb into my hard-won window seat, I glance over to Shiloh's house and notice it's completely dark. Where is she? Shouldn't she be home? She's a single mom, and it's after eight. Right now, on a normal day, she'd be getting the boys ready for bed, and the upstairs of her house would be lit up. But it isn't. In fact, no light is visible at all. *Stop*, I tell myself. It doesn't matter what she's doing. She isn't my concern anymore. Pushing her out of my mind the best I can, I holler at Lucas, "Dude, we're grabbing dinner before hitting the club, right?"

He nods. "Yes, we're headed to Steak & Co. before heading to Polaroid."

Dinner is amazing. The restaurant serves everything family style, so with four professional hockey players and one fit agent, our table is going to be covered in a ton of food.

"Guys, what should we order?" Lucas questions.

"Since we're getting steaks, we have to get the wild steakhouse mushrooms," Rocco declares.

"Anyone else want the cream-style spinach?" Ace asks. Both Rocco and Lucas grunt. *Apparently, that means yes.*

Rocco looks at me. "Since Lucas picked the place and both Ace and I have selected a side, you need to choose one too."

Looking at the menu, it all sounds appetizing, but nothing sticks out. "I guess I pick the garlic horseradish mashed potatoes."

With a full stomach, the rest of my night involves having a few drinks and seeing where the night takes me.

As we drive around downtown, I stare out the window, my thoughts again focused on Shiloh. Even though we never went out clubbing, everything makes me think of her. And right now is no different. Though she doesn't want me anymore, my desire for her is seemingly unshakable. I'd pay anything to spend the evening with her. To touch and grind up against her all night would be absolute ecstasy. Hell, at this point, I'd pay anything just to have a conversation with her, even if it's her yelling at me.

Lucas notices I've gone quiet before we walk into the club and he reaches over and punches my shoulder. I look at him, confused, and he gives me a sad, knowing smile. My pre-festivities buzz must have worn off because I realize he understands exactly how I feel. Two years earlier, he was feeling much the same when Samantha broke up with him. Heartbreak sucks. Acknowledging him, I grimace, then dip my head, knowing I have to get my shit together before we arrive.

Walking up to the bouncer minutes later earns us immediate attention.

"Lucas, Mika, Rocco, Ace," a group of ladies squeals. Lucas and I hang back while Rocco and Ace approach them. Selfies are taken and, before long, Rocco saunters back with a shit-eating grin plastered to his face. "It's a bachelorette party, and from the looks of it, they are ready to party."

When we finally enter the club, we're garnering attention from every direction. Thankfully, Rocco and Ace will happily absorb it. Being a professional athlete, it's something we've gotten used to, but ever since I met Shiloh, it doesn't capture my interest the way it did previously. Since meeting her, I've realized I've become more like Lucas and Connor. One woman is what I want, today and every day. In fact, since the 4th of July, I haven't paid any attention to any other females.

As we stride into the club, Rocco and Ace head one way toward the bachelorette party, and I follow Lucas and Christian as they make their way to the lower bar. It seems weird that they picked this bar since it was next to the dance floor. Are they planning to dance? With who? I can't believe either of them would screw up what they have with their women to dance with some rando. I mean, Christian isn't officially dating Monica, but that's because he's too chickenshit to admit that she's it for him. As far as I know, he hasn't been with anyone else since they hooked up right before Lucas and Samantha got engaged over a year ago. He's committed, he just can't admit it.

Being a few steps behind, I watch as they approach some ladies seated at the bar, and I can hardly believe my eyes. *Holy. Shit!* Am I watching two of my closest friends cheat on their women? Incredibly uncomfortable, my heart thunders in my chest as I further slow my approach. Panic sets in and a nervous sweat breaks out over my entire body. I don't want to witness this.

Frantically looking around for an exit, I need to get out of the club before I see anything else. Already having gone through my own relationship imploding, I'm not about to bear witness to my friends sabotaging their own.

Lucas is practically crawling on one woman, and my mouth flies open in astonishment. Wait, is that

Samantha? Taking another step closer, recognition spikes. Needing complete confirmation, I turn to look at Christian and notice he's whispering in the other woman's ear. She throws back her head in laughter, and I know immediately it's Monica. Unease plagues me. My eyes dart around, and I shift nervously. Is Shiloh with them? Is this the moment my mama had been talking about?

Needing a drink, I approach the recently vacated seat on the side of Samantha. A petite blonde in a tight black dress had just been sitting here, but she dashed off as soon as we approached. I hadn't seen her face, but I definitely noticed her. Her shape is burned into my memory and I can't shake the feeling of familiarity that licks down my spine. Was she with Samantha and Monica? If so, who was it? Still curious, it only makes sense that it was Shiloh. Had she seen me and run away? I don't remember the guys mentioning that they were meeting the girls tonight. What is going on?

Wondering where the mysterious blonde resembling Shiloh went, I run my eyes over the dance floor, but she isn't there. Turning back, I spot her on the other side of the bar. Confirmation is instant. It's Shiloh. And she looks fucking incredible. A goddess in black, she's sexy and sinful. Her hair is curled and I want to palm her soft waves. She's wearing her makeup dark, drawing me in.

Across the way, I stare at her like a stalker while she remains completely unaware. Being away from her for so long, my eyes eat her up, tracing over every curve, refamiliarizing myself. There she is, on full display for everyone, yet she is off-limits to me. Not wanting to accept it, my hand clenches into a fist. I'm desperate to touch her. It is unfathomable to believe it's been months since I've last been able to do that. In the short time we'd been together, I had gotten to know all of her. From the spots that make her flinch, to those that make her laugh, and my personal favorites, those that make her moan. Every part of her is perfect and mine. Or so they had been.

Shiloh orders a drink and my curiosity piques. What did she order? When the bartender hands her an electric blue shot, she wastes no time slamming it back. Setting the empty shot glass down, she wipes her lips and then heads for the dance floor. Watching her make her way into the middle of it, it takes all my willpower to remain where I am. I keep myself in check as I track all the attention she's getting that she is blissfully unaware of. Not wanting to cause a scene, I tell myself to calm down, even though the adrenaline that pumps through my body makes me shaky.

My eyes never leave Shiloh. My mama's reminder flashes in my mind again. *Take the opportunity*. I'm sure she hadn't considered stalking Shiloh through a dark, packed dance club as part of the scenario she envisioned when she gave me that advice. But I'm taking the moment. Shiloh has become my prey, and I'm more than ready to pounce.

Mesmerized, I watch as she closes her eyes and dances to the music pumping through the club. It seems the longer she dances, the more comfortable she becomes, and the more men pay attention to the way her hips sway back and forth in the most sensually provocative ways.

When it looks like a few of the men are going to approach her, I make my presence known. Stepping forward aggressively, I put myself between them and Shiloh. Seeing my size and the possessive expression on my face, they shy away.

The entire time dancing, Shiloh has kept her eyes closed, so she's unaware of how close I am to her. My body responds instantly to being near her and I have to fight myself not to reach out and grab her. Watching her move uninhibited is erotic as hell. Desperately, I want to be replicating her dance moves in my bed, naked. Thinking about how her body felt against mine, I grow obscenely hard. Recalling all the chemistry we shared makes my blood boil and my body heat. Truly, she was made for me and we fit together perfectly, like puzzle pieces.

Over the speakers, I recognize the beginning beats of Jason Derulo's "Talk dirty to me," and I know this is my moment. I step up behind Shiloh and lean forward, whispering in her ear, "Talk dirty to me." Her response is immediate. She shivers. Just like when I'd turn her on. It's a sign.

Wrapping my hand around her hip, I pull her back

into me. Her perfect ass rests against my raging hard-on, and for the first time in months, my life seems once again perfect. Shiloh is again right where she is supposed to be. With me.

When she registers the contact between our bodies, she lets out a throaty gasp and I swallow hard, worried she might pull away. But she doesn't. Instead, she continues to dance up against me, and our bodies grind against each other to a sensual rhythm only we can feel. I flex my hand against her hip, relieved I'm finally touching her. This is absolute heaven.

Finally, tucked into my body, is the woman I thought I'd lost forever. Looking at her face and noticing the smile across her lips, my heart hammers in my chest. Her smokey painted eyes are still closed and then it registers. Shiloh doesn't know it's me grinding up behind her. My stomach drops. What will her reaction be when the song ends? When she finally opens her eyes and reality comes crashing back in?

Chapter 29

Shiloh

Feeling the obvious reaction of the man behind me fills me with lust, and I push farther back into him, enjoying the feel of his impressively large, hard shaft rubbing against me. His firm grip on my hip feels possessive and drives me insane, causing me to grind harder against him. My skin overheats where his fingertips thrum, and my body becomes needy. Wanting this man's hands to cover every inch of me, I remain close, inhaling the smell of musk circling around us, reminding me of Mika's cologne. Strong undertones of amber and leather dance around me, enticing me. At the thought of Mika, my heartbeat picks up, but instead of panic, I feel desire and want.

When the song ends, I open my eyes, blinking slowly to adjust to the darkened room. Nervously, I glance over my shoulder, wondering how the image of the man I created in my mind compares to the one my body had melted into. When my eyes land on him, a loud gasp escapes my lips and my heart stops. Had I conjured him here? Was there something extra in that shot? Shaking my head to clear it, I realize it was Mika who had been dancing behind me. Now I know why it felt perfect, being in this man's arms.

His expression registers. He recognized me and danced with me on purpose. He wasn't surprised to see me. He knew when he approached me. He knew the whole time that he was dancing with me, while I was happily oblivious. Mika forces a hesitant smile, and my eyes fall to his lips; his soft, pink lips. Ones that I've missed for months. When he sees me focus on them, his smile turns to a sexy smirk that both aggravates and tempts me.

This whole time, dancing behind me was the man who even now has my heart. Having him near was familiar because when we were together, I'd loved it when he would spoon me. In his embrace, I'd never felt more safe and secure, just like here on the dance floor. But then New York happened, and that security was ripped away.

Thoughts of it all whip through my head like the winds of a tornado. Swirling and twirling, aggressive and abrupt. I have to know why Mika is here. Was this girls' night a setup? It feels beyond amazing to have him near me again, but do I want that?

Confused, I step away from him, and his tight, possessive hold on my hip slips. My heart shudders. In an instant, I feel like I'm losing him all over again. *Shit!* This encounter with him is going to knock me right back on my ass, back at square one. Guess what? Square one fucking sucks. All those months of trying to pretend that I didn't miss Mika was torturous, and I'm confident I won't be able to do it again. If I have any hope of surviving this, I need to get away. Now. Before my heart gets any more involved.

Without a word, I turn and run. And Mika follows me. Off the dance floor and through the various sections of the club, I run, probably drawing much unwanted attention.

Flustered, I scan back and forth, trying to determine the best route to an exit. I should probably head toward my friends at the bar, but I feel slightly betrayed. In my heart, I now suspect this has been a sneaky setup. And a question I need answered is: was Mika involved? I'd seen both Lucas and Christian at the bar, and neither Samantha nor Monica appeared surprised when they arrived. Scattered, unsure, and trying to save face, I school my emotions, roll my shoulders, and head in the opposite direction of our friends. I don't know where I'm going, but I'm getting away. Or at least that's what I hope.

The farther I push into the darkened club, the fewer people I encounter, and before I know it, I'm alone in an almost blacked-out room. My skin prickles and goose bumps cover my body as I slowly continue forward. "Breathe, Shiloh," I mutter to myself through chattering teeth.

Stomp, stomp. Mika's shoes slap noisily on the concrete floor as he pursues me. The sound echoes in the abandoned room, bouncing off the dark walls, making it sound louder than it is. If he catches up to me, what will happen? Uncertainty makes me fearful. But fearful of what? Mika doesn't scare me, but if he catches me, I'm afraid he'll get me to admit all the feelings I still harbor for him. I don't want him to know how badly I still want him. How much we still miss him. How much it hurt to lose him. But, as those fears run through my mind, I tell myself that too much time has passed and there is no way he still feels anything for me, still wants us. Well, maybe he feels something, considering all the stomping he's doing behind me. He's angry. But that doesn't make sense. His touch on the dance floor seemed full of passion, but it hadn't been driven by anger. No, it felt more like lust. So, what is going on? I'm not sure I'm ready to find out. Will I be able to handle it?

When I finally spot a green exit sign, I jet toward it, hoping for freedom. Just as I shove through the door and am taking a full breath of freedom, firm hands haul me back into the dark room, trapping me against a hard chest. Struggling to free myself from the large biceps that wrap tightly around me is pointless. My arms flail and a pathetic squeak falls from my lips. Still, Mika holds me against his heavily muscled body, refusing to give me any wiggle room. Our labored breathing is the only noise heard in the room.

After a few moments, the grasp across my biceps tightens, then releases completely. Did he hug me? Still facing away from him, I try my best to push down all the emotions I feel bubbling up inside me. Mika is taking deep breaths and exhaling loudly, making me pause my thoughts. Is he breathing through a panic attack? Our run through the club certainly wouldn't wind a professional hockey player. So, if it's a panic attack, what triggered it? Is it because he's angry? While we were dating, I'd seen Mika angry once or twice. All of those times, his anger had been because he'd been incredibly frustrated. Did I frustrate him? Is that making him angry with me? Because until now, that controlled, hostile energy had never been directed at me. Right now, being the object of his frustration, I can admit he's intimidating. He never intimidated me before. During our time together, we'd never fought or been cross with one another. Our personalities meshed so easily and effortlessly. But right now, at this moment, it feels different, charged with emotion that I can't tell is negative or not.

Slowly, I turn toward him, afraid to make eye contact. Instead, I stare at the floor, as if it's a previously undiscovered Picasso and I'm the art appraiser tasked with assessing its value. While focused on the scuffs on the floor, I see his foot edge into my vision. Sensing his body move closer to me, I back into the wall. Mika's muscular arms bracket me firmly to the cold cement. If this were any other man, I would feel trapped and scared, but with him I've only ever felt safe and protected. Even now. Why is that? In my heart, I know he would never physically hurt me. But emotionally, that proved to be another story. He had ruined me. So, now, what does he want? Needing to know, I hesitantly lift my eyes to his.

Chapter 30

Mika

Watching her flee from me is the final straw. Crazed, I chase after her. She is going to give me the answers I need. The answers I know I deserve. My heart pounds in my chest and I struggle not to go entirely alpha asshole on her, knowing I have the potential to scare her if I remain this agitated.

When she pushes through an exit door, I reach out and grab her arm, stopping her. My grasp isn't hard enough to leave bruises, but it certainly stills her. When I pull her in tight, she finally gives in, coming willingly. She feels so good in my arms, I just hold her for a moment, relishing the closeness before I let go.

After a while, she slowly turns toward me but keeps her gaze glued to the floor. *Shit!* She can't even look at me. This isn't going at all how I want. I step closer, and she remains where she is. Using my size, I back her up against the dark, abandoned wall. Glancing around, I notice we're alone. Running my eyes over her entire body, I search for telltale signs of her being afraid and see there aren't any.

Other than her inability to make eye contact, her posture seems mostly normal. She doesn't appear nervous or timid, just exhausted. Maybe our breakup has worn her out too. Shiloh looks thinner than she did months before, and that angers me. Has she been eating? Sleeping? When her back finally touches the wall, I place my arms on either side of her, boxing her in. A visible shiver travels over her body and her breathing picks up.

Suddenly intrigued, I angle my head at her. These aren't signs she is panicked. They're telling me she's turned on. Interesting. We hadn't explored much in the bedroom, as we hadn't been together long. And with kids around, it isn't as easy to be as adventurous as you might want. Maybe she likes to be controlled? I can definitely be the alpha man she needs if she finds that attractive. Before I let my mind wander too much, I need to fix things between us. Otherwise, there won't be this alpha male in her bedroom. Not if she doesn't permit me back in her life.

"Shiloh," I whisper, praying she'll look up at me. Seconds tick by agonizingly slowly as I wait to connect with her tender blue eyes. Her eyes are like the windows to her soul, her emotional polygraph, and I'm glad they will finally give me the answers I need.

"Shiloh. Please look at me," I plead. My voice is tinged with the despair I've felt deep within every facet of my body for the past five months. Her hurt compounds mine, and I know I'll never forgive myself if I don't fix things between us. She is my person, and I care more for her than anyone else in my life.

Desperately needing to apologize, I remind myself that whatever happens between us now is her choice. She can walk away from me if she needs to. Of course I hope that once I've apologized, she won't, but I have to be realistic. It could happen. Instead of walking away, I hope she lets me beg, grovel, plead, whatever she needs, to earn a second chance. Because the truth is, she's it for me.

When she finally looks up at me, tears leak from her eyes, and my heart continues to fracture. Our feelings are mirrored. Two broken souls, barely holding ourselves together.

Standing there, I fight the need to pull her into me, bring her closer. I want to fix it all. To annihilate all the pain that racks her body. More tears fall, and my hand rises to wipe them from her cheeks. My thumb sweeps gently across her skin, abolishing the wet reminder of her pain. Mind racing and heart beating wildly, I savor the simple contact she is allowing me. We stare at each other, the thumping noise of the club disappearing entirely. It's only us, broken, bruised, and baffled where we'll go from here.

Needing to try something, I say, "I'm sorry,

Shiloh." I look deep into her eyes while I apologize, needing to know she hears me. Shiloh blinks hard, really focusing on me. Her expression isn't as full of shock as it had been moments before. Now she seems filled with uncertainty. But why? Then I realize she's unclear about me. About my apology, my feelings, and about everything I've said and done. Feeling overwhelmed by it all, I take a step back, giving us both space.

An ache plagues my chest, tightening down, and the pain harnessed within it is one I've become very familiar with over the past months. It occurs whenever I feel afraid. That fit, because right now, I am terrified I've lost Shiloh forever. But have I? I don't know and won't until she answers. Standing there, I don't want to force anything between us. Shiloh couldn't feel trapped by me. I need her to want to be here with me. If she comes back to me, it has to be because she wants to, not because I coerced her.

We stand there for a few minutes, saying nothing, and it's torture. Then, her small hand reaches out to me and touches my chest, over my heart, right where it aches most. I look down at her, and she seems lost in her own feelings and thoughts. It's then I notice her other hand placed directly over her own heart. Unthinking, I move my hand to cover hers, and the warmth her hand radiates feels like a soothing balm, healing my fractured, broken heart. My feet bring me closer to her and her eyes focus on me.

Still, I haven't spoken, unwilling to disturb the magnetism that surrounds us. She shyly smiles at me, and my restraint shatters. Pulling her in and holding her feels unbelievable. Screw the earlier promises I made to myself. I need her near me, and I don't care what it will cost.

"Mika." Shiloh speaks softly against my chest. For months I've imagined I would never hold her again, but here she is. Seeing it as a positive sign, I nuzzle my nose above her ear and whisper, "Baby, I'm so sorry. I missed you so much." Holding her tightly against me, I know things haven't magically been fixed between us, but right now, she isn't running from me.

"I don't know where to begin," I confess to both of us in a strangled voice. The stress of the past few months and this moment is coming to a head, making me feel like a tightly wound spring. One wrong turn will destroy what I'm clinging desperately to.

In a quiet, patient voice, Shiloh tells me, "Start at the beginning, Mika."

Forcing a tight breath out of my chest, I start, "You know the game that Ace was injured in?" Shiloh nods her head. "That game was fucked up. The guy, Jeremy Kane, who took him out had been playing dirty the entire game, and I knew something bad was going to happen. I could feel it. And then it did. Watching Ace lie there on the ice, not moving, did things to me. Until then, I'd never considered hockey dangerous. Other than missing teeth, a little blood, and a broken bone or two, I hadn't seen anyone go down that hard."

"Oh, Mika." Shiloh whimpers in my arms. "That must have been so scary."

"It was. But it also made me angry. I wanted to pummel Kane, pay him back for the pain he'd inflicted on Ace. However, Coach warned us off of that. The referees came up with a bullshit penalty and that just made me angrier." I can feel myself getting worked up. Needing to calm down, I hug Shiloh. "When we returned to the hotel that night, Connor and I went to grab a drink. Then those puck bunnies approached. I knew they were trouble immediately, and I should have just got up and left, but I was trying to protect my image and not be the asshole so many people assume I am."

My chest is starting to feel lighter now that I'm finally able to talk to Shiloh about all of this. But there's more to this story.

"What happened next?" Shiloh encourages me to go on, like she knows the story already and she's just waiting to hear it from me.

"When they approached us, we tried to be respectful. We didn't engage or encourage them, but the blonde one was aggressive. When she touched me, I'd had enough, and I tried to remove her hand from me, but she took that as an invitation to push things further. It was during these moments that a newspaper photographer was poised and ready to capture the story they wanted to tell, one of me hooking up with someone while I was in the city." I growl the last part, disgusted by what lies they told and the damage it had done.

The last part of this story has to be told. "Shiloh, I didn't take that woman to my room. After I stormed out of the bar, I never saw her again. Please believe me. I'm sorry I didn't talk to you about this right after it happened. I know I made things worse, but I need to know you trust I didn't cheat on you."

Shiloh hugs me. "I know you didn't cheat, Mika. Several of your teammates, your coach, Christian, and Monica have pled your case." Relieved, it feels like a giant weight has been lifted from my shoulders.

Holding her tight, but understanding this conversation isn't over, I ask, "Do you want to get out of here?"

"Yes, please."

Grabbing her hand, I tug her from the darkened room. "I know just the spot." A few blocks later, I lead her into a 24-hour greasy diner. Over coffee and a shared piece of apple pie, we start our path back to each other. Or that's my hope as I stare at her across the booth.

Reaching across the chipped white laminate table, I thread my fingers through hers and my heart gallops in my chest. When I chance a look at her, I see her blue eyes are wide and expressive, and I know she's ready to hear everything I have to say. Not just about New York, but how I feel about her. Knowing I've wasted too much time already, I talk, holding nothing back.

"Shiloh, I've missed you so much these past few months. Life without you and the boys has been miserable. And it's all my fault. A misunderstanding started it all, but I couldn't figure out how to best explain what happened. I know I didn't handle it well and I hurt you. I am so sorry about that. But most of all, I'm sorry I didn't fight for you. You are worth more than that, and I let my fear control me. I was too scared you'd never forgive me for what happened, so I didn't do anything. You know I didn't cheat on you. I'd never do that to the woman I love."

After I pour out my heart, I sit there, silently hoping she'll forgive me and we'll move past this. Shiloh's hands are still intertwined with mine, making me hopeful. Then I see a tear fall from her eye and my heart flinches. With the next silent seconds, I prepare myself as best I can for the impending delivery of her dismissal. The longer I sit there, the more I worry. Did she hear my confession of love? I hadn't really intended to tell her for the first time since our breakup like that, but I just blurted it out. Had doing that sealed my fate? I didn't regret it, because after what we've been through, I'm not sure I'll get another chance to tell her, and I want her to know exactly how I feel. Shiloh remains quiet, and I question if that is a good or bad thing. Honestly, I don't know.

Shiloh releases one of my hands, and my stomach clenches with unease. With it, she sweeps away another tear that escapes. I hate to see her cry. She grabs her napkin and wipes at her nose before slowly taking a sip of her coffee and looking back at me. This is torture.

Finally, a timid smile appears on her face and she whispers. "After the New York trip and the newspaper story, multiple people, including Connor, Christian, and your coach, reached out to me, telling me it was a misunderstanding. However, the only person who didn't was you. Yes, you texted initially, and when I responded, just having been completely blindsided, you walked away. From me. From the boys. Mika, you broke our hearts."

Tears now stream down her face and, along with her words, shred the rest of my fractured heart. The one I thought we were taking strides to repair.

Will we ever be able to get past this? Lowering my head, I confess, "I'm so very sorry, Shiloh. You and the boys are the last people I'd ever want to hurt. You mean the world to me. And you're right, I didn't stay. I walked away like a coward because I thought you were done with me and it was pointless to try. I've learned since then. I'm not walking away from you ever again. That is, if you'll give me a second chance. What can I do to make this better? Will you ever be able to forgive me?" I can hear the desperation clinging to my voice. I don't care who sees me. I will do anything for her forgiveness and another chance.

Still holding my hand, anchoring me to the table, Shiloh sniffs and then confidently answers, "Mika. I know you're sorry, and I believe you that nothing happened with that woman. But I needed time to deal with what happened, your reaction, and my own feelings about everything. And I didn't want to do that in front of anyone, especially the media."

I nod my head, completely understanding her concerns. Being a professional athlete makes me the target of so many, and I don't want Shiloh or the boys to get dragged into the negativity that easily follows. Weeks after the article and pictures were published and my life exploded, the newspaper printed a tiny retraction. In it, they explained they had learned that the puck bunny who'd made the accusations was found to have sold multiple fake stories recounting trysts she'd had with other professional athletes. In my case, on the night in question, someone at a party on the other side of town had photographic proof she wasn't in my room with me. But the damage had already been done.

Over the past few months we've spent apart, I've had ample time to examine my feelings for Shiloh, the boys, and what I want for us. If we can move past this, I'm ready to go all in. I just need to know where we stand. Will she tell me? I told myself if Shiloh was over me; I have no other choice than to move on.

Without her, however, there'd really be no moving on. I love her and that isn't something you get over. Ever. But here and now, I have to know what her decision is, because not knowing is killing me.

And whatever she decides will impact my life greatly.

Living next door to a woman I love and want so badly is physically and emotionally destroying me. The longer I can't have her, the worse it gets. As the months passed, I even considered transferring teams or at least moving to another section of the city. The only things that prevented me from doing that are that I love my team, my house, and the woman and her kids next door. No matter how much it hurt, I'm not ready to give up. On her. On us. On the family I now dream about. More times than I can count, Samantha and Monica informed me, through Lucas and Christian, that Shiloh still loves me. That I had to be patient. I hope what they said is true. Because permanently walking away from her will be the end of me.

"Shiloh, I have one important thing I need to know," I nervously state. Shiloh doesn't know how much power she holds over me or that she can finish me with minimal effort. So here, sitting in a greasy diner at two a.m., I am giving her the opportunity to do just that. In all honesty, what do I have to lose? *Her. Forever.* Breathing out deeply, summoning my strength, I ask, "Do you still have feelings for me?"

She stares at me across the retro booth, pushes her coffee cup to the side, and lets out a deep breath. My heart spasms and then drops. Dread ravages my gut. *Here it comes. The letdown. Man, I feel like shit.* I look around, panicked. Maybe I can dash out of here before she answers? *No!* I need to man up, hear her answer, or I'll never be able to move forward with my life. I wipe my sweaty hand on my jeans while I anxiously wait. Looking into her eyes, I will them to give me a hint of what she'll say. They don't, but then she speaks.

"Mika, this is complicated. You are dangerous to me." Her confession knocks the wind out of me.

"Dangerous? I don't understand," I rasp, totally confused.

She releases my other hand and grabs her ceramic coffee mug and fiddles with the handle. "Yes, I do still have feelings for you. I have missed you terribly. So have the boys. But what happens if we don't work out? What happens if we get even more attached and you decide you didn't sign up for an instant family?" The tremble in her voice tells me how worried she is. Shiloh is the strongest woman I have ever met. She protects her boys with a fierceness that is both awe-inspiring and incredibly sexy. I understand her trepidation. While we were still together, I'd had similar fears that I hadn't been brave enough to share with her.

My brain urges me forward; it's now or never. Man up!

"I understand your concerns. Really, I do, and I wish I could give you the words or promises that would give you a one hundred percent guarantee, but I can't. What I can do is tell you how I feel and share what I'm thinking and hope that you accept it." My confession leaves me feeling like I'm standing on the jagged edge of a cliff, teetering as the dirt loosens below me.

"Okay," she says.

I blow out a nervous breath and move my hands back onto the tabletop, hoping to center myself. "I'm still madly in love with you." I hear her gasp, and I instantly freeze. Apparently, when I'd alluded to that earlier, it hadn't fully registered. Not knowing how the rest of my confession will go, I'm suddenly even more nervous. But I have so much more to say. Will she give me the chance? I look at her hesitantly, trying to gauge if it's okay to continue. She hasn't run from the diner yet, so that's a good sign, right? Plus, she's smiling; another good sign. For the first time in months, I feel like I'm on a winning streak. Pushing forward through the nerves and discomfort, I continue, "I have missed you and the boys terribly. Having you ripped from my life felt like someone tore my still beating heart from my chest, leaving a desolate cavern in its place. I've just been going through the motions. I've been numb. Babe, I know that you, Sam, and Lian are a package deal, and I am signing up for it all. I want you all."

Letting the full weight of my last words fill the air between us, I pause before I continue. Shiloh's smile grows wider and her eyes sparkle, and I see the moment she understands what I mean.

"Unfortunately, I'm a professional athlete, and until I retire, my life is not entirely my own. I don't want to live another day without you three, but you have to make the best choice for you. You have to weigh whether or not this—us—is worth the cost of having the media in your life. I can't promise you I'll never appear in the papers, but I can promise you I'll be faithful to you. I will honestly tell you anything that is going on. I'll do my best to make sure you are well protected." It feels incredible to finally get all my thoughts out. Now, I just hope Shiloh will accept it all and take me back.

Instead of answering right away, Shiloh reaches her hands across the table and intertwines them with mine again. My heart expands, filled with renewed hope. Still worried, I stare into her eyes and will her to speak.

"Hearing you say you love me makes me so happy. I've wanted to hear those words again from you for so long, and after what happened between us, I was confident I wouldn't." She stops for a moment and hangs her head, making me insecure. I shift in the booth, hoping to alleviate the unease I feel.

"Even after learning the truth about New York, I feared the intensity of my feelings for you and the hold they had on me. I felt like I was drowning and there weren't any life preservers available. Making it worse was thinking that after I pushed you away, you'd realized I wasn't worth fighting for. It confirmed my fears when you didn't even try to save our relationship. Not wanting to feel that anymore, I convinced myself that I needed to move on. In fact, that's what tonight was about for me. But now, here you are, and I'm relieved."

The words she says are hard to hear until she gets to the end. Without argument, I could say Shiloh's right. I didn't fight for her. Honestly, I didn't think she wanted me to, but now hearing her words, and seeing the pain stretched across her face, I know there's nothing more she wanted. I'd let her down again, and her plan was to move on until I showed up and started fighting. Squeezing her hands, I confirm I'm here with her now. I've learned my lesson. I'll always fight for her.

"Apparently, I was wrong about everything. I was wrong about you, how I dealt with everything, how I thought I could move on, everything. Mika, I am so sorry I never gave you the opportunity to explain after New York. I thought thinking you'd hooked up with someone was better than if you'd told me you wanted to break up. I was trying to protect myself from something I thought was inevitable."

While Shiloh pours her fears out to me, tears stream down her face and splash on the aged table between us. I don't want to let go of her hands, but I can't handle the tears, so I release her, stand up, and join her on her side of the table. I wrap my arms around her tight. Being here with her feels right, perfect, and I just hold her as she sobs into my chest. She shakes as waves of sadness move through her petite frame. Wishing I could wipe all her sadness away, I just hold her tighter, pulling her closer into my embrace. I can't take away her sadness, but I can be there for her, helping her through it, showing her I am serious about my commitment to her and the boys.

When she begins to calm down, I kiss the top of her head tenderly. I pull back and let her catch her breath. Swiping the fresh tears from her stained cheeks makes my heart ache. Shiloh feels this way because of me. Right here and now, I vow to never again hurt her like I have.

Reaching over to the napkin dispenser, I pluck a few thin napkins from it and hand them to her. She laughs, then buries her head into my chest while she blows her nose and cleans up her face. She's embarrassed, and I promise to be her safe harbor. Always and forever, I plan to be her strong and steady.

Hours after arriving at the diner, we make up. Now, as we dine on greasy cheeseburgers, we talk, laugh, and reconcile. This food isn't a typical part of my regular season diet, but I would do anything, eat anything, to prolong this moment. Plus, I have to admit the burgers, crispy fries, and rich chocolate shake are perfection, the best meal I've had in forever, hands down.

That night, when we entered the diner, we were uncertain of where we stood. By the time we leave, it isn't just a new day, but a new start for us. We ride home in an Uber I order, and we hold hands the entire way. Having her this close to me again replenishes my weary soul.

When the Uber driver drops us off and I know

she'll be going to her own house, even though it's only next door, it hurts. My heart is still raw, and I can feel a slight, tender ache. It's nothing like I'd endured before, but it's still noticeable. I don't want to let her go, but we have to face reality. Shiloh has to get the boys after a night off, and we both need time to rest and reset. Before she climbs out of the car, we share an innocent kiss, and it is, without a doubt, the best kiss of my life. It's full of forgiveness and hope, dreams and wishes, innocence and love.

Even though I'll be seeing her soon, I'm hesitant to have her walk away. My mind is plagued with worries. *What if she doesn't come back?* Then I remind myself we came up with a plan to move forward. We both admitted we want to be together, but we agreed we need to take it slow. Shiloh told me she needs to work on rebuilding trust, which I understand from seeing what her ex put her through and what she thought I'd done. Plus, we don't want to overwhelm the boys. Although it feels wrong, I agree to hang back, despite my heart screaming the opposite. Honoring Shiloh is what I need to do, and I'll do whatever it takes so we can rebuild what we had.

A life without them is terrible, and I never want to experience that again. Because I felt what it was like without them. I was missing a piece of me, a piece I'd been completely unaware of before meeting them.

Chapter 31

Shiloh

Heading into the city to meet Susan, Samantha, and Monica at the hotel for brunch, my nerves spike. What am I going to tell them about last night? Honestly, I'm still trying to wrap my head around it.

I know I don't want to say too much because little ears could catch it and I'm not sure how Sam and Lian will react. Maybe later tonight the girls and I can share a Zoom call after the boys are in bed and I can fill them in on the club, diner, and everything else.

Mika and I are back together.

Just thinking about it causes a wave of happiness to crash over me. Hearing him confess his love for me again was indescribable. I never thought I'd hear him say those three words again, and I couldn't hold back, confessing the same. After our talk at the diner, we're ready to move forward, slowly.

We have a lot to work through yet, and he has a lot of rebuilding to do with the boys. They're too young to understand what happened, but they were both affected. Sam had been grumpy and sullen for months, quick to anger and lash out, especially at me, as if he felt I was the one to blame for his pain. And Lian had thrown temper tantrums every time we'd go out front, trying to make his way to Mika's house, demanding to be seen. It will take time, but I have faith that we can find our way back to where we were before.

My mind wanders to the sweet kiss he gave me just as I was about to exit the car, which then brings me back to that darkened room at the club when he had me pinned to the wall and the not-so-sweet thoughts I'd had.

Fantasies I never considered had filled my head, and hopeful images flooded me. His powerful hand around my throat, lightly squeezing, my legs kicked out wide as he thrust into me roughly from behind.

I'd pictured Mika as a commanding, dominating alpha partner. He'd never been that in the bedroom, not that we'd had enough time to explore fantasies and kinks since we hadn't been dating that long.

I wondered if that was something he'd ever entertain. The idea of him like that excited me. It still excites me. My skin becomes flushed as I envision it all again. Apparently, the darker romance books I've been reading are sinking into my subconscious.

I release a dreamy sigh as I continue my drive to the hotel.

Susan has her suite decked out with flowers and a brunch spread that would make a king jealous. The boys squeal their excitement at seeing me, but their attention wavers when Monica lifts a stainless-steel dome revealing a plate piled high with chocolate chip pancakes. Walking over to check out the food, we all gasp at the enormous variety before us; scrambled eggs, mini quiches, bacon, sausage, silver-dollar-size pancakes in both regular and chocolate chip flavors, yogurt parfait, and fresh fruit. We fill our plates high with food, then we sit around the round dining table and enjoy each other's company.

When we've all had our fill of the delicious food, Susan, Sam, and Lian disappear into the bedroom and emerge a few minutes later with handmade cards and a wrapped package. Confusion marks my face as I wonder what they're up to. Unwrapping the gift proves to be quite the challenge. Apparently, the boys had helped, and it seems like an entire roll of scotch tape was used. My breakfast knife provides assistance in getting into the box.

Once I finally unwrap and open the box, I pull a gorgeous frame out. In it is a picture that Samantha took of me and the boys. Tears well up in my eyes as I stare at the treasured gift in my hands. "Thank you, Susan. Thank you, too, Samantha and Monica. I couldn't have survived these last few months without you, or your love, support, and encouragement."

And it's true. If it weren't for them, I don't think I'd be where I am right now—happy and ready to move forward with the man I love.

Chapter 32

Mika

When Shiloh and I first started dating, we'd moved fast, and I'd adapted to quasi living with them in only a few weeks. But this time around, we intentionally move slower. It seems, though, despite that, time passes quickly. Days turn into weeks. Weeks morph into months. And before long, I again practically live with Shiloh and the boys.

The transition back to us was rough at the beginning. Our breakup caused deep hurts for both the boys, and they weren't so accepting of me. In fact, they initially rebelled. Sam refused to engage with me at all for the first month, and Lian threw a fit every time I tried to help Shiloh with anything around the house.

Normal tasks like making dinner, bedtime, or watching them so Shiloh could have some time to herself became a battle zone. But we were committed to making us work and turning the four of us into a family. I won't say it was easy—it wasn't—but being together was everything. I even started hosting sleepovers at my house. While Sam, Lian, and I would play, watch movies, and goof off, Shiloh would take long, hot bubble baths in my soaker tub. Then at night, after tucking the boys into the beds I'd ordered for the spare rooms, I'd tuck Shiloh into my bed. It was the best of both worlds.

Four months after we started dating again, I officially moved in. I still kept my house next door, but when I wasn't traveling, I slept over every night. The memories we were making cemented us together. Every trip to the park, every movie we enjoyed while snuggling on the couch, even the visit to a farm we'd taken where Horace the goat tried to eat Lian's hat right off his head. Together, we were building something real, lasting, and so damn good.

A month after I move in, I take the boys to Sprinkles 'N Scoops for some serious conversation. After ordering a scoop of rainbow sherbet for the boys and a Dutch chocolate for me—Shiloh got me hooked and now it's the only thing I get—I ease us into things. "Hey, guys. How's your ice cream?"

Lian, who's doing more playing than eating, informs me, "It's my favite."

"Favorite, Lian. It's your favorite," Sam, the big first grader says. Lian shakes his head of messy curls. He's wearing a smile that's pure magic as he stares at his brother.

"I'm glad, Lian. Sam, how's yours? Still your favorite?" I ask, curious. Recently Sam is changing his mind about a lot of things, and it wouldn't surprise me if this was one example of that.

Shrugging his shoulders, he replies, "I don't know. I still like it, but maybe I'll try a new flavor next time."

"That sounds like a good idea. Change can be difficult, but sometimes it's really great."

I take a deep breath before continuing with, "Speaking of change being a good thing, was it a great change when I moved in?" Without hesitation, both boys nod their heads. They love our morning routine of getting ready. On days that I'm in town, after they're dressed, we hop down to the kitchen to pack lunches and have breakfast. Like the big boys they are, they love to help. Yes, it makes for a messy and chaotic experience, but it's one I wouldn't change for the world.

"You know what would be another great change?" I ask, wondering if at least Sam is following along.

"Getting a puppy?" Sam answers confidently.

"A puppy?" Lian squeals and then barks at me. Being used to his silly behavior, I just smile.

"No, we aren't getting a puppy. I was wondering if you'd think it was a good thing if I asked your mom to marry me?" Silence fills the surrounding air. *They probably didn't understand what I was asking.*

"You want to marry our momma?" Sam asks in a

timid voice that makes him sound far younger than he is.

Nodding my head, I answer, "I do. I love your mom very much."

In that same small voice, Sam questions, "What about us?"

The sad expression he's wearing tugs at my heart. "Sam. I'm not sure I fully explained myself. Yes, I want to marry your mom because I love her. But I love you and Lian too, and I want us to be a family."

Sam stares at me with a blank expression on his face. "You want to be our daddy?" Hearing the tremble in his voice makes me even more sure that this is what I want. There is nothing more. I want that to be a husband to Shiloh and a dad to Sam and Lian.

"Yeah, Sam, I'd like to be your dad. That is, if you'll let me."

Hearing that, Sam's frown turns into a smile seconds before he launches himself at me. Holding him tightly, I ask, "So is that a yes?" Sam hugs me tighter before he pulls back and gives me a giant grin, showcasing his two missing front teeth. Lian, completely unaware of what's happening, is staring at us from across the table.

Sam understands what I'm saying and gives me his approval. Lian happily agrees too, basically mimicking his big brother. For me, it's a win-win. Sam and Lian both help with my surprise proposal about a month later.

* * *

Christmas Morning

The morning starts early for me. As it's my first Christmas with kids, the excitement and anticipation made it almost impossible to sleep. Last night, Shiloh had surprised us all with matching jammies, and we posed around the eclectically decorated Christmas tree for a selfie. After putting out the reindeer feed, an oatmeal and glitter mix Sam had made at school, we filled a plate with cookies and carrots before heading off to bed.

Now, I'm staring out the kitchen window at the frost-covered grass while I'm enjoying a cup of coffee before the boys wake up.

"Mika," a sleepy voice calls from the top of the stairs. Abandoning my cup on the counter, I go in search of Sam. Sure enough, he's clutching his lovie in one hand while rubbing sleep out of his eyes with the other.

"Morning, bud. How'd you sleep?" He's alone, so Lian must still be sleeping.

"Did Santa come?" he asks with hushed excitement.

I motion to the living room. "Come on down. We'll check it out before your mom and Lian wake up." He rushes down the stairs and toward the living room. I have to almost jog to keep up.

Standing in front of the tree, Sam looks all around. "He came, Mika!" His excitement is palpable, and suddenly I wish Lian and Shiloh were awake so we could open gifts.

"Sam, do you want to go make coffee for your mom and chocolate milk for you and Lian? I bet they'll be up soon." Just as we're finishing the drinks, Lian and Shiloh saunter into the kitchen.

The next hours are beyond chaotic as the boys quickly tear through their many green and red-wrapped gifts. Their overfilled stockings are a whole other shit show. Whoever decided to put candy in plastic candy canes never had kids. Those tubes are impossible to pry from their hands once they unwrap them. Thankfully, they hold up to the death grip of a three- and six-year-old, so we don't have to deal with sugar comas at seven a.m.

Once we set aside all the toys that need batteries or assembly, pick up all the shredded wrapping paper and decimated boxes scattered around the family room, I suggest Shiloh go take a long, relaxing shower.

My plan is to make breakfast and get the boys ready for the day while she has a moment alone. Being completely comfortable with me, Shiloh doesn't hesitate a bit, accepting my offer of help. She kisses me tenderly before heading up the stairs toward the master bathroom. The boys and I follow behind and move over to their bedroom.

When I pull out the special shirts Samantha

helped me order online, Sam and Lian whoop and holler. The shirts aren't all that fancy, but they're perfect. They read *Momma, will you marry our Daddy?*

About a month ago, after I'd asked for their permission to marry their mom, Sam and Lian started calling me Daddy. And although Shiloh was nervous it had scared me, I assured her that nothing had ever felt more natural or right. As far as I was concerned, they were my boys, and I loved them completely. In fact, I couldn't wait to marry Shiloh and have more children. Being an only child, I'd always wanted a big family, and now it was happening.

Once dressed, and with teeth brushed and room tidied, the boys and I head back to the kitchen to prepare breakfast. When I planned my proposal out, I stuck to simple because, honestly, that's what works best.

Playing in the NHL means I'm away from home for days at a time, and I've learned to take advantage of every moment we have, often relying on the simplest option. Thankfully, it's Christmas time, and I've been able to use the extra time home to get everything I planned accomplished.

As I pull food out of the fridge, I reflect on all the fun family adventures we've already had. So far, we've enjoyed lazy mornings, movie nights, and wild outings like skating and sledding. Shiloh and Sam are out of school, so we kept Lian out of daycare and have had a fabulous time together.

Lian, "the climber," pulls himself up into his chair while Sam and I assemble everything we need. Arms loaded carefully, Sam carries plates, napkins, cups, and utensils to the table while I follow with chocolate chip muffins and a fruit salad. Sam sets the table while I return to the kitchen for yogurt, granola, and OJ. Moments after we've set the table, Shiloh walks into the kitchen looking dreamy. Her signature scent of vanilla and citrus follows her and makes my mind spin. This woman, she is my everything, and I can't wait to make her mine.

Scheming with young kids makes pulling off surprises interesting. Fortunately, the boys haven't blown it yet, although we've had some close calls. Anxious, I'm hoping to get through the next few moments before Shiloh notices the boys' shirts.

Sam leads Shiloh to her chair and then shuffles over to his. Returning to the kitchen, I grab two mugs from the cabinet, fill them with coffee, and check that I have the ring in my pocket one last time. Before turning to the table, I roll my shoulders, take a deep breath, and try to shake out my nerves.

I sit Shiloh's mug down in front of her, ensuring that she'll be able to read it, and then walk to my chair. When I sit down, I notice she's staring at me, a twinkle in her eye. Reaching over, I grab my coffee mug and hold it up. "You have to try the coffee. I got a new flavor, caramel-vanilla cream." A wide smile spreads across her face.

Excitedly, I watch as Shiloh's gaze returns to the mug, reading it carefully. Her face scrunches like she's confused and I nod to the boys. Along with the shirts, I had a special mug made for today. It reads *We have a question for you.* Sam and Lian carefully stand up on their chairs and proudly display their special shirts. Shiloh, seeing their movement, looks up from the mug. Her beautiful face, still scrunched with question, softens when she reads the boys' shirts.

She immediately turns toward me, and I'm already kneeling next to her with the ring box opened, revealing a two-carat diamond solitaire ring. Her hand flies up to her mouth, and a gasp sneaks out as she looks at me, then over to the boys, who are smiling with pride.

When her eyes return to mine, they are wild with emotions. A lone tear slips out and makes its way down her flushed cheek. Without thinking, I reach for it and wipe it away, then set my hand on her thigh. Before I lose my nerve, I speak, breaking the silence of the room.

"Shiloh, you are my everything. From the moment we met, I was drawn to you. My attraction to you is so far beyond the physical. You inspire, challenge, encourage, forgive, and love me. Unconditionally. I never imagined I would have a family, and because of you, I do. Sam and Lian are mine. I love them so much and I can't wait to spend forever with you all. That's if you'll have me. Will you make me the happiest man in the world and marry me? Psst... the boys already gave their permission."

Shiloh doesn't make me wait long for an answer as she throws herself at me.

"Is that a yes?" I question as I breathe into her hair.

She nods and then pushes back, wrapping her hands around my face, pulling me in for a kiss. At that moment, she makes all my dreams come true.

Chapter 33

Shiloh

Christmas morning was an absolute surprise for me. Presents and stockings go smoother than ever before. Having a second adult to assist with gift distribution, unwrapping, and cleanup is incredible.

After the chaos of the morning and a refreshing shower, we sit down for breakfast. Mika pours a fresh cup of coffee into a new mug and brings it out to me. Commenting that I should try the new flavor he brewed, I reach for the mug and notice the words on it. They're confusing. *Can we ask you a question?* While I try to figure it out, I sense Sam and Lian stand up on their chairs. Knowing that could be dangerous, my eyes flick up to check on them. But before I can fully assess their safety, my eyes are drawn to the words spread across their tiny chests. I read, *Momma, will you marry our Daddy?*

Being in education, I know the power of words, but until now, I never imaged six simple words changing my life forever. Tears in my eyes make rereading their shirts more difficult. When I finally manage, I look over to Mika, who is no longer in his chair. Instead, he's kneeling next to me with an open ring box displaying the most beautiful ring I've ever seen. And then he delivers a speech that leaves me breathless and without words. When he's done, I can hardly contain my excitement, and I fly out of my chair and toward him. Mika grunts when I slam into him, and he wraps me in his big, muscular arms before whispering his need for my answer. Of course, I say yes. Mika is the man of my dreams, and I can't wait to spend the rest of my life with him and our boys. That's what he said; he considers Sam and Lian his. I'm so glad to hear that because I have one more Christmas surprise for him and it coincidentally relates to what he just did.

After finishing breakfast on our first Christmas together as a family, I give Mika the best gift I could think of. Seated on the couch, relaxing while the boys play with new toys, I hand Mika a large envelope stuffed full of paperwork.

"I have one more gift for you. I hope you like it."

Mika removes the thick packet of paperwork, and I watch as his eyes scan the documents. A giant smile spreads across his handsome face as he continues to read what is written. Anticipation about his reaction builds up within me, and I fidget with my fingers.

When Mika finishes the first page, he lowers the document and looks at me with tears in his eyes. "Is this for real, Shiloh?" he croaks out. I nod, and a tear slips down his cheek. Crawling toward him, I settle next to him and kiss it away.

"What do you say? Do you want to adopt the boys?" I hesitantly ask. My decision to visit a family lawyer a month prior was based on the fact Sam and Lian had been calling Mika Daddy, and he'd insisted he wanted nothing more than that. Hearing him with them, watching them together, I couldn't ask for anything better. Mika had truly become their daddy, and here I am offering to make it official

A look of confusion covers his face. "Really? It's this easy? I just sign this document and they're mine?"

"It is," I promise him. Knowing he's probably wondering how it happened, I explain how I visited a family lawyer who completed the paperwork easily since Trent had already signed over his rights.

Mika lays down the paperwork and pulls me into his lap. He leans forward and tenderly kisses me with such passion. Knowing we're in the company of little people, we keep the kiss G-rated and Mika whispers we'll do a better job of celebrating later. And then he thanks me.

Chapter 34

Mika

After I proposed on Christmas Day and Shiloh surprised me with adoption paperwork for the boys, time flies by at warp speed. The adoption proceedings are going great and we'll sign official documents before the judge the week after our wedding. Then we'll all officially be Popov-Stevensons.

*** * ***

Wedding planning goes smoothly, as we don't want a huge event. A few months after I proposed, we hold a small ceremony and reception in the backyard of my house. Only fifty of our closest friends are in attendance. Lucas and Christian are my groomsmen, and we're dressed in beige linen suits with navy-blue ties. Samantha and Monica are Shiloh's bridesmaids and wear navy-blue dresses that match us. We also dress Sam and Lian to the nines, wearing beige linen pants, white button-up shirts and navy-blue suspenders. The boys' role in the wedding is helping us with a colorful sand pour. Shiloh explained it was to symbolize the joining or blending of our lives.

Since Shiloh's parents and grandparents are deceased, Coach Tristan offered to walk Shiloh down the aisle. I'd already been on the Steel for a few years when he'd been hired as the coach. He isn't that much older than us and has often taken the role of big brother. Thankfully, over the past few years, he's become friendlier and easier to tolerate. In fact, when Lucas worked on team building his first year with the team, Coach Tristan was often among the chaos, living it up. Because of that, our personal relationship has gained depth, going from coach/player to friends. So, when the New York scandal had taken place, Coach had been the one to tell me that second chances are worth fighting for. And here I am, proving just that, and he's there beside us, participating fully.

Since our wedding venue is my backyard, we could have it any way we wanted it. We tossed a lot of ideas around initially, but finally settled on a simple theme. Neither of us are religious, so we asked my mama to perform the ceremony. She'd come in from Boston a week beforehand. In fact, over the past few months, she's made the trip to Chicago several times, as she was desperate for grandkids and she couldn't wait to get to know Sam and Lian. They loved her immediately, their first meeting a few months ago, going better than I could have hoped. Sam and Lian already affectionately call her Baba, which is short for Babushka, or Grandma in Russian. When she's in Boston, we FaceTime often, and both Sam and Lian count down days until her next visit.

Following the simple vow exchange, the catering team sets up tables and chairs for a wedding picnic. Shiloh was adamant that if we were having a picnic, we'd forgo the red and white checkerboard table cloths for the more classic and elegant white. It's a wedding after all, not a hoedown. Wildflowers adorn each table in large jars. They fill a buffet table with fabulous tasting food. Shiloh and I picked the menu, deciding to upgrade from burgers and hot dogs to grilled chicken, steak, and salmon. Multitudes of side dishes like green salad, orzo pasta salad, mac and cheese, baked beans, veggie and fruit trays, and kettle chips cover every inch of the buffet table. Instead of a traditional wedding cake, we went with wedding cupcakes in both vanilla and chocolate, decorated with the opposite flavor frosting, and they are simple but divine. The boys and I may have snuck an extra or two all under the guise we were celebrating.

When the festivities are over, we're all wiped out. Because it isn't doable right after the big day, we plan to take a honeymoon/family vacation after the season ends. Shiloh and I sneak off for the rest of the wedding weekend because my mama offered to watch the boys. I doubt they'll even miss us. Baba has big plans: visits to the park and the aquarium, movies, and homemade pierogies. Shiloh and I easily escape without tears and have a great rest of the weekend wrapped around each other, occasionally coming up for air and food.

Chapter 35

Shiloh

Our wedding is everything I could have hoped for. Simple, fun, and memorable. We take our vows in front of our closest friends and then celebrate after. The day is relaxed and enjoyable, rather than stuffy and stiff. Overall, it is perfect and so is my dress. I selected a simple ivory-colored tea-length dress. When the reception started, I changed from my heels into ornately decorated ivory Chucks. The guys all wear beige linen suits, and my ladies don dresses in navy blue that match the guys' ties and their Chucks. Stealing the show are Sam and Lian, dressed to match the groomsmen, but instead of a coat and tie, they wear navy-blue suspenders. The wedding and reception are pretty low key, and everyone has a great time.

We won't be heading off to an official honeymoon

until later. Mika, the boys, and I are going on vacation to Maui—a familymoon—after the season ends, and I am definitely looking forward to it. It will be the boys' and my first plane rides, and even though that petrifies me, Mika assures me we'll be fine. We're all looking forward to playing in the ocean, soaking up some sun, and visiting some of the well-known tourist hotspots.

Until then, we have this weekend. Following our ceremony and reception, Mika's mom offers to take the boys for the rest of the weekend. It's our first time alone together in what feels like forever, and we embrace it fully. We rented a suite in the heart of downtown Chicago and play the part of tourists. We go to the Willis Tower Skydeck and stand in the glass box one hundred and three stories above the ground. It's terrifying and I have a death grip on Mika's hand most of the time. Then we go to the Navy Pier and ride the Centennial Wheel before we take a dinner cruise on Lake Michigan. Everything is great, but the thing I love the most is the alone time. It isn't about all the sexy fun we have. That's phenomenal, but being able to connect fully with my person without interruption is amazing.

And speaking of phenomenal sexy fun, our wedding night is incredible. Mika brought silk ties and a blindfold that he uses on me. When he first ties my wrists together and pushes them above my head, I'm nervous. I've never done anything like this before. But when he pulls a feather out of his bag and begins tracing it up and down my legs, making goose bumps spread across my heated skin, I'm transported to bliss. Fluttering the feather across my stomach makes me feel like I have hundreds of butterflies trapped inside me, trying to break free.

Squirming on the bed, I pull at my hands to reach for Mika, and a deliciously warm tug reminds me I'm restrained. A whimper falls from my lips as Mika traces the pointy edge of the feather around my nipple, making it pebble immediately. My back arches, chasing the buzz that moves through my body toward my center, which is throbbing in protest, begging to be touched. I'm on sensation overload.

When Mika slides a silk mask over my eyes, taking away my sight, I worry I'll miss the visual stimuli. But I don't even notice. Every reaction I have is instantly more intense. The pulsing and throbbing in my clit aches for relief, and I try to press my thighs together, hoping to ease some of the delicious pressure. Seeing that, Mika stops me, prolonging the release I'm desperate for.

I can feel the heat of Mika's body as he hovers over me. After teasing me to the edge time and time again, when I almost come several times, he finally succumbs to my whimpers. Lowering himself on top of me, his soft skin brushes against mine, lighting me up like an arcade game. I'm sure sirens will blare when my body reaches its high score. Mika lowers his lips to mine and kisses me slowly, teasing me. Frustrated, I nip his lower lip and he growls at me. Feeling stubborn and needy for my release, I suck his lip into my mouth and he comes with it, turning our kiss into one that is messy, aggressive, and passionate.

When we're both panting, Mika pulls back and lines up his cock with my center. Slowly, he pushes inside of me, causing us both to release a deep groan. My arms tug at the restraints, and Mika growls, reminding me to stay still. He rolls us to the side and pulls my legs up so he can change the angle of his thrusts, hitting me deeper. After his third deep stroke, the orgasm that has been flirting with me rips through my body like a wildfire in a patch of dried brush. Destroying me in all the good ways. Shortly after, Mika topples over the edge, finding his own release. Staying inside me and continuing to thrust, he kisses up my neck to my earlobe. Pulling the flesh into his mouth, he sucks it and then releases hot air into my ear canal, setting off a quiver that travels down my spine. He whispers, "You are mine forever, Shiloh. I love you completely." Again, my body shivers involuntarily. I have never had someone command me before, and shit, is it sexy. Not long after, Mika takes off the blindfold and silk ties and pulls me into his body. We spoon in bed until we both pass out, completely sated.

The next morning, as I lie in bed in our suite, I reflect on those months without Mika. I'd missed everything about him, but the thing that I'd missed more than anything else had been the way he made me feel—so loved and protected. Yes, the sex was amazing.

I mean, come on, a muscular god who knows what he's doing? That's every woman's fantasy. But what was even better was the assurance that I was exactly where I was supposed to be with the person meant for me. And Mika was definitely my person.

Chapter 36

Mika

It's Friday and I'm in town for the entire weekend. What the boys don't know is that when Shiloh and I had been talking about this weekend, we'd decided to make our sleepover at my place the entire weekend. You know, test out the bigger space and see how it feels. While unpacking everything from our visit to the store earlier for sleepover necessities, Sam catches me off guard. "Daddy, why do we only do sleepovers over here at your house? It's so much bigger. Since you and mom are married, why don't we live here?"

Scratching my head, I don't really know how to answer him. "Sam, that is something your mom and I have to discuss. But aren't we lucky that we have two houses to choose from?" Trying to distract him from further questions, I remind him we need to set up the living room for movie viewing because I ordered new blankets for the boys to snuggle with. He runs off and I put the last of the groceries away.

"No way!" he shouts from the living room. *Must have found them.* Smiling to myself, I round the corner and there stands Sam, proudly wrapped in his new Teenage Mutant Ninja Turtle blanket.

"You like it?" I question.

His eyes grow big as he nods his head up and down. "Yes. It's awesome. Thank you."

"I'm so glad you like it. Do you think Lian will like his?" Sam's face falls. *Oh, no.* Worry wraps itself around my heart. Sam sets his blanket down and slowly walks over to the other bundle.

"*Paw Patrol*," he whispers to himself.

Turning back to me, he says, "Daddy... Lian is going to love it." Pushing out the breath I was holding, my heart beats a normal pace again as I try to regulate my body. Relief overwhelms me.

"That's great. I'm glad."

"We're here," Shiloh announces as she and Lian push through the front door.

"In the living room," Sam and I holler back.

"Daddy, daddy," Lian calls as he makes his way through the house toward us, the slap of his naked feet echoing off the wood floor. Tossing his new blanket over my head, I do my best to remain still and hide in plain sight. Sam follows suit and does the same. I hear Lian stop and squeal, "Momma, where?"

Seconds later, when Shiloh enters the room, I hear

her giggle. "Lian, where are Sam and Daddy?" Almost as if I could see him, I know he's lifting his arms up to shrug.

"Seems like they're hiding. Do you want to find them?" Shiloh asks.

"Momma, hep," Lian tells her.

"Yes, Lian. Momma will help. How about you look over there and I'll look over here." Hearing Shiloh step closer, I try not to laugh. When she's right next to me, she whispers, "Hi babe." Then she moves by Sam and whispers to him, "You're doing great being still, Sam."

"Momma!" Lian hollers from the other side of the room. And Sam laughs, shaking his blanket. "Sam, zhat you?" Lian says while tugging on my blanket. It's hot and stuffy in my hiding place and I need fresh air.

Lifting the blanket off my head, I shout, "Surprise!" Lian claps his hands and joyfully squeals. Picking him up, he throws his arms around my neck and hugs me. It is one of the best feelings in the world.

"Where's Sam?" Shiloh asks.

"Sam, brufher. Where?" Again, the blanket starts to shimmy and shake. "See you," Lian calls out, letting everyone know he knows where Sam is hiding. When Sam finally removes the blanket, Lian excitedly says, "Brufher." They aren't just brothers, they are friends. What could be better?

Later that night, when the boys are passed out after our carpet picnic dinner and movie, Shiloh and I are snuggled up in my California king bed and I mention what Sam had asked about regarding why we didn't live in my house.

"Is that what you want, Mika?" Shiloh asks.

"I don't know. I see two sides to it. Your house has sentimental value but is rather small and in need of repair on multiple fronts. This house is larger, so it can accommodate a bigger family one day, and it's newer, so we aren't having to face expensive repairs anytime soon. But it's devoid of personality, kind of a large bachelor pad." Instead of saying anything, Shiloh looks like she's considering both sides of the argument. "You know," I tell her, "we could move into this house and fix up your grandparents' place so we could put it on a vacation rental site."

"Wouldn't that be expensive?" Shiloh questions.

"Well, I'm assuming you don't want to sell it. So we invest money in it now, then the income from having it be a rental property pays you back. Before long, you'll be making money off it and we can put that in the bank for the boys' college fund."

"That's really smart. Let's do that. But maybe in a few months, when life isn't so busy."

Having a plan feels great. We'll move into my house after the hockey season ends, but for now the Steel are still in the running for the Stanley Cup. Unfortunately, it isn't looking as good as it had in the years when we'd won it.

* * *

After previously winning the Stanley Cup two times years before, this isn't our year. We lost before the play-offs. Instead of sulking, we take our familymoon to Hawaii. We visit Maui. It's my second time being on the beautiful Hawaiian island. The first time was for Lucas and Samantha's wedding. Even though it had been a tough time in my life, I loved Maui. When we were planning our familymoon, I knew I wanted to bring Shiloh and the boys here so we could make some great memories for their first real vacation—*our* first real vacation.

We rent an Airbnb that's right on Charlie Young beach in Kihei. Every morning, the boys and I walk up to the ABC store to buy fresh-cut fruits and wraps to make a picnic lunch. Our plan while on the island is to discover as many beaches as possible. We find one closer to Wailea that Shiloh loves, called Mokapu. While she sits and enjoys the sound of the ocean waves crashing, the boys and I explore and play catch with a football. Neither boy is athletically inclined yet, but that would come with age, so instead, we do lots of splashing and running in the waves.

On day three of our find-the-best-beach quest, Lian declares he wants to see turtles, and since the TMNT are Sam's favorite heroes right now, it becomes my mission to find them. And I do. In Ho'okipa, we see large green sea turtles and a lot of surfers.

"Turtles!" Lian shouts from his car seat as we park our rental car in the upper parking lot. Looking out, I see we are next to a high cliff overlook, which instantly makes me nervous considering our mischievous climbing toddler. Before we'd left Chicago, we'd purchased a hiking toddler carrier backpack. Mainly, we planned to use it for easier travel through the airport, but today seems like a perfect excuse. The reason we park in the higher lot is that the lower lots are filled.

"Turtles!" Lian again shouts from the back seat.

"Hold on a second, buddy. I've got to get your backpack out first," I tell him.

"No! I walks," he demands as Shiloh is getting him out of his car seat.

Like the fantastic mom she is, Shiloh just shakes her head and calmly says, "Lian, it isn't safe. There is an enormous cliff and lots of walking ahead before we get to the turtles. Wouldn't you rather have a ride from Daddy?" Digging out the backpack, I wait to hear his response, but it's silent. *Oh shit, is he doing one of those breath-hold temper tantrums? I've heard they're the worst.* Closing the trunk, I peer over at Lian and expect him to be bright red, but to my shock, he's wearing a big smile and appears happy. *Guess I'd be happy if someone carried me around too.*

Once everyone is ready, we begin the hike down to the lifeguard station to read all the rules about keeping our distance from the turtles.

When we're actually close enough to see them,

Lian excitedly says, "Wonder which one is Crush." Glancing at Shiloh, I'm confused.

She laughs and whispers, "It's from the movie *Finding Nemo*." I've yet to see that one, but I know we will add it to our repertoire soon.

We visit Lahaina a few days later, where we eat gigantic cups of shaved ice under the largest banyan tree in the United States. That same day, we visit the best family activity on Maui: the Maui Ocean Center. Everyone loves it. We all stay in the tunnel, watching the sharks and stingrays swim overhead for at least an hour.

On our last night, we go to a luau and stuff ourselves full of kalua pig, dance the hula, and watch in awe as the fire dancers pull off amazing moves. My favorite part beside the food is when the boys tried to hula.

"Look at me dance, Momma," Sam says as he gyrates his hips side to side.

"That's great, Sam. Can you move your hips in a circle like the dancers?" Shiloh swishes her hips back and forth, and I'm mesmerized by the sensuality of it.

"Shiloh," I say in a low growl as I lean in closer. Her eyes flick up and she gives me a sultry smile that makes me wish we were alone. The restraint it takes me to shift focus and not go full caveman would earn me honorable mentions.

Sam continues to swing his hips, occasionally getting them in a circle. "Way to go, Sam. You got it."

Lian steps in front of Sam and declares, "I try." Muffling my laugh proves difficult as Lian channels an animatronic Elvis Presley. *Watch out, ladies. These boys have got the moves.*

Later that night, after the boys are in bed and after Shiloh gives me a personal hula dance, she surprises me by telling me she wants to expand our family to five. I'm totally on board with that plan, especially if it takes months of trying. It's a sacrifice I'm willing to make.

We return to Chicago relaxed, sun-kissed, and ready to enjoy the entire summer before having to jump back into school, work, and hockey.

* * *

Over breakfast on the morning of the 4th of July, two years after we met, Shiloh presents me with a box. Knowing it isn't my birthday, I look at her expectantly, silently asking if I'd forgotten an anniversary. She recognizes my uneasiness immediately and laughs. "It's not our anniversary. But it is a special gift for you."

Still leery, I shake the box, but nothing happens. Again, I look at Shiloh, but she gives no further direction or instruction. Sam and Lian are busily scarfing down the pancakes we made and pay me no attention. For good measure, I shake the box again before I slowly unwrap it. It's a shirt box, and I wonder what's inside.

Finally, I pull open the box and push back the

tissue paper. My fingers graze something soft and white. It looks like a small towel. Still confused, I pull the item from the box. It isn't a towel but a small piece of clothing. Much too small for me. Then something occurs to me. I glance at Shiloh for confirmation, but she says nothing. She does, however, wear the biggest, brightest smile across her beautiful face. Her hands are clasped together, and she appears to be holding her breath in anticipation.

Slowly, I unfold the white cloth and realize it's a baby onesie. Plenty of my teammates have become fathers over the past few years. I had been to a handful of baby showers, so onesies aren't entirely foreign to me. Turning it over, I read what it says: *Daddy slipped one past the goalie.* A loud laugh falls from my lips, grabbing the boys' attention, causing them to drop their forks. Assuring them I'm fine, they return to their pancake massacres. When they're again preoccupied, I look at Shiloh, and when our eyes meet, the truth sinks in. *We're having a baby.*

I pump my fist in the air and then rush over to her. Sweeping her up in my arms, I hear a whoosh. She'd expelled the breath she'd been holding. Had she been worried about my reaction? Really? Needing to know, I set her back on her feet, push her chin up, and look deep into her eyes. Then I ask, "Really?" She nods, and I kiss her with an intensity that is unmatched. "Thank you, thank you, thank you," I say when I finally pull back from the hottest kiss I've ever had. Hugging her, I whisper against her head, "You have made me the happiest man in the world."

After we eat breakfast, we busy ourselves around the house until it's time to head to Lucas and Samantha's for their annual Independence Day barbeque. We'd met each other on this day, two years before, and now we're a growing family.

The barbeque is an absolute blast. Since many of our teammates are having children, it's become more family friendly. Lucas and Samantha are expecting and are due around the new year. Connor brought his boys, and I know they'll play with Sam and Lian. It's like they've grown up together, even though they obviously haven't. Of course, there is the pool, which is filled with a horde of floating toys. Lucas also set up games like cornhole, giant Jenga, and yard Yahtzee, which keep us busy for hours.

Christian, Samantha's brother and sports agent representing most of us, grills burgers and hot dogs. I make a beeline for him so I can say hi before I have to head into the pool with the boys. I swear my boys are part fish; that had become apparent in Hawaii.

"Christian. My man. How are you?" I offer him my hand.

"Great, Mika. How was Maui?" he asks with a sly smile on his face.

Shaking my head, I answer, "You know, we had the boys with us. No crazy shenanigans."

He stiffly laughs. "Shit, I forgot. I knew you were

on your honeymoon, but I forgot you turned it into a family vacation. How'd the boys like it?"

Pushing my sunglasses on my head, I feel a smile spread across my face. "They absolutely loved it. I wasn't sure they'd even want to come home. Every day, we went to a new beach, trying to find the best one. We visited the Maui Ocean Center, and we spent an hour watching the fish, sharks, and manta rays in their tunnel tank. We had to promise the boys something from the gift store to lure them out of the aquarium. Lian fell asleep on the drive back to our rental, hugging his stuffed tiger shark. In fact, he tried to bring it today to show you and Monica."

Christian smiles widely. "Lian is awesome. I think he's become one of my favorite people. When Monica and I watched him and Sam a few weeks ago, he made me laugh the entire time. In fact, we're inviting everyone out to Monica's family's farm in two weeks, including Sam and Liam. They'd love the cows."

Nodding my head in agreement, I ask, "What's going on at the farm? Special celebration or something? We've never been invited out there before."

He shifts his weight, suddenly nervous, and hollers out to Monica. "Monica, you want to tell Mika what's going on at the farm in a few weeks? I told him the whole family is invited and that the boys will love the cows."

My eyes flick over to Monica, who is lounging in a chair next to Samantha. Her cheeks are flushed and I can't tell if it's from the sun or embarrassment. *It isn't that hot yet. What can she be embarrassed about?* Monica stares at Christian and they have a silent conversation with their eyes. Uncomfortable, my eyes travel between them, questioning what's happening. Finally, Monica rises from her chair and comes over to the grill, joining Christian and me.

"Mika, you and Shiloh and the boys definitely have to come out to the farm. We're hosting a celebration and a barn dance. It'll be lots of fun and we'd love to have you there. Samantha, Lucas, Coach, and some of the other guys are coming too."

Thinking it sounds fun, I answer, "I'll just need to talk to Shiloh, but I'm sure we'll be there. What do you wear to a barn dance?"

Monica laughs. "Nothing too fancy. Slacks and button-ups for the guys and a summery dress for the ladies."

"Great. Sounds fun. What's the celebration for?" I ask, genuinely curious.

Both Monica and Christian become shifty, and Monica quickly excuses herself, explaining she needs to replenish the drink container and buffet table before Samantha tries. As she scampers off, I turn to Christian to get my answer from him. He looks nervous and guilty. *What is going on?*

Christian clears his throat. "Your trip to Maui sounds amazing. What else did you do? Luau, surf lessons, snorkeling, parasailing?" His questions fly from his mouth at rapid speed. *He's definitely avoiding my question.*

Confused about his obvious redirection, I shrug my shoulders and tell him more about our vacation. How Sam had impressed all the hula dancers at the luau with his moves. And Lian had regaled the lifeguards with his turtle knowledge at the beach when we'd seen the turtles. Although we'd only stayed on the island for a week, we'd squeezed a lot into that time.

We eventually plan to visit again. *And with another kid in tow.* Shiloh's breakfast announcement comes rushing back, and it feels like I'm high. She made me so happy. Thinking about her makes me want to be near her. I glance around the backyard just as she and the boys are exiting the pool house, decked out in swimsuits and float vests. Knowing I want to help, I motion over to them and make my excuses to abandon Christian. He waves me away, knowing where my alliances lie.

Chapter 37

Shiloh

Telling Mika this morning that I was expecting was thrilling. I knew he'd be excited, but his reaction was so much more than I could have wished for. He had been talking about making a baby since I told him in Hawaii that I was ready to expand our family. And trying had been so fun. It was tough to pinpoint the exact time of conception since Mika and I have basically been horn balls since we returned from vacation, having sex whenever the mood struck us. Sometimes that required us to be fast and clever since we had two little guys nearby most of the day.

When I'd gone to my doctor's appointment to confirm the pregnancy, I was overjoyed when I saw the flashes of the baby's heartbeat on the screen of the ultrasound machine—it was still too early to hear it yet, but the tech assured me it was strong.

I know Mika will be an amazing father. He already is with Sam and Lian. This is an exciting time in our lives and I'm so ready for the adventure ahead, just me and my family. Going through what we had, I'm so glad that Mika hadn't checked out of our lives for good. We were made for each other, and our future is bright.

Epilogue

Mika

May 2025

After putting the boys to bed and checking that our three-month-old daughter, Aurora, is still asleep, I go back down to the kitchen to check on Shiloh. When I'd left, she was lounging on the couch watching Netflix, but while upstairs I heard her head to the kitchen and get out a pan. The faint smells of melted cheese waft upstairs, and I suspect she's making herself a grilled cheese sandwich. Shiloh hasn't told me she's pregnant again, but her insatiable appetite in the bedroom and for grilled cheese is making it hard to deny. She was the same way when she'd been expecting Aurora.

The thought of another child fills me with unspeakable excitement. We hadn't planned to have another so soon, but I'm not about to complain.

Shiloh is remarkable. The way she loves our kids, the way she loves me. Words can't do it justice. I'm constantly in awe of her. In fact, one of my favorite things to do is to watch my wife when she doesn't think anyone is around. She is beautiful, but when she's pregnant, she is breathtaking.

From the tender touches she makes to her stomach to the contented smile that always graces her lips, she is magical. Having the knowledge of what her body is again undergoing—making another little miracle—is incredible. She is a living work of art. Timeless and priceless.

Trying to remain silent while I sneak toward the kitchen is tough, especially when I finally get there and see something that steals my breath from me. In front of our gas stove stands my irresistibly sexy wife, dressed in a simple, light-blue cotton chemise that highlights her perfect curves. Tied in a loose braid, her blonde hair reveals the curve of her neck that I love to nuzzle my nose into. Shiloh is busily making herself a night-time snack, something she's been doing a lot of recently.

Her back is to me, and not hearing my approach, I take more than a moment to appreciate everything. I run my eyes over every curve and valley. Stopping to appreciate my favorites: the bend of her knee, the curve of her shoulder, the width of her hips. I know all of them intimately. I've loved on every one of them and been gifted her response to each. The moans, breath holds, shivers, giggles, they all light me up inside.

She's never been sexier to me than she is right now. I don't need fancy lingerie or vapid sexual advances to entice or intrigue me. With her, it doesn't take much to get my blood pumping. Every part of Shiloh is desirable, even the stretch marks she always tries to hide from me. To me, they aren't flaws, only evidence of her love for our kids. They make her more attractive to me. Shiloh is one of a kind, an original, and undeniably irresistible.

With the flick of her lithe wrist, Shiloh turns off the burner, ending the near-silent hum of the gas. After she plates the sandwich, she slowly turns toward me, wearing a knowing smirk. She knew I was watching. Apparently, I wasn't as stealthy as I thought.

During our entire relationship, she caught me often, just watching her. Instead of it bothering her, she's amused by my fascination with her. Watching her is my kink, and I love the fact she's into it. More often than not, it becomes a game between us. She'll bend over and jut her hips out, tempting me, and I'll try my best to remain still while my body radiates with anticipation and want.

She licks her glossy lips and eyes me seductively. "Want to share?" she offers. Her voice is saucy, dripping with desire, as she holds out the plate.

Set on the plain, white porcelain are two perfectly

toasted grilled cheese sandwiches. The smell accompanying them is rich, and I know they'll be as amazing as they look. As if on cue, my stomach growls loudly and her blue eyes sparkle, dancing with amusement. As she laughs and clutches her slightly protruding belly protectively, my belief that she is, in fact, carrying our newest little creation in her womb is confirmed.

Thrilled, and smiling widely, I pat my stomach and answer, "With you? I'd love to. But how will I ever repay you?" My question comes out in a husky tone as I waggle my eyebrows at her suggestively.

Still balancing the plate, Shiloh taps her finger to her chin, weighing her options. While biting her lower lip, her eyes hungrily roam over my body. Holding my breath in excited anticipation, I can hardly wait for her response.

"I think I can come up with something," she seductively replies, then winks. And it's like a direct check to my heart. Still, after all this time, this woman can bring me to my knees, and she is all I want. Forever.

* * *

Thank you for reading *Checked By You*, the second book in the Chicago Steel series. I'd love to hear your review of Mika & Shiloh's story.

If you'd like another peek into the Chicago Steel world, visit my website at https://907publishing. wixsite.com/my-site and subscribe to my newsletter.

As a subscriber, every month, you'll hear the latest and greatest in the Steel World, and you'll learn about any extra sneak peeks that will go straight onto my website.

While there, check out the extended epilogue for *Checked By You*.

Acknowledgments

When I was dreaming up this series, I honestly didn't have any idea what it took to write a book, publish it, and market it. Guess what... I still don't. I hoped that my love for the stories swirling in my head would propel me forward, and it certainly did. However, I discovered there were bumps, big and small, along the way. Those bumps forced me to sit up, evaluate, and make changes. Shortly after I released my second book of the Chicago Steel Series, Checked By You, I made the tough decision to pull the books out of publication and hire a developmental editor. As a fledgling indie author, I didn't have the guidance of an agent or publishing house to advise and guide me in my deci-sions. Basically, I was doing it all and still am. I knew to hire an editor and book designer, but I was confident I could handle the rest. And I can now admit, I bit off more than I could chew. I jumped before I was ready. Looking back, it has been a painful lesson to learn, but it was so invaluable. As I hone this craft and grow into the author I strive to be, I am confident there will be many other learning opportunities for me. I'm hoping that you, my reader, will hang on for the ride. As always, I love to hear your reviews, even the negative ones.

So many people have encouraged me along this journey, and I find myself truly blessed. I've been surprised and delighted when pieces and parts I'd been struggling with just popped into place after a conversation with someone who loves this world as much as I do.

Thank you to Karen Hulseman (Feed Your Dreams Designs), who keeps me laughing, questioning, challenging, and creating at every turn. You are so much more than what your business card says. You are like the Mary Poppins of Romanceland.

Thank you to Shauna (Ink Machine Editing), you keep me focused and I so appreciate that you stepped outside of the editing to question me. I know that wasn't your job, but I cannot say thank you enough. And you catch all my blunders. You are awesome.

Thank you to Nicole (Emerald Edits), who offers guidance, care, humor and, most importantly, direction. You are a gem and I appreciate your willingness and availability to answer all my questions.

Thank you to Darren, Zach, and Kadin for being my biggest cheerleaders. When I need to hide in my office to get some words down, thank you for understanding. Thank you for asking how it's all going. Thank you for being invested, even if it isn't something you are truly interested in. I love you three. You are my world and I wouldn't be able to do this without you.

Thank you to those who chose to pick this book up.

I hope you fell in love with the story as much as I have. Thank you to all those who've left reviews, either privately or not. Your support and encouragement mean the world to me. Be blessed.

Don't forget to read *Hooked By You*, the first book of the Chicago Steel series with Lucas and Samantha. It's on Kindle Unlimited. Here's a blurb to tease your palate.

Lucas

She's a goddess in heels. Absolute perfection. Well, almost.

Samantha Fox is the heiress of Fox Sporting, my new management team. As one of the best wings in the NHL, I have never shied away from a challenge, and she is definitely a challenge. But if her company representing me doesn't stop me from wanting her, the fact she's engaged should, right?

But the noticeably absent sparkle from her left ring finger makes me question. I vow to myself that I'll find out what that's all about. And if she's single, I plan to make her mine. Or at least, mine for the night. I just need one taste of the divine.

Samantha

Off-limits. That's what he is. Lucas Bouchard is the prestigious new client acquired by my family's company. From what I know, not only is he an amazing hockey player, he's a humble and generous philanthropist too. Also, he's a walking aphrodisiac.

It doesn't matter that I've just broken off my engagement to a cheating, using loser. Every time our eyes lock, I find myself captivated. But he's not for me. No matter how many times I remind myself of this, though, it doesn't compute. Plain and simple, I want him. And keeping my distance might prove impossible.

Also by Jessica Buss
Chicago Steel Series

Hooked By You (Lucas & Samantha)

Checked By You (Mika & Shiloh)

Clipped By You (Christian & Monica)

Speared By You (Tristan & Stephanie)

Coming Soon

Slashed By You

Delayed By You

Tripped By You

Blocked By You

About the Author

Jessica Buss was born and raised in Anchorage, Alaska. She is married to her high school sweetheart and has two sons. Although she has both her bachelor's and master's degrees in Psychology, she stepped away from that field to be a stay-at-home mom. Now that her kids are growing up and she's getting more time to herself, she's giving this writing thing a chance.

https://907publishing.wixsite.com/my-site

www.ingramcontent.com/pod-product-compliance
Lightning Source LLC
Chambersburg PA
CBHW071448140726
47997CB00005B/1635